NEW DEAL FOR DEATH

ALSO BY ELLIOTT ROOSEVELT

Murder in the West Wing
Murder in the Red Room
The President's Man
A First Class Murder
Murder in the Blue Room
Murder in the Rose Garden
Murder in the Oval Office
Murder at the Palace
The White House Pantry Murder
Murder at Hobcaw Barony
The Hyde Park Murder
Murder and the First Lady
Perfect Crimes (ed.)

ELLIOTT ROOSEVELT

NEW DEAL FOR DEATH

A "Blackjack" Endicott Novel

St. Martin's Press   New York

AS ALWAYS AND FOREVER TO MY WIFE, PATTY

NEW DEAL FOR DEATH. Copyright © 1993 by Elliott Roosevelt. All rights reserved. Printed in the United States of America. No part of this book may be used or reproduced in any manner whatsoever without written permission except in the case of brief quotations embodied in critical articles or reviews. For information, address St. Martin's Press, 175 Fifth Avenue, New York, N.Y. 10010.

Production Editor: David Stanford Burr

Design by Judith A. Stagnitto

Library of Congress Cataloging-in-Publication Data

Roosevelt, Elliott, 1910–1990
        New deal for death : a "Blackjack" Endicott novel /
Elliott Roosevelt.
                p.   cm.
        "A Thomas Dunne book."
        ISBN 0-312-09267-9
        1. Roosevelt, Franklin D. (Franklin Delano), 1882–1945—
Fiction. I. Title.
    PS3535.O549N48   1993
    813'.54—dc20   93-7434
                                                     CIP

First edition: July 1993

10 9 8 7 6 5 4 3 2 1

Chicago

THE DEMOCRATIC NATIONAL CONVENTION
JULY 2, 1932

I pledge you, I pledge myself, to a new deal for the American people. Let all of us here assembled constitute ourselves prophets of a new order of competence and courage. This is more than a political campaign; it is a call to arms. Give me your help, not to win votes alone, but to win in this crusade to restore America to its own people.

It was triumph and bedlam all mixed together in one great, gaudy, noisy night; and for a time it seemed the applause would never die down, the tumult never be quieted.

The nominee was the irrepressible, ebullient Governor of New York, Franklin D. Roosevelt. He spoke to ten thousand people. No. He spoke to ten *million*. Estimates had it that

1

ten million people would tune their radios to hear this speech. Governor Roosevelt tuned his speech to reach *them,* the radio listeners, more than to reach the cheering throng in the convention hall. He was a master of radio oratory, and millions who had never heard him before were getting their first sample of the inspiring, persuasive voice of this brilliant new-style politician.

Inspiring . . . Persuasive . . . Not to everyone.

In New York, Al Smith sat in the bar at the Union Club, chewed on a cigar, and sipped rye. Bitterly angry that he had been defeated in his bid for the nomination, he had refused to move for a unanimous vote for Frank Roosevelt, had left Chicago, and come home: the Unhappy Warrior.

In Detroit, Henry Ford ordered posters, already printed, put up in every area in every Ford factory, saying that if times were to get better and unemployment not get worse, President Hoover must be reelected.

In Washington, Herbert Hoover listened to the Roosevelt speech. He considered Franklin D. Roosevelt flashy, trashy, and insincere.

New York Mayor Jimmy Walker was in Chicago. The Roosevelt nomination was bad news for him. It was a defeat for Tammany Hall and just about ended any chance he had of using political clout to prevent an investigation of corruption in his administration. He drank whiskey and pondered his future.

Sitting comfortably in an overstuffed chair in an unlocked cell in Atlanta Penitentiary, Al Capone was angry. This was not supposed to happen! Roosevelt was not supposed to happen. Somebody had screwed up.

Arthur Flegenheimer—better known as Dutch Schultz— was on a train rushing back to New York. The election of this man Roosevelt was going to mean *Repeal*—repeal of Prohibition and the return of legal beer—and that was going to ruin a lot of guys' businesses. There was only one sure way to prevent it, and Dutch Shultz had come to Chicago to do the necessary. Trouble was, not many guys understood, and they'd double-crossed him. Charlie Luck—Lucky Luciano—had done it to him in New York. So had Frank Nitti and Murray the Camel in Chicago.

Of course, the kingpin had been that bastard Endicott. It had been Endicott—sticking his nose in everywhere, talking to Charlie Luck and to Nitti and Murray the Camel—who'd screwed everything up. Roosevelt's hoity-toity pal. Old school chum. Top hat. Rich guy. Sailor, flier, race driver.

Endicott . . . Jack Endicott. They called him Blackjack. Not because he carried a blackjack but because he won money playing blackjack. He was a smart player, consistently beating the odds. He was a smart guy. Dutch was sorry he hadn't gotten rid of him when he had the chance.

John Lowell Endicott sat in the box that had been reserved for Al Smith and his wife and would have been theirs if Al had not left Chicago in a huff. Sitting beside him was a woman wearing a heavy veil. Both of them were acutely conscious that binoculars were focused on them from many points in the hall. They knew they were being studied by reporters in the press galleries. Blackjack Endicott did not care if he was identified. He was anxious, though, that the woman should not be.

In a press box above and behind, a young reporter handed his glasses to an older reporter. "Have a look, sir," he said. "Maybe you can figure it out."

H. L. Mencken, the Sage of Baltimore, sighed impatiently, put his cigar aside, and squinted through the binoculars. "Never saw either one of them before," he said. "Why's it bother you guys so much?"

"They are saying the man is John Endicott, from Boston. He's supposed to be a close friend of Governor Roosevelt."

"The woman," said Mencken, "is wearing a heavy veil for one of three reasons. She's in mourning, she's somebody else's wife, or she's somebody's girlfriend. In any case, a gentleman won't ask. An ethical reporter won't write about her. Personally, I have a more important story to cover here tonight."

The young reporter put his binoculars under his chair. He would feel self-conscious if he took even one more look at the veiled woman.

A few delegates on the floor—not many—recognized John Lowell Endicott and waved at him. None of them could identify the veiled woman. None of them could approach, either. The box was guarded by special security men, uniformed and plainclothes, and no one could come near enough to stare through the veil or hear the conversation between Blackjack and the woman.

"They don't guess what courage it takes for him to do what he is doing," she said quietly to Endicott.

They had watched James Roosevelt help his father lock the steel braces on his legs, understanding as very few in the huge crowd did. With the braces locked, Governor Roosevelt's legs were like two wooden legs that were not hinged at the knees; and he had lurched forward to the podium, in an awkward and painful gait. During most of his speech he clutched the podium with both hands. If he let go, he could lose his balance and topple over.

The crowd well understood the Governor was crippled. He played his part so well, with so much courage, that they supposed he was not in the least pain.

They were wrong.

They did not dream of another pain the Governor suffered. When he first reached and clutched the podium, the crowd had given him a standing ovation. He stood smiling, glancing around the hall, raising an arm to wave at this one and that. But Jack had understood he was searching. The Governor had scanned the boxes until finally his eye had lighted on this box. Suddenly, he had beamed. His great smile had broadened, and he had nodded and waved and bowed slightly. He had spotted her, the woman sitting beside Jack Endicott. Jack had managed it! He had brought her here! Frank Roosevelt's triumph was sweeter.

The woman seated beside John Lowell Endicott was the woman Frank Roosevelt loved. She was Lucy Mercer Rutherfurd.

It was not difficult to understand why Frank loved Lucy. In some ways she was like Eleanor—that is, she was tall, had light-brown hair and blue eyes, and like Eleanor she was of an aristocratic lineage and had been afforded the education and training that implied. She was possessed, though, of a grace that poor gawkish Eleanor had never managed to attain. She had exquisite taste in clothes, in vivid contrast to Eleanor, who chose hers so maladroitly that she sometimes wore outfits that were utterly grotesque. Lucy spoke in a low, almost suggestive voice, in contrast to Eleanor's nervous, high-pitched squeak. She was naturally, effortlessly enchanting.

He was not scornful of Eleanor Roosevelt. He understood, though, that a person had to know Eleanor well before her splendid qualities came out. A person had to be tolerant of her idiosyncracies before he could appreciate her. To appreciate Eleanor, you had to know her well. To appreciate Lucy, you had only to see her.

Frank Roosevelt had loved Lucy for more than twenty years. They had fallen in love during the war, when the Governor was assistant secretary of the navy. Eleanor knew. She had found out by reading his letters. Their love had been subdued by Lucy's religion and by Frank's ambitions and his financial dependence on his mother. Then—Well, if Frank Roosevelt had not become a captive of his wheelchair, God knew how the relationships might have worked out.

Jack Endicott and Lucy Rutherfurd remained in their box until the convention was gaveled to adjournment. It had to meet again in the morning to nominate a candidate for Vice President, but for tonight the delegates and everyone else burst onto the streets of Chicago, looking for fun. The job had been done! Governor Roosevelt was the candidate! Happy Days Are Here Again!

"Airport, boss?"

The cab was not just any Chicago taxi. This one was driven by Oscar Carter, a Negro Jack had guessed to be about fifty years old. For the past few days his cab had been Jack's, hired by the day. Carter had been invaluable to him. Oscar Carter was the man who had subdued Bo Weinberg, Dutch Schultz's chief gunman, during last night's little war on the lakefront—the quick, decisive battle that had put an end to the Dutchman's scheme to harm the Governor. Oscar Carter was the man who had kicked Bo Weinberg in the face and then broken his nose by grinding his heel on it.

"Airport, my friend," said Jack. "With a little stop—"

"Figured that," said Oscar Carter. "Little stop . . . Where at, boss?"

Downtown. In the Loop. Quietly and quickly, the motorcade carrying the Governor of New York to the first post-nomination gala pulled away and came to a stop in a side street. The taxicab sat at the curb, waiting.

Cops and security men surrounded the two cars, but on orders from the Governor they backed away a few yards. Lucy left the taxi and went to the limousine. In the backseat she had a few minutes alone with Frank Roosevelt. Jack Endicott stood beside the cab, smoked a cigarette, and waited.

"Boss," said Oscar Carter. "You the damnedest man—"

Jack seized Carter's hand. "Oscar," he said. "*You* the damnedest man. You have any interest in coming back to Boston with me? I mean, you have any interest in working for me, permanently?"

"I'd have to fly in that airplane, yours?"

Jack laughed. "No. Drive for me. But mostly be a man I can trust. It's hard to find a man you can trust. You have to test them. You've tested out damned well, my friend."

"Like I said, you the first white man in my whole life that ever called me friend," said Oscar. "Hell, boss . . ."

"We'll work it out," said Jack. "Tonight, I've got to get that lady back to Indianapolis. She's not supposed to be in Chicago."

"I bet you sayin' her husband don't know."

Jack nodded. "Her husband doesn't know. His wife doesn't know. You want to grasp how much I trust you? That's it. I've let you see and know something almost no one knows."

Oscar grinned. "I know somethin' about a man doin' what his wife don't like. Now, Mrs. Roosevelt, she's a fine woman, from all I hear. But—"

"The lady in the limousine is—"

"A lady," Oscar interrupted. "Leave it at that. But, boss—you gonna fly that airplane *in the night*?"

"From here to Indianapolis," said Jack. "Follow the beacons all the way. It's not so far."

"In the night? You flyin' in the night?" Oscar asked. "You doin' that for the Governor . . . I understand. So's the lady's husband won't know she was here tonight. So's Mrs. Roosevelt won't know. You got . . ." He turned and stared at the limousine. "I guess she's got the same kind of guts you got. Me, I wouldn't want to fly—"

Jack clasped Oscar's upper arm. "You would if . . . You would if for some reason—"

"Hope the reason never comes," said Oscar.

"It may," said Jack. "I have a feeling the Governor may need us again before this thing is over."

"Nothin' like bein' a part of—what you call this, boss? Bein' a part of history?"

Lucy Mercer Rutherfurd left the limousine and walked back toward the cab.

"Let's don't be too dramatic, my friend," said Jack Endicott. "I'll see you at the airport . . . Let's say noon tomorrow. Sometime tomorrow I'll take off for Boston, weather permitting."

"I'll drive the cab to Boston," said Oscar.

I
.

"A taxi, sir?" asked Drake, Jack's manservant.

"No, thank you, Drake. I'm going to the club first and will walk there."

"Very good, sir. If I may— If I may, sir, you have a bit of dust on your hat that I did not notice earlier. May I?"

John Lowell Endicott took off his silk hat and handed it to Drake. The moment gave him time to check himself one last time in the tall pier glass beside the door. He was wearing white tie. He turned the white carnation in his buttonhole a quarter turn to the right. Drake had fixed it nicely, but it could be improved. He ran his index finger over his mustache, settling into place the whisker or two that had strayed since he'd combed it with his tiny mustache comb.

"You are not improving yourself," said a low, suggestive female voice behind him.

Jack turned and grinned at his daughter, Marietta Biddle

Endicott, an eighteen-year-old beauty of whom he was very proud. "Your evening?" he asked her.

"More innocent than yours, I imagine," she said. "I'm going to a movie with Freddie, followed by dinner. If poor Freddie had anything evil in mind, he wouldn't know how to effect it."

"Don't be so sure," he said. "There's a hell of a lot of evil in innocence."

She laughed. "And a hell of a lot of innocence in evil," she said. "The boundary is ill-defined, as you've always told me. Don't worry. Freddie is a virgin, I imagine."

"As you are not, p'raps," he said.

Marietta's face was much like her father's: strong and handsome rather than delicately beautiful. Jack had no doubt that his daughter was beautiful, nor did anyone else who took a second look at her; but her beauty was earthy and uncomplicated. Her mother, from whom Jack had been divorced for six years, did not see Marietta as beautiful. She was not modish enough to suit her mother's tastes. She would not have her eyebrows plucked. She wore her dark brown hair longer than was chic in 1932 and refused to let anyone touch it with a curling iron. Her makeup, when she wore it at all, was never anything more than a light lipstick and maybe a touch of rouge.

"Were *you* a virgin when you were eighteen?" she asked.

"As a matter of fact— Never mind. That's a subject a gentleman does not discuss with a young lady."

"If you told me, you'd have to tell me who." She chuckled. "Something else you won't discuss."

"I'm walking to the club," he said. "Will you walk with me that far?"

"I should be honored," she said.

They left the house together in the peace of a summer evening: he in white tie and tails, wearing his high silk hat and carrying a cane; she in an apricot-colored knee-length silk-satin dress, with a burnt-orange cloche on her head.

John Lowell Endicott usually enjoyed a quiet walk along the sidewalks around Boston Common. On a summer evening it was particularly pleasant. The summery odors of leaves and new-mown grass mingled with the perfume of the fine Havana cigars gentlemen smoked as they walked. They tapped their silver-topped ebony canes on the bricks, which, with the clicks of the ladies' heels, set up a gentle, arhythmic dissonance that mingled with the murmured greetings they exchanged.

The ancient dignity of the Common was diminished now by another dissonance: the quiet entreaties of men and women begging—begging for anything, a simple handout, a day's work, anything to buy them bread. They had begun to appear around the Common about two years ago. The police kept them quiet but did not—maybe could not—drive them away. Jack Endicott carried quarters and dimes in his pockets and handed them out as he walked between his home and the Common Club. About half the people he knew did the same. The other half cursed the supplicants and threatened them with their canes.

For Marietta these people had been a condition of life since she was sixteen. She had come home from college in the spring of 1930, and there they were. Her first reaction had been that the police should drive them away from the neighborhood. A year later she had firmly declared herself a socialist, arguing that only socialism could cure the ills of society. Jack had invited Norman Thomas to dinner so Marietta might meet and talk with a real socialist. She had learned that what she and her college friends called socialism was only cant, that real socialism and the real solutions were far more complex than was dreamed on campus. She knew as well as her father did that his quarters and dimes solved nothing. Petty charity, no matter how humane, would not solve the nation's problems.

There was an old curse—"May you live in interesting times." They did.

A man coming toward them was smiling and was obviously about to greet them.

"Who is he?" Marietta asked quietly. "Quick."

"His name is Lansky," said Jack Endicott. "Meyer Lansky. He's from New York. He and his wife have a spastic child, and they've moved to Boston so the little boy can be treated by Dr. Carruthers at Children's Hospital."

"How do you come to know him?"

"I did him a favor. There was some anti-Semitic prejudice against renting a Jewish family an apartment in the area of the Common. He came to the bank, looking for someone who might help him, and Uncle Henry ushered him to my desk."

Meyer Lansky walked up, beaming, sweeping off his hat with his left hand and extending his right to be shaken. "Mr. Endicott!" he said. "It's a pleasure to see you. I hope you're enjoying the evening."

Jack shook Lansky's hand. "Mr. Lansky, may I present my daughter, Marietta?"

Lansky bowed. "I am honored," he said.

Meyer Lansky was only about five feet three inches tall, yet he was an impressive man with a studied dignity, wearing a black double-breasted suit with thin white pinstripes, a silk shirt, and a conspicuously expensive gray silk necktie. His dark hair was naturally wavy, and on the right a little of it had fallen over his forehead when he'd removed his hat. His features were regular, except for his rather weak chin. He was smiling, genuinely friendly; and yet, looking closely, Jack and Marietta could see a menacing coldness.

"How is your little boy doing at the hospital?" Jack asked.

Lansky's smile faded. "I don't know," he said. "I always have hope. I'll take him anywhere, any hospital, to be treated by any doctor. So far—" He shrugged.

"Well, my best wishes," said Jack.

"Thank you, Mr. Endicott," said Lansky soberly, his smile then returning. "You've been very kind to me and my family."

"I'm glad I could do a little something for you, Mr. Lansky."

"Well— I imagine you'll be leaving for Saratoga soon. The season opens next week."

"As a matter of fact, I *will* be going over to Saratoga Springs," said Jack. "You guessed right."

"It wasn't a guess, exactly," said Lansky. "Everybody who is anybody goes to Saratoga in August; and, Mr. Endicott, you *are* somebody."

Jack and Marietta both grinned. "I bet *you're* going to Saratoga Springs," said Jack.

"Right. I own a small interest in one of the lake houses. Maybe you've heard of it. The Piping Rock."

"Of course I've heard of it," Jack said. "In fact, I've been there. I don't go to Saratoga Springs just to see the horses run, y'know."

Lansky laughed. "Or to bathe in the sulphur water, either."

"No, b'god! Won't go near the stinking stuff."

"Well . . . I'd appreciate it if you would be my guest for an evening—maybe more than one evening—at Piping Rock. I'll be staying at the Grand Union Hotel. If you call or leave a note for me—"

"I am stopping at the Grand Union myself," said Jack.

"Fine. Then maybe I can do you a small favor. Nothing like the big favor you did me, but something, anyway."

"I'll look you up, Mr. Lansky," said Jack, and with a nod and smile he terminated the conversation.

"It's been a pleasure to meet you, Miss Endicott," said Lansky, and he bowed and walked away.

Marietta waited until Lansky was definitely out of ear-shot, then said to her father, "If he couldn't lease an apartment in Boston, how can he stay at the Grand Union?"

Jack smiled tolerantly. "His kind owns Saratoga Springs," he said.

"Jews?"

"No. He—"

"You mean gangsters?" she interrupted. "Is that what he is?"

"I'm not sure," said Jack. "The day after I helped him about his lease, he came in the bank carrying a small leather satchel, like a doctor's bag, and deposited a hundred thousand dollars—cash."

They walked on toward the Common Club. Two taxis were waiting there. Jack put Marietta in one of them and sent her on for her date with Freddie Adams.

Dropping his hat and stick with the attendant by the door, Jack climbed the broad, carpeted stairway to the bar. The bar had once been on the first floor but had been moved to the second when Prohibition went into effect. If ever police or federal agents had the temerity to enter the premises of the Common Club, the door attendant would step on a button hidden under the carpet and sound a raucous buzzer in the bar. By the time the intruders reached the second floor, the club's stock of liquor would have disappeared behind a panel and as many gentlemen as wished would have retreated out a rear door, leaving others who would confront the trespassers with intimidating indignation. Or so they had rehearsed. In fact, no policeman or Prohibition agent had ever visited the Common Club, and the members enjoyed their drinks as they had always done.

The room was lighted by bulbs burning inside milk-glass globes. Heavy dark-red plush drapes covered the tall windows. The walls were of dark wood paneling. The long bar was massive, its heavy wood deeply carved with images of Bacchus and bunches of grapes. There were no tables, chairs, or stools. Gentlemen of the Common Club drank standing at their bar. The wall behind the bar was dominated by a large painting of a nude girl reclining on a couch, holding a glass of wine in her hand and staring invitingly at the gentlemen across the bar. She was the only female who ever entered the bar.

Jack's uncle Henry Endicott was at the bar. So was George Saltonstall, tall and toothy, amateur sportsman and professional innocent. John Cabot and Charles Adams were there, too. All wore dinner clothes like Jack's. It was their custom to gather here for a drink about this time of evening, before going on to dinner.

"I haven't seen you since the Democrats nominated your chum Governor Roosevelt," said the wispy gray John Cabot. "You are pleased, I suppose."

Jack Endicott nodded at the bartender, who had just poured him a Black Label over ice and added a touch of water. He picked up the drink and saluted Cabot. "I am pleased," he said. "If for no other reason, I'd rather have a friend in the White House than a man I don't know."

"Let us arrange for you to meet Herbert Hoover," said Uncle Henry. "That way you can join the rest of us in supporting a sound man who's sound on money and a whole lot of other things—as opposed to this odd Democrat who makes vague promises about a 'new deal' and all that. You're a lifelong Republican, Jack. You should be for Hoover."

"I'm afraid Herbert Hoover has not been a very effective President," said Jack.

"Better to endure evils while evils may be endured than fly to others that we know not of," said Uncle Henry. He was twenty years older than Jack and twenty pounds heavier. He shared with Jack's late father a tendency to pontificate, only he did it in a booming voice. "Your man Roosevelt could turn out to be another Wilson. First he'll damage business with a lot of silly 'reforms,' and then he'll get us into war."

"Who in the world could we possibly fight?" asked John Cabot.

"Oh, he'll find somebody. Mexico . . . Canada . . ."

"It would be worth our while to fight Russia," said Cabot.

"Or Guatemala," said Uncle Henry.

"Not Guatemala," said Jack. "They'd beat us. Our army has been reduced to so low a state, we'd be hard put to defend ourselves against Guatemala."

"It had better be in good shape," said Uncle Henry. "I hear more and more talk of a mob of veterans marching on Washington to demand prepayment of the veterans bonus."

"That cannot be tolerated," said John Cabot.

"Anyway, I understand your friend Roosevelt is in town," said George Saltonstall. "Will you be seeing him?"

"As a matter of fact, yes. He's speaking tonight at the Copley. I'm seeing him later in his suite."

"At least," huffed Uncle Henry, "you're not going to hear all the Democrats make speeches."

"I listen to as few speeches as I possibly can," said Jack.

It was almost midnight when Jack Endicott rang the bell at the door of the Roosevelt suite at the Copley Plaza. The ring was answered by Missy LeHand, Governor Roosevelt's long-time personal secretary and confidante.

"Come in, Jack," she said. "The Governor has been waiting for you. The Missus has gone to bed, and Eff Dee is sitting with Louie Howe."

"Good to see you, Missy," he said. "Did Eleanor know I was coming?"

Missy smiled and nodded.

Most men have friends their wives dislike: the old school chums that remind them of their youth and sometimes inspire them to deviate from the paths of rectitude. That was how Eleanor Roosevelt saw John Lowell Endicott: as a man insufficiently serious, inadequately dedicated, a rogue and bon vivant, the very kind of man she did not want her husband to cultivate. If she had not gone to bed, she would have made a stiff, artificial effort to be cordial to him. He was glad she had spared herself the effort and spared him the awkwardness of it.

Missy, who was no girl but a mature woman, wore an ivory silk crepe dress that flowed down over her generous figure like the water from a shower. She was more the slave

of fashion than Eleanor or Marietta and so had her blond
hair cut short, above her ears, and curled. She wore dark red
lipstick and small rimless eyeglasses.

"Jack!" cried Governor Roosevelt. "Come in! Have a seat
and a drink! You've had your dinner, I certainly hope."

"Oh, yes," said Jack. He crossed the parlor to the Governor and shook his hand, then the hand of Louis Howe, before
he sat down on the couch that faced the Governor's wheelchair. "Wouldn't mind one of these finger sandwiches,
though."

"Missy, pour Jack a Scotch," said Governor Roosevelt.

Frank Roosevelt had worn black tie for the political dinner downstairs. So had the hunched, wizened, gnomelike
Louis McHenry Howe, Frank's dedicated friend and political
mentor. Twenty years ago, when Howe was a political reporter in Albany, he had decided the young state senator
Franklin Roosevelt was a coming man and had attached
himself to him. When Frank went to Washington, appointed
Assistant Secretary of the Navy by President Wilson, Howe
went, too, as assistant to the Assistant Secretary. He had
remained a loyal friend through Frank's ordeal of infantile
paralysis. Most of what Frank knew of politics—and everything Eleanor did—had been learned from Howe. Jack liked
the man and respected him immensely.

"How's it going, Louie?" Jack asked Howe.

Howe thrust a hand toward Frank Roosevelt. "The next
President of the United States," he said flatly.

Howe lit a cigarette off the end of the one he was smoking.
He was a chain-smoker, literally, and consumed four or five
packs of Sweet Caporals a day. As a result he suffered from
emphysema, and his racking cough often interrupted his
conversation and his work, though never his concentration.

"Jack," said Frank, "I don't think I've thanked you sufficiently for what you did for me earlier this month." He shrugged. " 'Sufficiently?' A man couldn't thank you sufficiently. There is no way I could thank you enough. No way."

Jack reached up and took the Scotch and soda that Missy had poured for him. *"Au contraire,"* he said. He liked to drop the occasional foreign expression into his conversation. It was an affectation, he knew, but he enjoyed doing it. "I'm glad to have been able to do something for you."

"I might damned well be dead if it hadn't been for you," said Frank. He, too, lit a fresh cigarette. He didn't smoke nearly as much as Howe but did enjoy his Camels, which he smoked at the end of a long black holder. "Those fellows had it in mind to kill me."

He was talking about the Dutch Schultz scheme to assassinate Frank Roosevelt before he could be nominated. Some men in the mobs saw the likely repeal of Prohibition as ruinous to their most profitable business, bootlegging, and had determined to rid themselves of the man who would probably make it happen. Frank had called on Jack to find out as much as he could about the conspiracy. Jack had done more. He had destroyed the conspiracy. Not all mobsters liked the idea of assassinating a candidate for President, he had discovered. He'd had the help of some of the most powerful figures in organized crime.

"I wish you could have taken an active part in it, Frank," said Jack, sipping Scotch. "How else is a man going to become an acquaintance of men like Lucky Luciano, Frank Costello, Joe Profaci, Albert Anastasia, Al Capone, Frank Nitti, Murray the Camel Humphreys . . . ? Not to mention Polly Adler, the world's most famous whorehouse madam. I got an intimate look into an element of American life that most of us read about in the papers and don't really believe is out there."

"I understand Mr. Luciano asked a price for his help," said the Governor.

Jack laughed. "Yes, he asks that President Roosevelt not appoint Tom Dewey United States District Attorney. I assured him you would not."

Frank Roosevelt tipped back his head and laughed heartily.

"I understand," said Missy, "you got a look at 'café society,' too."

"Oh, yes. The Stork Club. And a cheap little ex-con named Sherman Billingsley. I had the pleasure of seeing Lucky Luciano break his nose."

"Question," said Louie Howe. "Is it over? After all, Dutch Schultz is back in New York, big as ever."

"Not as big as ever, Louie," said Jack. "There'll be a problem down the road, but maybe we don't need to worry about it during the campaign. Men like Dutch Schultz and Al Capone are . . . Well, how would you put it? Crooks. Cheap little crooks. Not very smart. A man like Luciano is something different. He and men like Frank Costello in New York and Frank Nitti and Murray the Camel in Chicago are smart. Their idea is to *organize* the rackets. In the kind of organization they're thinking about, there's no room for wild men like Dutch Schultz and Al Capone. They are going to eliminate men like Schultz. I'd guess Dutch Schultz doesn't have very long to live. One of these days, Luciano—or somebody designated by him—will have control of everything Schultz ever had. Capone . . . He thinks he still runs things, from his cell in Atlanta. He doesn't."

"Odd idea," said the Governor. "Organizing— The Sicilians?"

"Mostly," said Jack. "Frank Costello's real name is Francesco Castiglia. Luciano, Profaci, Anastasia . . . all Sicilians. Their idea is to organize crime the way a business is organized and run it quietly, with as little publicity as possible. That's why Al Capone will never get back to Chicago alive. He made too much noise."

"Anyway," said Governor Roosevelt cheerfully, "the campaign is off to a good start. I have a lot to thank you for, Jack—not the least of which was that daring nighttime flight to and from Indianapolis."

"That was a pleasure," said Jack.

The Governor glanced at the three others: Jack, Howe, and Missy. He sipped from an old-fashioned. It was his nightcap, instead of the martinis he favored at the cocktail hour. "A man is lucky to have friends like the three of you," he said solemnly.

"I want you to know you can call on me for any help I can give you," said Jack.

The Governor grinned. "Except to enroll in the Democratic Party."

"I don't think that would help you," Jack laughed.

"Well, God forbid I have to ask you to risk your life again."

Still smiling broadly, Jack nodded. "I'd just as soon not have to do that again," he said.

The taxi he had hailed in front of the Copley dropped him in front of a house on Spruce Street, one block from Beacon Street and Boston Common. The greenish glow from a gas mantel lighted the ivy-clad bricks, the worn-down stone of the steps and stoop, the wrought-iron railings, the white double doors, and the brass number plate and knocker.

Jack tapped with the knocker. After a long moment, the door opened, and Charlotte Wendell extended her hand and drew him inside.

"I was beginning to wonder," she said.

They had dined together, and then he had dropped her at home while he went to pay his call on Governor Roosevelt. She was still dressed in the wine-colored silk gown she had worn for dinner.

"I am sorry," he said. "I did say, though, I'd have to spend half an hour or so with Frank Roosevelt."

"Well . . . You're here, anyway. I had Alicia make a pot of coffee before she went to bed. Brandy?"

"Just a spot, p'raps. I had a Scotch with Frank."

Charlotte Wendell was the widow of a college friend of Jack's. Before Jack's divorce from Cynthia, Bob and Charlotte had met socially with some regularity. When couples divorce, friends tend to side with one party or the other. Bob and Charlotte had not done that; but Bob, a proper Bostonian, had felt a bit embarrassed to associate intimately with anyone who had been divorced. It was only after Bob suddenly and tragically died that Jack and Charlotte could revive an old friendship—though of course it was revived on a radically different basis.

She put down the silver tray and coffee service on the table in front of the couch, then went for the brandy and glasses. When she returned and sat down beside him, she kissed him on the neck before she turned to pour coffee.

Charlotte was a handsome woman. Forty years old, a blonde, she wore her hair cut more than stylishly short,

leaving even on top just enough to be brushed in a small
swoop across her right forehead, otherwise as short as a
man's. Her eyes were blue but narrow and slanted, like an
Oriental's, and they were her most characteristic feature.
Her mouth was small, her lips thin.

The wine-colored silk gown she had worn to dinner left her
arms and shoulders bare. The ankle-length skirt was slit to
the knee and above. She pulled the slit back to expose her
right leg: top of stocking and bare skin above.

That was how it was between them. They had not declared love but were as casual with each other as though they
had. Jack draped his arm around her shoulders and pushed
his hand into her dress to fondle her breast, and her reaction
was to draw a deep breath and close her eyes.

"Are you coming to Saratoga Springs with me?" he asked.

"Do you insist on driving that damned Bugatti?" she
asked.

"Of course. I'll ship our trunks. They'll be waiting at the
hotel."

"And I'll be living in sin with you? Sharing a room?"

"Sharing a suite. I'm sorry, but the hotel is booked solid.
Marietta will be using the second bedroom."

"I suppose I could sleep on the couch," she said in a
throaty, erotic voice.

"Sure. That'll be just fine."

"You bastard! I think you'd let me."

He squeezed her breast. "Not in ten thousand years," he
said.

"You would if my tits were little."

"You misjudge me, m'dear. I respect all your parts, not
just your tits."

"Including my mind, of course."

"Including your mind, certainly."

She got up. As he watched she lifted the wine-colored dress over her head. She was wearing loose pink silk tap panties. Her dark stockings were held up by thin black lace garters around her legs. As he knew, she was wearing no brassiere.

"Do you know what Bob did when I undressed in front of him?" she asked.

"I'm not sure I want to know."

"He looked away and pretended he didn't notice. I can't be so evil as to suggest I'm glad he's gone, but I'm glad I have room in my life now for a man who's not frightened by—"

"Charlotte."

"Jack."

"I don't want to talk about what Bob did. I don't want to talk about him. He was my good friend, and I'm terribly sorry he's gone."

"You feel no guilt about us, for God's sake!"

"No, none at all. None at all. Come here. . . ."

II

The Bugatti was an open, four-seater sports touring car, capable of racing; and Jack did in fact race it. Painted royal blue and lovingly waxed by the garage where it was kept and serviced, the car gleamed and attracted admiring attention wherever he took it. A round nickel-plated headlamp was mounted on each front fender. The wire wheels were painted butter yellow—six of them, four mounted and two carried on the rear as spares. The control panel and steering wheel were of polished wood. The cockpit, which seated the driver and one passenger, was upholstered all around in tan glove leather—as was the deep, more commodious passenger compartment behind.

The roads between Boston and Saratoga Springs were all but perfect for the Bugatti. Not just fast but nimble, it obeyed Jack's practiced driving and reached speeds of nearly eighty miles an hour on some of the rural highways. A Massachusetts policeman on a motorcycle took out after it at one point, but he gave up after less than a mile, when the odd little sports car he could not identify was out of sight.

Marietta sat in the front beside her father. Charlotte sat in the rear. Marietta was jubilant. Charlotte tried to conceal her motion sickness. Jack studied the road ahead with grim intensity and adjusted his speed to the curves. They passed everything: other cars, trucks, farm wagons . . . Jack was an artist with his horn and sounded a half-musical warning. An occasional driver elected to challenge him, but that driver did not know what he was challenging, car or driver. The Bugatti sped past, Marietta waving.

Some of the scenery along the way was memorably beautiful. Most of it was drab. Most of rural America was drab. Its monotony was relieved by signs.

Everyone enjoyed the doggerel of the white-on-red Burma-Shave signs:

SHE LOVED HIM MUCH

SHE TRULY DID

BUT SUFFERED FROM HIS STUBBLE

UNTIL HE LEARNED TO CUT IT SMOOTH

SO NOW THEY KNOW NO TROUBLE

BURMA-SHAVE

Barns badly in need of paint were painted free of charge for the farmers by a company from Wheeling, West Virginia—black with blue borders, then with great yellow and white letters legible from half a mile away:

CHEW

MAIL POUCH TOBACCO

TREAT YOURSELF TO THE BEST

Other signs were peeling paper posters attached to barns and other farm buildings. They advertised things like CLAB-BER GIRL, a brand of baking powder, and BROMO-SELTZER, a headache powder.

Not all the roads were hard-surfaced. A few miles here and there were paved only with gravel, and vehicles were trailed by great thick plumes of choking yellow dust. The Bugatti loved gravel. It was designed to cope with the sliding a car could do on loose gravel. Jack and his two passengers were not so pleased with the dust.

As they approached Saratoga Springs, New York they began to encounter trucks carrying racehorses, also big Packards and Cadillacs carrying revelers to the season. There was some honking of horns: not warnings but greetings from people who recognized Jack Endicott and the Bugatti and ordered their chauffeurs to honk. It was fun to swing out and pass those big cars. Even the faintly nauseous Charlotte joined in waving and grinning at the people in the limousines.

"Everybody who is anybody goes to Saratoga in August," Meyer Lansky had said. He'd only repeated a cliché that circulated among all the people who could afford it. It had been so for nearly a hundred years now. The racing season at Saratoga was where fashionable people went in August. If they needed to rationalize the extravagance—which many felt they did—they talked about the therapeutic value of soaking in and drinking the nauseous sulphur water that flowed from the springs and gave the town its first cachet and its name. Like Marienbad and other European spas, like White Sulphur Springs in West Virginia, Saratoga Springs attracted people who persisted in believing its malodorous mineral waters were really a cure for many ailments.

By 1932 it was fully understood that the real attraction was gambling, on the horses or on the tables, plus eating and drinking and being seen—and for a few, the joys of the company of the jolly ladies who thronged the town from every part of the country during the August season.

Local officials pretended they did not see the illegal gambling, drinking, and whoring. Local citizens fronted for most of the operations, and the town reaped a tidy profit, not the least part of it from payoffs. Hundreds of others had jobs for a month. Some had jobs to which they didn't even need to report.

The Grand Union Hotel was one of the largest in the world. An immense white frame building situated on some seventeen acres of downtown land, it was characterized by the sine qua non of nineteenth-century resort hotels: a broad shady porch that extended more than a hundred yards, where guests strolled, rocked in wicker chairs, smoked, snacked, and took the air.

The Endicott Bugatti was recognized by the doorman, who trotted forward to help Mr. Endicott and his ladies out of the car. He summoned other attendants to lift the three light bags that were all the luggage they had carried in the car. He tsk-tsked over the dust that had settled on the Bugatti during the drive and promised Mr. Endicott the car would be meticulously cleaned and polished in the hotel garage—immediately.

"I won't need it this evening, Paul," said Jack.

"It will be ready when you wish it," said the doorman.

John Lowell Endicott did not need to check in at the Grand Union. The bell captain left his station to escort Mr. Endicott to his suite. It was of course the same suite Mr. Endicott had occupied since 1921, with new drapes, freshly

aired, and adorned with baskets of flowers. Two bottles of
champagne were brought in on the heels of the bell captain
and the guests, together with hors d'oeuvres of caviar and
smoked salmon. The trunks had arrived yesterday and had
been unpacked into the bureau drawers by the maids.

"God, how I like your style!" Charlotte laughed as soon as
the staff had left the suite. "Bob could have afforded it
maybe. But—" She shook her head. "—didn't know what
money was good for."

"A little is good for things like this," said Jack. "You
must not bankrupt yourself for it."

"My father," said Marietta, "would consider Buckingham
Palace ostentatious. Wouldn't think of living in it. Ostentatious."

Jack, in his driving clothes—khaki riding breeches and
soft leather boots, a white cotton turtleneck, and tweed
cap—tossed his cap aside and lectured his daughter. "Going
out around Boston Common in evening clothes is not dangerous, not yet. But flaunting enough diamonds at your throat
to feed twenty families for a year is damned foolishness," he
said sternly. "How would you feel if your family were hungry and here came enough gaudy jewelry to solve all your
problems and the problems of fifty other people—all that
money doing nothing better than decorating some old bat's
wrinkled neck? A guillotine could be set up on Boston Common. Don't forget it."

Charlotte leaned back wearily on a couch. "Is that the
kind of thing you hope your friend Governor Roosevelt will
cope with?" she asked.

Jack nodded. "If Frank Roosevelt staves off revolution in
this country, he will have a claim to the title of one of the
greatest Presidents we've ever had."

Marietta stared at the ice buckets and the champagne for a moment, then said, "Maybe we should enjoy what we have while we have it."

"We can still be enjoying it twenty years from now," said Jack, "if we do in the next five years what civilized people have to do to help the many who are in need."

"What an introduction to a sybaritic week," said Charlotte.

"*Après nous, le déluge,*" said Jack. "But not necessarily. So no need to expect the worst. Let's open the champagne. Two weeks from now I'll return to worrying about the state of the nation—and maybe helping Frank to do something about it. For right now . . . let me gain strength."

The dining room in the Grand Union served fourteen hundred people at a sitting. Two hundred fifty waiters worked to serve efficiently—many of them literally trotting through the back halls to carry food toward the tables.

Men in white tie, women in every shade of silk, hung with glittering jewels, sat beneath crystal chandeliers, at tables set with linen and heavy silver. They scanned menus as big as newspapers. Those who did not want to spend twenty minutes studying the menu might elect to accept the **Menu Suggestion** of the day. It was:

Hors d'Oeuvre à la Française

Coquilles Saint-Jacques à la Mode de Saint-Malo

Salsifis aux Fines Herbes

Contrefillet Grillé Maison

Pommes en Liard

Salade de Saison

Le Plateau des Fromages

Pâtisserie Parisienne

Glaces Variées

Corbeille des Fruits

A wine list was put beside a gentleman at each table. That cocktails were not served in the dining room was not a concession to Prohibition but in conformity to the tradition that hard liquors were taken in the bars before dinner, not at table.

The first thing everyone did once seated was to glance around, to see who was sitting nearby.

A handsome young man with dark curly hair parted in the middle nodded at Jack and smiled. Jack had noticed him on the porch when they arrived in the afternoon. He looked then as if he'd just come in from a round of golf. He had been dressed in plus-fours, argyle socks, and a white knit shirt. Now he was in white tie like all the other men, and he was comfortably confident that almost no one recognized him. He was Julius Marx—Groucho. His brother Arthur sat at the same table, even less likely to be recognized. He was Harpo. They were with their wives.

Sitting at another nearby table were the all-time great golf champion, Bobby Jones, and tennis champion Ellsworth Vines.

A handsome man passing by on his way to his table paused for a moment to shake the hand of John Lowell

Endicott. He was Richard Whitney, president of the New York Stock Exchange. He went on to sit down with Charles G. Dawes, a Chicago banker and former Vice President of the United States.

Mayor Jimmy Walker walked by on his way to sit down with Al Smith. He did not elect to say hello to Jack Endicott.

"My father came here every year," said Charlotte. "For the horses. Really. He enjoyed the racing. I mean, he loved the whole scene. I doubt he ever placed a bet."

"So did my father," said Jack. "And my grandfather. He used to talk about how southern families came here and brought their Negro servants with them. Abolitionists used to try to persuade the slaves to escape, telling them they were in free territory—and, not only that, they were very close to the Canadian border. A few did escape, but most of them were just confused, as he told it."

"It was the Southerners," said Marietta, "who brought casino gambling to Saratoga Springs. They liked to play the games they played on Mississippi riverboats."

"Who brought the ladies of the night?" Charlotte asked.

"They will appear wherever there's a clientèle for them," said Jack.

"Apparently there's no law here," said Charlotte.

"Wherever there's this much money, there's no law," said Jack. "That's not a cynical opinion. It's just an observation. And there's a lot of money here, waiting to be shaken loose."

Jack had studied the menu and was ready to order. He did not accept the "suggestion" but ordered a platter of assorted Lebanese olives in oil, to be shared, and rolled smoked salmon for his appetizer. Omitting soup, he ordered *la rogonnade de veau mijotée à la Lyonaise,* Liard potatoes, new lima

beans, and a Riviera salad. Charlotte asked him to order the
same for her. Marietta asked him to order a rare fillet of beef
for her entrée. He ordered a bottle of Châteauneuf-du-Pape
and a bottle of Chablis *grand cru.*

Another grand tradition of Saratoga Springs was that
smoking was done in the smoking lounges of the great hotels,
never in their dining rooms. In fact, in the midst of gambling
and prostitution, tradition insisted that ladies did not smoke
at all. Tradition suggested that even men smoked only cigars, perhaps pipes, but never the low-class form of tobacco:
cigarettes. When from time to time men and women slipped
out for five minutes, it was understood by their table com-
panions that they had retreated to a porch on the rear for a
quick smoke.

Marietta and Charlotte were acutely uncomfortable with
this tradition.

Marietta wore an apricot-colored silk dress, trimmed with
white organdy. The sheer organdy was meant to suggest
modesty covering the depth of her décolletage. Charlotte's
liquid-silk lime-green gown did not cover her arms and
shoulders. In her own décolletage rested the almost-famous
Lanier Emerald, set in white gold and hung from a white-
gold chain. The interbreasts valley in which it nested was
unfashionably deep, filled with an accentuating shadow.

"I hope we—" Jack began to say, but he was interrupted
by a modest smattering of applause rising from the tables
near the nearest door.

A tall man, spare and erect, glancing around with piercing
eyes, had just entered the room, and a few people had recognized him. He was a man in his late fifties. His hair, though
still thick and dark, was retreating from his forehead. On his
arm he escorted an exquisite young woman: diminutive, as

erect as he was, wearing her black hair in two braids down her back. Though her skin was milky white, her eyes suggested she was Oriental—as did her costume, a jade-green silk jacket elaborately embroidered with gold and silver thread, with a slim black silk skirt slit to four inches above her knee.

The applause spread, and at some tables people chose to rise.

"Who the hell—?" muttered Marietta.

"General Douglas MacArthur," said Jack. "The girl is his mistress. He brought her to the States from the Philippines. This must be one of the few public appearances she has ever made."

Two weeks ago, General MacArthur, Chief of Staff, United States Army, had led Third Cavalry in the attack on the Bonus Army and had driven the veterans out of Washington. If not many Americans chose to applaud him for that, certainly this crowd did; and he walked majestically into the dining room, nodding just a little, acknowledging the applause but not seeming to bask in it.

The girl—her name was Isabel—clung fearfully to the general's arm.

Jack did not stand. As MacArthur passed two tables away, Jack raised a hand in a sort of half salute and smiled at him. The General returned the same gesture. The two men had met in France in 1917 and had seen each other half a dozen times since.

"Is there anybody you don't know?" Charlotte asked dryly after the General and Isabel had passed by.

"There are some people here I wish I didn't," said Jack.

"How about the little man from Boston?" Marietta asked.

She nodded across the room, where Meyer Lansky had just entered and stood looking around.

"Dapper little fellow," said Charlotte. "Who is he?"

"I'll tell you later," said Jack as he saw that Lansky had spotted him and was coming toward them.

Meyer Lansky crossed the room quickly, his smile spreading as he came. He was not alone but was followed by another man, taller than he was. Jack knew who the other man was; but, before he could tell the two women, the men were at the table.

"Mr. Endicott! It's nice to see you! And your lovely daughter. It's nice to see you, Miss Endicott."

Jack reached up to shake Lansky's hand. "Let me introduce Mrs. Charlotte Wendell," he said.

"Honored, Mrs. Wendell," said Lansky. "And let me present my business associate Charles Luciano. I understand you and Lucky have met, Mr. Endicott."

Jack shook hands with Luciano. "Absolutely," he said. "It's good to see you again, Charlie."

Lucky Luciano was a young Sicilian with a swarthy complexion and wavy black hair. His right eyelid drooped, probably because a knife cut that had left a thin scar had severed a nerve, giving him a menacing expression.

"Glad to see you, too, Jack," said Luciano. He nodded at the two women but did not extend his hand toward them. "Nice to see you, too, ladies."

"I wasn't aware you were a friend of Lucky's until just now when we walked in here," said Lansky. "When I said I was coming over to say hello to you, he said he would, too."

"Charlie was a big help to me a month or so ago, in a matter I think we had better keep confidential," said Jack.

"Odd, isn't it," said Lansky, "how friends sort of— What

would you call it? Form networks? Interlacing networks. You can never guess who are the friends of your friends."

Jack smiled at Luciano. He wasn't sure just how seriously to take Meyer Lansky and was looking for a signal. He didn't get one.

"You remember," said Lansky, "you are invited out to the Piping Rock. Any night, Mr. Endicott. Any night."

"I'll be there," said Jack. "Probably tomorrow night."

Two uniformed parking attendants competed for the privilege of driving the Bugatti from the door of the Piping Rock to a place in the parking lot. The doorman, somehow, knew Jack Endicott had arrived and welcomed him by name.

The Piping Rock Casino was not a single building but a complex of low buildings laid out in a Spanish or Moorish style. Hidden from the road by a grove of trees and from the lake by another, it featured peach-colored stucco, orange tile roofs, rooftop shrubs, balconies, windows covered with wrought-iron grillwork, the whole lighted in the evening by dim floodlights casting a gentle yellowish glow.

Most of the parking was behind the buildings, but the biggest Packards and the Rolls-Royces were parked in front—as was Jack's Bugatti. Guests arriving at the Piping Rock were to understand from their first glimpse that this *was* someplace; it was not no place.

Marietta and Charlotte were back at the hotel, annoyed. Jack had emphatically refused to take them to Piping Rock this evening, saying he might take them another evening, after he had checked the place out. He had gone back to the suite after dinner, changed into black tie, and driven out so as to arrive at the casino a little before eleven.

He had no stick to check, no hat; but even his momentary stop in the reception area was enough for Meyer Lansky, who emerged through a door and strode toward him, smiling and extending his hand.

"No ladies?"

"Not tonight. Another evening maybe."

Lansky nodded and smiled knowingly. "Another evening, dinner," he said. "We do it well here. If you like to gamble, we can do that. But I wonder if you wouldn't like to see the show."

"Show?"

"Well . . . We have a show for the gentlemen, the gentlemen who don't bring their ladies—if you understand me."

"Mr. Lansky, I never turn down an opportunity to see a show that is for the gentlemen and not the ladies."

Meyer Lansky gestured toward a solid oak door studded with imitation hammered-iron nails. "Mr. Endicott. I will call you Mr. Endicott, but I would appreciate it if you would call me Meyer."

"No deal. Only if you call me Jack."

The showroom was at the top of a flight of stairs and down a corridor Jack guessed led toward the rear of the building. It was not a large room: seating maybe fifty at a dozen tables. Jimmy Walker and Al Smith were at one of the tables, but neither of them elected to greet Jack Endicott.

"That's the kind of lowlife I have to put up with in New York," Lansky muttered under his breath.

Jack laughed. "Meyer," he said, "I think you and I could become friends."

"Maybe not, exactly," said Lansky. "But Charlie Luck told me you were a man I could trust."

"Did he tell you how he and I became acquainted?"

Lansky looked up at the waiter who had come to their table, then to Jack. "Your pleasure?" he asked.

"Well . . . I've had dinner—"

"Let me order for a man who's had dinner," said Lansky.

"I place myself in your hands, Meyer."

"Stolichnaya," Lansky said to the waiter. "Very cold. You know how. With plenty of ice to keep it cold. Tin of caviar. Biscuits. Smoked salmon. Capers. The works."

"I believe I'm about to add something to my education," said Jack.

"I was born in a town called Grodno," said Lansky. "You've never heard of it. You shouldn't. A Russian town. Worse, a Jewish town. I was named Mei'er. It means 'the bringer of light.' The family name was Suchowljansky. The Russians made it difficult for us. My grandparents left for Jerusalem. They died there, both of them, within a month after they arrived. My father decided to try America instead. I was ten when I arrived here. I spoke Yiddish. Russian vodka? My friend, I never tasted it in Russia. But it is good. I assure you about that."

"You speak English with no accent," said Jack.

Lansky lit a cigarette. "That is no problem," he said. "You can get rid of an accent if you want to get rid of it."

Jack followed suit. "I guess Charlie told you about how he helped me with the problem I had."

Lansky nodded. "I knew nothing of that when I came to you at the bank in Boston," he said. "And you know nothing of me, I guess. But I'm going to tell you what you did, Jack. You befriended a Russian Jew from New York and helped him get a place to live near the hospital where his son is being treated. In fact, I think you did more than that. I have an idea you called Dr. Carruthers and told him to take my son for a patient—"

"Meyer—"

"I've been successful in business, Jack," Lansky pressed on. "I can buy most of what I want. But I couldn't buy your friendship. You *gave* it to me. You know, when it comes down to it, what you can buy is not nearly as important as what you can't buy."

In the anticipation of encountering Meyer Lansky at Saratoga Springs, Jack had made inquiries about him. He knew what business the man was talking about when he said he'd been successful. He was a professional gambler. Very likely, too, he was a partner in a major distillery, making tens of thousands of gallons of illegal alcohol. Jack had not been surprised when Lansky appeared in the dining room with Lucky Luciano, nor when he introduced Luciano as a "business associate."

Lansky seemed dead serious about what he'd just said about friendship, so Jack nodded and said, "That's true."

"Charlie Luck told me over dinner last night something about how it is between you and Governor Roosevelt. I guess he did the Governor a favor, indirectly."

"He did. The Governor knows about it, too."

Lansky frowned in thought and pursed his lips. "Maybe *I* can do something for Governor Roosevelt," he said.

"You understand I'm not a part of the presidential campaign," said Jack. "I'm a Republican."

"I understand. I'm not talking about a contribution. I'll make that, but I'm talking about something else. We—"

He stopped abruptly because a man had walked up behind him and given him a friendly but firm pat on the shoulder.

"Can I join you, gentlemen?" the man asked.

"Uh . . . sure, Frank. Sit down," said Lansky. "Jack, this is one of my partners in Piping Rock. Frank Costello. Frank, say hello to Mr. Jack Endicott. Jack's a friend of mine from Boston."

Frank Costello was a handsome young man, well built, with dark hair neatly slicked back. As he shook Jack's hand, he said, "We've met. Remember? The Metropolitan Hotel in Brooklyn."

"I remember," said Jack.

Costello grinned at Meyer Lansky. "You may think your friend here is just a Boston banker. That's what Fine Louie thought when he took the contract to kill him. You still carry the biscuit?" he asked Jack.

By "biscuit" Costello meant a pistol, and Jack shook his head.

"Louie Feinman?" asked Lansky. "You're telling me *Jack* killed Fine Louie?"

Costello nodded. "The Dutchman sent Fine Louie to drop Jack. It didn't work out that way. Jack dropped Fine Louie. Charlie sent Polly to get Jack out of there before the cops came."

"Charlie promises that we can trust Jack," said Lansky.

Frank Costello put his hand on Jack's arm. He was a man who liked to touch his friends. "Come to *my* club sometime," he said.

"Do you know which club is Frank's?" Lansky asked Jack. "The Copacabana. Look at the silverware. Frank brings Copacabana silverware up here every summer."

"I learn something new every day," said Jack.

"You'd make a great rabbi," said Lansky. "Do you plan

to gamble while you're here?" he asked. "I hear you play a mean game of blackjack."

"While I'm in town," Jack said.

"Piping Rock is honest," said Lansky. "If you want to gamble—"

"I understand."

"Stick to blackjack," said Lansky. "It's the only game where you have any chance at all. We don't cheat at Piping Rock. I absolutely insist on that. We don't cheat. If the word gets around that your games are not honest, you are out of business. A lot of greedy men have gone out of business in Saratoga over the years."

Jack smiled. "The house doesn't have to cheat to win," he said.

"You understand it," said Lansky. "An absolutely honest roulette wheel collects two-point-seven percent of what's bet every night, no matter what. There's no getting around that. How people bet makes no difference. That's the way the odds are set. Twiddling the wheel is stupid, when you're going to collect two-point-seven on every night's play. Crap table? Depends on how smart the player is, but the smartest player will drop a percent and a half in the long run. A stupid crapshooter? My God! Horses? You might as well light cigars with your money. No book ever closes a single day in the red. No book."

"But blackjack?"

"Put aside the card counters," said Lansky. "We've pretty much put them out of it by playing with two or three decks. A smart, honest player . . . He can play something very close to even odds. Not quite, but close. A really smart player, playing a long time, will come out about even. Some nights he'll win, some he'll lose, and in the end it comes out about even. We don't make much on it. What we do make, we make on the dummies who get their emotions into it. You know why we keep blackjack tables going? Because the smart players who play blackjack and tell about their winnings over the dining tables at the Grand Hotel bring us the suckers who'll play the games that don't need brains—and lose."

"Besides," said Jack, "blackjack is *fun*. Win a little, lose a little, you had a good time."

Lansky nodded. "Gambling wrenches a man's guts out, Jack. Stick with your blackjack and have fun."

"Whatever you do, don't bet on the horses," said Frank Costello.

The super-chilled vodka, the caviar, and the rest of what Lansky had ordered were brought to the table. Jack's education was indeed augmented. The vodka was so cold that it had thickened, and it could be drunk only in tiny sips. It was the perfect accompaniment to the caviar. White wine was bland compared to half-frozen Stolichnaya.

The band—two cornets, one trombone, two clarinets, three saxophones, a piano, and drums—shrilled a fanfare, and a show began. To Jack's surprise, the first performer was Rudy Vallee, who trotted on the small stage of the stag bar and introduced himself with his signature line: "Heigh-ho, everybody! Heigh-ho!" He was performing in the main dining room of the casino and three times each evening took off ten minutes to appear in the stag bar. He sang "Good Night, Sweetheart," and "The Whiffenpoof Song," then paused at the edge of the spotlight's circle to welcome the next performer.

She was Nellie Nelson, onetime featured singer of the *Ziegfeld Follies*, now a little older, a little slower, and visibly ravaged by something, probably liquor and cigarettes—a thirty-five-year-old woman past her prime. On the stage of the stag bar at Piping Rock, Nellie Nelson appeared in the cold, hard glare of a limelight, dressed as she had once appeared on the stage of the *Follies*—but somehow very different—with her generous white, pink-nippled breasts bare. She sang songs from the *Follies,* and soon she was joined on the little stage by four stark-naked chorus girls who danced and postured around her.

Fortunately, the audience liked her. If her performance was demeaning to her, at least she had the compensation of knowing she was remembered and appreciated. Jack, who had seen her several times on the New York stage, did her the courtesy of keeping his eyes on her throughout her performance and not turning to Lansky or Costello when they tried to capture his attention. He applauded her, not with excessive enthusiasm but with respect, and she noticed.

When she left the stage, Costello touched his arm. "We can set up a room for you," he said. "Champagne and Nellie."

"Thanks, I brought my own," said Jack.

"Not exactly," said Lansky. "He brought a fine lady."

"Thanks, Meyer," Jack said. "The little joke was inappropriate."

Nellie Nelson came to their table for a moment, not having received a signal not to. She was dressed as she had been on stage. She was a strawberry blonde, with faint freckles on her cheeks and on her breasts. Lansky poured vodka for her, and Jack spooned caviar onto her plate. He lit her cigarette.

"This is high livin'," she said as she spread a cracker with caviar. Jack had not realized she had a southern accent, which did not sound in her singing voice. "Girl grew up on fatback and collard greens—"

"Nellie has many personas," said Meyer Lansky. "I know for a fact she has never been south of Fulton Street."

"Have so," said Nellie. "Where you think Bensonhurst is? Dumb Heeb."

"I saw you in the *Follies*," said Jack.

Nellie lifted her tiny glass of vodka. "There's a gentleman," she said. The southern accent was gone. "Boston, I bet. You people talk funny."

"We spend our whole lives tuning our accents," said Jack. "Your typical native Bostonian takes his 'dag for a ray-ad in the kay-ah'—meaning he takes his dog for a ride in the car. Then he goes to Harvard and learns to speak of the 'Haa-vad yaad'—which is an arrogant affectation for 'Harvard campus.' " He shrugged. "Talk funny, Nellie. Join the crowd."

"Given a night with you, I bet I could learn to talk Harvard," said Nellie.

"Unfortunately, that will not be tonight, Nellie," said Lansky.

"Aww . . . Well—"

Seeing her begin to push back her chair, Jack spooned more caviar onto her plate. "We enjoy your company," he said.

Maybe he shouldn't have said it. Being treated civilly, she was immediately self-conscious about her naked breasts. She tied her napkin around her throat, then looked at it and decided that was ridiculous, and tore it off and returned it to her lap. "Y' never quite get used to it," she murmured to Jack.

He nodded sympathetically.

"Hey, Jack," said Costello. "Here's another friend you oughta meet. Benny Siegel. Hey . . . He's got a nickname. 'Bugsy.' Don't ever use it. The guy goes wild when he hears that name."

Benjamin Siegel was an exceptionally handsome, square-jawed young man.

"We've been friends since we were kids," said Lansky.

Siegel sat down beside Nellie Nelson and cupped her left breast in his hand. "Introduce me," he said to Lansky.

Lansky paused for a moment, fastening a cold eye on the bigger, younger man. Siegel released Nellie's breast and shrugged.

"Benny, this is Mr. Jack Endicott. He's a friend of Charlie's and a friend of mine. He's also the man who dropped Fine Louie."

Siegel started visibly. "I thought . . . Charlie . . ."

Costello shook his head. "Jack."

Benjamin Siegel nodded and visibly amended his judgment of the proper Bostonian. "Pleasure," he said. Only then did he reach to shake Jack's hand. "Don't often meet a guy like you."

It was interesting to Jack to see how Meyer Lansky could dismiss two men like Frank Costello and Benny Siegel. He was smaller than either one of them, quieter, better spoken, better mannered, and he had the aspect more of a small-time accountant than of a powerful man in the rackets. Yet, when he suggested that he would like to speak alone with Jack Endicott, the others left the table, and neither seemed to take offense.

"I said I'd like to do a favor for Governor Roosevelt," said Lansky when he and Jack were alone. "Let me say something, in case it's not clear. Men like Charlie Lucky and myself, Frank Costello and Bennie Siegel, make our living outside the law. I don't have to tell you that. We serve you drinks here. That's against the law. We offer gambling here. That's against the law. If you'd like an hour, or a night, with a charming young girl, we can provide that, and it's against the law. Men on your side of the law—and after what Frank tells me about Fine Louie, I'm not one-hundred-percent sure which side that is—buy the commodities and services we well. That's our business. We provide what people want."

"A rationalization, Meyer," said Jack.

Lansky shrugged. "Who's the criminal?" he asked. "The man who sells the bottle of gin, or the man who drinks it? The man who puts down a bet, or the man behind the table who takes it? The man who gives a girl money to have sex with him, or the girl who takes the money and does it?"

"There *is* a difference, Meyer," said Jack.

"There is," Lansky agreed. "And you know the difference. Evil men have dominated our line of business for a long time. Violent men. That's coming to an end. I swear to you, Jack: I have never killed anyone, or authorized anyone to do it, or condoned it."

"I've heard this before," said Jack.

"And you don't believe it," said Lansky. "Let us make our record. Give us a chance."

"You don't owe me a record," said Jack. "I'm drinking your vodka, eating your caviar . . ."

"I said I could do something for Governor Roosevelt," said Lansky. He waved off a waiter who had come to offer something, more likely a word than service. "I'm going to give you some information. I can't vouch for it. But, knowing what I do about the origin of this information, I suggest you take it seriously, Jack."

Jack raised his glass and took a small sip of the still-supercold vodka. "Meyer," he said. "The last thing I would do is take you less than seriously."

Lansky nodded soberly. "Men like Dutch Schultz," he said, "aren't the only ones in this country who are worried about the possible—shall we say probable?—election of Governor Roosevelt as President of the United States. For many men, a lot is at stake in the preservation of what we may call the status quo. Some of them liked the idea of the nomination of Speaker Garner. An old-line southern Democrat. Business as usual. Nothing changed but the names. Al Smith . . . Well, I hardly need tell you. Al plays ball. But Roosevelt . . . They're not sure. Some of them are very upset."

"Can you be specific?"

"Yes. Specific. Do you know how they run things in Los Angeles? I mean in Hollywood? Pictures are made by slave labor, Jack. What goes on behind the cameras is anything but glamorous. Anything but."

"I know about the contracts," said Jack. "I mean the star contracts, that make the stars property to be traded like slaves."

"Not the half of it," said Meyer. "My friend Siegel has been going out there. He thinks there is money to be made in Hollywood. He comes back with stories of corrupt labor unions. You know, it takes thousands of people, tens of thousands of people, to make pictures. It takes carpenters, painters, electricians . . . Putting aside the special skills, the set designers, the makeup artists, the cameramen, and all that . . . putting them aside, you still need a lot of ordinary people that pound nails, slap on paint, twist wires, push dollies, carry loads . . . Those people want decent wages, insurance against injuries, provision for retirement, and all that. So they have unions. They have labor unions, it says here in small print. But they don't have unions, really, because their unions are the creatures of the producers. The phrase is a cliché, but there's an unholy alliance between the producers and the heads of the so-called unions. It's wildly profitable for both sides. The producers get cheap labor. The union leaders get big payoffs."

"Governor Roosevelt means to look into things like that," said Jack.

"That's exactly the point," said Lansky. "He's got a reputation for being too close to men like Senator Robert Wagner and Congressman Fiorello La Guardia. The Governor has dropped around some words about a 'labor bill of rights'—maybe called a 'national labor relations act.' That's got some men in California very upset. Benny Siegel came back with the story that the Californians don't mean to let it happen."

"Meaning—?"

"I don't know how far they're willing to go. One thing was mentioned. The Governor has a son in California."

"What would they do to his son?"

"Jack . . . I don't know. I'm reporting rumors. The story is, they don't mean to let Governor Roosevelt break up their sweetheart deals, no matter what they have to do."

III
—

Charlotte was asleep when Jack returned to their room at the Grand Union. She wore a black silk nightgown redolent with perfume that filled the air, since she slept in the warm night with no sheet or cover over her. She had smoked a cigarette not long before. Its odor, too, was on the air.

Jack looked around for the butt. People had died from smoking in bed. Charlotte was no fool, though. He found the butt, still hot and issuing a tiny stream of smoke, well crushed in an ashtray.

"Your gangsters show you a good time?" she asked abruptly.

"I thought you were asleep."

"Who could sleep with you prowling around the room? How much have you had to drink?"

"Too much, but I can still prowl around quietly. You weren't asleep."

"So—? I was asleep. I wasn't asleep."

He sat down on the bed beside her. "It was an interesting evening," he said.

"You had a telephone call a couple of hours ago. It was Governor Roosevelt, calling from Albany. He wants you to call him, but not tonight."

Jack glanced toward the door. "Is Marietta in her room?" he asked.

Charlotte nodded. "I gather she had a dull evening."

Jack began to undress. Charlotte left the bed and came behind him to help him loosen his black tie. "Good," he said in response to her comment that Marietta had had a dull evening. "The girl has too much fun. If I'd taken her to Piping Rock tonight, either she'd have lost a thousand dollars at the tables or she'd have won a thousand, which would have been a favor to me for which I'd have been obligated."

"She plays a wicked game of blackjack," said Charlotte. "She cleaned Freddie and his mother and me out of about thirty dollars apiece."

"Serves you right for playing blackjack with her," said Jack. "She learned the game from me. She can beat you without cheating—and given the chance she'll do that, too."

"She'd have beaten the house," she said.

"Not so easy," said Jack. "In a friendly game the deal passes. The dealer always has a little advantage, especially if he plays by the house rules and always takes his hit on seventeen and never on eighteen. In a house game, the deal and the advantage stays with the house dealer. You can win if you're damned good and have a little luck. Let me guess. You played with one deck."

"What else?"

"Marietta counted the cards. She knew what had been

played and what was left in the deck. You didn't stand a chance."

"Is that cheating?"

"No. You could have done the same thing, if you'd concentrated enough. I'm going to have to speak with my daughter. She'll get her legs broken if she's not careful."

Jack opened a bureau drawer to take out his white cotton pajamas, but Charlotte stepped behind him and gently pushed his arm back, to drop the pajamas again into the drawer. "Too hot," she whispered as she pulled her nightgown over her head.

He stretched out on the bed beside her. It *was* hot. She switched off the light.

"If you go to Albany, will you take me with you?" she asked, quietly speaking toward the ceiling. "I'd like to meet your friend the Governor."

"Why not?" said Jack. "I can drive down there in an hour or so."

"I have friends who'll think I've lost my mind, wanting to meet the Democratic candidate."

"They won't know," said Jack.

"Oh?"

"No." He rose on one elbow. "You and I have become . . . more than friends in the past month or so. If you are going to meet Frank Roosevelt and hear what he and I talk about, you have to keep every word confidential. I'll have to assure him that he can trust you, and that means trusting you to be one hundred percent circumspect. You can't even tell anyone you met him, much less anything we said. I don't know why he wants to see me, but I imagine whatever it is will be a confidential matter."

Charlotte reached up and caressed Jack's neck and shoulder. "Do *you* trust me?" she asked. "I mean . . . are you sure about me, that much?"

"Yes."

"I respect your trust, Jack. I'm grateful for it."

Franklin D. Roosevelt laughed. "Confidential, indeed! There *are* reporters lurking about, you know. You hardly come incognito when you arrive in a royal-blue Bugatti!"

They sat down in wicker chairs on the shady veranda where the Governor sat in his wood-and-steel wheelchair and had been working when they arrived. He was wearing a rumpled cream-white double-breasted suit and a white shirt visibly wilted from the heat and humidity.

Missy LeHand was there. She had been taking shorthand on a pad, had risen as the guests came out, and now stood leaning against the porch rail. Her violet-colored cotton dress was wilted, too.

"Frank," said Jack, "I want you to understand I trust Charlotte completely, and you can, too."

"Well, it's a pleasure to meet you, Mrs. Wendell," said Governor Roosevelt. "And if Jack takes you into his confidence, I shall, too."

"Please, Governor. Call me Charlotte."

"On the condition that you call me Frank," said the Governor grinning broadly. Then he did something characteristic of him: He tucked a Camel into a black cigarette holder and lit a smoke. "I must warn you that I've asked Jack here to discuss something unpleasant. You may not want to hear it."

"I, uh . . . am not afraid, Governor."

"All right then. But remember, I'll call you Mrs. Wendell if you won't call me Frank."

Charlotte smiled. "Frank . . ."

The Governor carried a small watch in his breast pocket. It was attached to a short chain that ran from the buttonhole on his lapel. He pulled it out and checked the time. "Well, it's a little early in the day for it, but what would you say to something tall, cold, and refreshing?"

"Porquoi non?" said Jack. Why not?

Missy took the cue and went in the house.

"General MacArthur is at Saratoga Springs," said Jack. "Quite the man of the hour. He's even had the audacity to bring the little Filipino girl with him and show her off in public."

"Pinky will slap his hand," said Governor Roosevelt.

"Excuse me," said Charlotte. "Who's Pinky?"

"The general's mother," said the Governor. "She lives in his official quarters in Washington. I'm surprised he came to Saratoga Springs without her."

Jack grinned and said to Charlotte, "She went to West Point with him, you know. She lived the entire four years in the old Craney's Hotel, right at the end of the campus. He's never gone anywhere without her—geographically or careerwise."

"Speaking confidentially," said Governor Roosevelt, "Herbert Hoover and Doug MacArthur have done me a big favor. They could have left the Bonus Marchers encamped in Washington. They weren't hurting anything, really. But I was being pressured to make a statement, that the bonus should be paid or not be paid. That put me between a rock and a hard place. If I'd said yes, the bonus should be paid now instead of when it comes due, I'd have been accused of fiscal irresponsibility, because the government doesn't have the money. I'd also have been accused of caving in to the demands of . . . well, of rioters, in effect. And if I'd said no, I'd have been accused of insensitivity to the plight of needy veterans. So Hoover sent the army to drive the Bonus Marchers out of Washington, and MacArthur carried out his orders with a cool efficiency that shocked the nation. In the hullabaloo, the idea that I should take a position was entirely forgotten."

"God looks out for little children, drunk men, and the United States of America," said Jack.

"In which of these categories do you put me?" asked the grinning Governor.

"All three," Jack laughed.

Missy returned and was followed shortly by a butler carrying a tray on which stood four tall, sweating glasses—Gin and tonic, with slices of lime.

"Well," said the Governor, raising his glass. "To us and ours."

He had decided, obviously, not to raise his unpleasant subject until they had enjoyed their drinks.

"Will you be campaigning across the country, Frank?" Charlotte asked.

The Governor nodded. "By train. All across the country. Jack Garner tells me that all I have to do to be elected is stay alive. He's not the only one advising me to run a front-porch campaign. But I won't do that. I don't want the American people getting the idea that I *can't* campaign."

"No one—"

"*Franklin*. Oh, hello, Jack. I didn't know you were here. It's pleasant to see you."

"It's pleasant to see you, Eleanor. Let me introduce Charlotte Wendell."

Mrs. Roosevelt nodded at Charlotte. "How nice to meet you," she said.

The First Lady of the State of New York wore a long, slender beige dress, decorated with a double column of black buttons that began at the neckline and ended at the hemline, halfway between her knees and ankles. She also wore a black straw hat with a veil that hung over her forehead, not below her eyebrows, plus flat black shoes. The woman had utterly no sense of style, Charlotte immediately concluded. The outfit could not have been more ill-chosen if a political enemy had meant to make a grotesquery of her.

"Would you like a glass of lemonade, Babs?" asked the Governor.

Mrs. Roosevelt looked at their glasses and raised her eyebrows. "Limeade," she said. "Thank you, no. I'm on my way to a tea being given by the ladies of the Westchester County Democratic Club. They are asking for a statement from you. They want to know if you mean to balance the federal budget."

"My position hasn't changed," said Governor Roosevelt. "Deficit spending would destroy this nation's economy. Permanently. We can't borrow ourselves out of this Depression."

"Then I will quote you as so saying."

The Governor nodded.

"It is nice to have met you, Mrs. Wendell, and nice to have seen you again, Jack. I have other meetings later and probably will not be back in time to say good night."

"Don't get me in trouble, old girl," said the Governor.

Mrs. Roosevelt's chin jerked up. "Have I ever?" she asked.

"Figure of speech, Babs."

"Oh . . . Yes, of course. Well, I must be going."

Governor Roosevelt watched her stride through the French doors into the house, and all of them heard her heels on the floors inside as she hurried to her car and her appointments.

The Governor sighed. "The curtain of confidentiality now comes down," he said.

The others nodded. Missy went so far as to step inside the double doors to be sure no servants, or even a reporter, were lurking. Coming back outside, she closed the doors.

"I had a telephone call yesterday from my son Elliott, in California," said Governor Roosevelt. "He is deeply troubled. An accusation is being made that he is the father of a child being carried by a girl in Los Angeles."

The Governor paused, and Missy spoke. "Which is only half of it," she said.

The Governor nodded. "Yes. The other half is that the girl is only sixteen years old. It has been suggested to him that he may be charged with statutory rape."

"B'god!" said Jack.

"Elliott is a headstrong young man," said the Governor. "You know he refused to go to college. *Refused*. He is capable of mistakes. He has made some, and he'll make more. But he assures me, on his word, that he never met this little girl, much less engaged in intimacy with her; and I believe him."

"Let me guess," said Jack. "You've not told this story to Eleanor."

The Governor shook his head.

"Who has contacted Elliott?" Jack asked. "And saying what?"

"He's received two telephone calls," said the Governor. "The first was from the girl's mother. The second was from the girl herself."

"They haven't gone to the authorities?"

"No. Or apparently they haven't."

"In other words, they want . . . What? Money? Have they mentioned money?"

"Elliott says no."

"Then they want to damage your candidacy," said Jack. "It's an odd coincidence, but I was warned about this. Not about this specifically but about an attempt to get at you through Elliott. Frank . . . We've made some strange friends. The same people— The same *kind* of people who helped me with the Dutch Schultz business brought me the warning."

"Who wants to damage him?" asked Missy.

"People who are making a lot of money off the status quo," said Jack. "Prohibition. Who has it benefited but bootleggers? They don't want it repealed, and we saw what some of them are willing to do to prevent it. In California some of the big producers are making fortunes with sweet-heart contracts between the studios and the labor unions. They see you as too cozy with men like Norris and La Guardia. They don't want another Norris-La Guardia Act. Frank, when you said something about a 'bill of rights for labor,' you raised some hackles. From Dearborn, Michigan, to Los Angeles, California. Wounded in the pocketbook, some people can get pretty vicious."

"Jack . . ."

"The answer is yes. I'll be in Los Angeles in a few days."

"I hate to ask you," said the Governor. "You've done

enough for me, risked enough. But . . . who else can I trust so completely."

"Trust me, too, Frank," said Charlotte.

The Governor looked quizzically at Charlotte.

"I'm going to California with him," she said. "He didn't know it until this moment, but he can't talk me out of it."

"People used guns the last time around," said Governor Roosevelt. "Worse than that. They dynamited a yacht and killed all the people on board."

"Frank . . . Since my husband died, my life hasn't had much meaning. Is that a cliché? The trouble with clichés is, they express the truth. Anyway . . . Well, I should amend the statement. It didn't have much meaning until Blackjack Endicott picked up the pieces of Charlotte Lanier Wendell and started sticking them back together. And there's something more to having your pieces put back together than just . . ." She hesitated and blushed. "There's something more to life than sitting around playing cards."

"We'll discuss it later," said Jack firmly.

The Governor smiled. "I'm not sure you've got anything to discuss," he said. "Charlotte seems to have a firm personality."

"A woman can be a big help to you in dealing with a situation like this," said Missy.

"Think of this, too," said Charlotte. "If *I'm* going to California with you, it may help you prevent Marietta from coming."

Jack glanced into the faces of all three. "You seem to be coming at me from all sides," he said.

* * *

The main room at Piping Rock suggested only a posh night-club. Only the knowledgeable guests realized that casino gambling and high-price prostitution flourished in other parts of the sprawling Moorish complex.

Jack and Charlotte arrived for dinner. Dinner was simpler at Piping Rock than in the hotel, but the simple food was excellent: roast beef, steaks, chops, lobster, shrimp, all expertly prepared and served—with of course a choice of wines. Since many of the guests would leave large amounts of money at the gambling tables later, the menu prices were low.

"I sometimes wonder," said Charlotte as she sipped vintage Bordeaux, "who is really inconvenienced by Prohibition. I can't remember ever wanting some wine or a cocktail and not being able to get it."

"It's enforced in the Bible Belt," said Jack. "And in the hookworm belt. Where it's God's will, b'god."

"Well, I thank God I've never been either place."

"A couple of Prohibition agents tried to seize my yacht a few weeks ago, contending I was using it to smuggle in liquor."

"What'd you do?"

"I threw the more obnoxious of the two off the gangplank and into the drink. Twenty members of the Yarmouth Yacht Club were prepared to testify I did it only in self-defense, having been assaulted."

Charlotte laughed. "You know, I could fall in love with you."

Jack stared at her, eyes wide. "I thought you had," he said blandly.

"You egomaniacal bastard!"

A red velvet curtain swept back. Rudy Vallee strode onto

the stage, saxophone under his left arm, baton in his right hand, and raised the baton to cue his band. "Heigh-ho, everybody!" he cried. "Heigh-ho!"

The audience applauded enthusiastically, and the band swung into his theme music, "The Whiffenpoof Song."

Charlotte nudged Jack. "Who . . . ?" She nodded toward a big, brassy woman who had just entered the room. "A lot of people seem to know her."

"Her name is Texas Guinan," said Jack. "She runs a very big pub in New York."

"I noticed," said Charlotte, "that the silverware here is from another very big pub."

"In the racing season, *this* is a very big pub."

Rudy Vallee, with a fine sense of the public mood and the oncoming repeal of Prohibition, sang "There is a Tavern in the Town" and won raucous applause.

"Times change," Jack said to Charlotte. "I'm revealing how old I am, but I remember when that was called 'The Drunkard's Song' and was sung by drys to warn people of what terrible things resulted from drinking."

"It's evil to have fun," said Charlotte. "You're a Bostonian. You should know that."

"I'm a slow learner," said Jack.

The chorus dancers in the main room were not nude, as those in the stag bar were. But these, twelve of them, wore costumes that exposed their breasts. They were in fact a part of the chorus line from *Earl Carroll Vanities:* four blondes, seven brunettes, and a redhead, each a distinct personality, no way uniform. Their costumes varied, too, though all featured hip-high skirts, and all danced with furs around their shoulders. Ten of them wore hats. Their hairstyles varied widely, as did their makeup. On no signal, never simultaneously, they threw their furs back to reveal that they wore nothing else above the waist.

As the chorus line performed, Meyer Lansky slipped onto a chair at Jack's table. He said nothing as the performance continued, but a waiter brought another bottle of Bordeaux and four clean glasses.

"I hope you are enjoying," said Lansky when the curtain closed and the lights came on.

"Meyer, you are a perfectionist," said Jack.

"It's a great pleasure to see you again, Mrs. Wendell," said Lansky. "I've asked our next performer to share a glass of wine with us before she goes on stage."

It was quite obviously Meyer Lansky's wish to remain inconspicuous, even anonymous, at Piping Rock. When Frank Costello entered the room, a few people recognized him as the proprietor of the Copacabana and a notorious New York gangster. When Lucky Luciano walked in, a murmur went up across the room. Lansky was able to walk in unrecognized—though, as Jack understood, his interest in Piping Rock was as great as any other man's.

When Jack had made inquiries about Lansky, he had learned some other things about him—that he was regarded as a master of organization, for example, shielding himself from trouble with the law by creating several levels of business structure between himself and activities like gambling, liquor, and prostitution. He was said also to have a photographic memory, to keep his accounts in his head, making no paper records that could be seized. He was the quiet, shrewd, behind-the-scenes man. He was the businessman of the rackets.

"The problem you told me about, in California . . . It's come up," said Jack. "I'd like to talk to you about it."

"Certainly," said Lansky. He glanced at Charlotte and added, "A little later."

"We can talk in front of Charlotte. She's made herself a partner of mine."

Lansky nodded. "But we'll be interrupted. I invited a young lady to join us for a glass of wine."

The young woman appeared a minute later, and Lansky rose and introduced her as Marlene Dietrich.

"Es freut mich, Fräulein," said Jack. He kissed her hand.

"Meinerseits," said Dietrich casually.

Although she had appeared in several American films lately, Jack had seen Marlene Dietrich only as the sultry café singer in the German film *The Blue Angel*. That was her persona, which she had not yet escaped. There was no reason why she should. She was a huge success in the role she had chosen for herself.

"Are you going to sing for us, Miss Dietrich?" Charlotte asked.

"Yes. They pay me to do it, can you believe?" replied Dietrich. She retained a German accent but only a faint one, and she spoke in the low, velvety voice that was another of her characteristics.

Jack reached to light her cigarette, which gave him an opportunity to stare at her for a moment. Her hair was straw-yellow. Her eyebrows, plucked into two thin lines, were darkened with pencil. She wore kohl and mascara. Her mouth was small and sensitive. All of these things were secondary, though, to the exquisite beauty of her thin, bony face.

"Are you another of the partners here?" Dietrich asked Jack.

Meyer Lansky laughed. "Jack Endicott is a vice president and director of First Boston Provident Trust, a very large bank."

"Oh! A banker!" exclaimed Dietrich in mock innocence.

"Actually," said Jack, "I'm not very active in the business. I inherited from my father enough of the bank's stock that they have to give me a title. My uncle Henry, my father's brother, runs the bank, and I don't interfere."

"Jack is a yachtsman, a racing driver, a flier, a—"

"A playboy, then! How interesting!"

"He has a serious side, too," remarked Charlotte.

"A man of many parts," said Dietrich.

They drank a toast in champagne, and shortly Marlene Dietrich left the table. She went backstage and in three minutes reappeared, having changed that quickly into her costume. She wore a glittering silver top hat, a blue-and-white feather boa around her shoulders, and a short black dress, with a skirt cut so short that it barely covered her hips but displayed the famous Dietrich legs in dark stockings.

Another man directed the Rudy Vallee orchestra, and Dietrich was backed up also by a chorus of four young women in costumes similar to but briefer than her own.

The audience loved her. Jack wondered for a moment how the men who ran Piping Rock had persuaded her to appear on this stage. As if he read Jack's mind, Meyer Lansky answered: "We pay her a lot of money."

She concluded her performance with "Lili Marlene," a soldiers' ballad that had been the favorite of the German soldiers in the Great War, with a tune so haunting that Allied soldiers picked it up as well and asked that it be sung in their own languages. It would have the same impact in another war.

When she reached the final lines of each verse, many of the audience joined in singing. She received a standing ovation.

"Would you rather talk in the office?" Lansky asked after Marlene Dietrich had left the stage.

"Not unless someone more is about to join us."

"I have issued no more invitations."

"Charlotte and I met with Governor Roosevelt this afternoon," Jack said. "You told me the other night that some kind of effort against the Governor might be made through his son in California. It's true, apparently. His son Elliott has had calls alleging that a sixteen-year-old girl is pregnant by him. The Governor is certain that's not true. But—"

"I'm not surprised," said Lansky. "That's exactly the kind of tactic the people I told you about would try. And I warn you—it's just an opening gambit. Worse will follow."

"What you are saying is—" Charlotte ventured.

"Labor racketeering," said Lansky. "Using the unions. Uh—I do not represent myself as a square citizen." He glanced around the room, then settled his eyes on the bucket of champagne beside their table. "I supply you champagne. That makes me a criminal. You drink it. That makes you criminals. In another group of rooms, you can gamble. That makes me another kind of criminal. You gamble, and that makes you another kind of criminal. Forgive me if I rationalize. But I only offer you a product or service you want and that you can afford. A man who exploits labor unions takes bread and milk from the mouths of children. I don't like it. Anyway—"

"Anyway, there it is, huh?" said Jack. "They do it."

Lansky shrugged. "Dutch Schultz is a thug. He'll kill to keep his share of the business he's in. But what's his business? Supplying beer to people who want to drink beer. There's no union member who comes home with less in his pay envelope because he wants to drink beer. If you want beer, you may have to pay too much for beer that's not very good, because of Dutch Schultz; but if you have to be a member of a union to work in a certain trade, you wind up paying dues to sustain a union that sells you out to the bosses."

"And there is very big money in it," said Jack.

Lansky nodded. "Yeah. And what's more, the Coolidge and Hoover administrations have never cared. Exploit labor. Exploit their unions. Make big profits. After all, the business of the country is business, and what's good for General Motors is good for the country."

"Where do I start, Meyer?"

"Start to do what?"

"I'm going out to California—"

"So am I," Charlotte interrupted.

"—to look into this matter about Elliott Roosevelt and the girl. Where do I start?"

Meyer Lansky used his finger to draw a circle on the heavy linen tablecloth. "Well," he said, obviously hesitant, "I can make a phone call or two and get you in to see a man called Big Dick DiCalabria. His real name is Antonio DiCalabria; and, I'm sorry Mrs. Wendell, but the nickname refers to his male anatomy."

Charlotte shrugged. "I'll be surprised if it's true."

"Let's hope you have no occasion to find out," said Jack.

"DiCalabria is an important man in Los Angeles," said Lansky. "I'll phone him tomorrow."

IV

A wit had observed that a hog could cross the country without changing trains, but people couldn't. People could, though, cross the country in great comfort, even luxury.

Having left Saratoga Springs after only four days there, Jack and Charlotte boarded a train for New York on Monday. Marietta, protesting angrily, went out to Yarmouth and took up residence aboard the ketch that was named for her: *Marietta*. Jack and Charlotte took the Twentieth Century Limited to Chicago and there transferred to the California Zephyr, where they occupied a roomette listed in the names of Mr. & Mrs. John Lowell Endicott. The railroad would not rent a roomette on a train to a man-and-woman couple who were not husband and wife.

Calling once again on his good Republican friend Congressman Joseph Martin, Jr., of North Attleboro, Jack had secured an FBI report on Antonio "Big Dick" DiCalabria.

* * *

DICALABRIA, ANTONIO SALVATORE, AKA
BIG DICK, AKA MICHAEL SALZA. b. Montecor-
vino Rovella, Italy, 1895 (?), entered U.S., New York,
January 18, 1899, naturalized June 22, 1919 under
name Michael Salza. U.S. Army, June 25, 1917–February 3, 1919, as Michael Salza, awarded Distinguished Service Cross for gallantry in action.
Honorably discharged, corporal, infantry. m. (1)
Maria Pozzuoli, May 25, 1919 (2) Angela Block, Octo-
ber 3, 1924. Father of Antonio, b. August 8, 1919;
Maria, b. April 28, 1920; Vincenza, b. February 21,
1921; Michael, b. March 7, 1922; Floria, b. June 12,
1923.

—Arrested March 3, 1912, NYPD, assault. Served
30 days, House of Detention.

—Arrested May 11, 1912, assault with deadly
weapon. Served six months, House of Detention.

—Arrested January 30, 1913, assault. Charge
dropped, want of evidence.

—Arrested April 8, 1914, attempted murder. Sentenced two years, Sing Sing. Released December 1,
1916.

—Arrested July 4, 1920, U.S. Immigration, false
information on naturalization application—false
name, omission of criminal record. Held for deporta-
tion. Awarded adjusted naturalization on basis of war
record.

—Arrested December 11, 1920, violation of National Prohibition Act. Charge dismissed for want of
evidence.

—Arrested March 2, 1921, violation of National
Prohibition Act. Dismissed for want of evidence.

—Arrested May 3, 1922, assault on Prohibition
Agent. Sentenced 30 days, House of Detention.

—Arrested November 22, 1925, Los Angeles, California, violation of National Prohibition Act. Dismissed for want of evidence.

It was a very different record from the file on Meyer Lansky, which Jack had asked for at the same time. Lansky had been arrested twice in 1918 and once in 1928. In 1918, as a sixteen-year-old boy, he had been charged with felonious assault, which charge had been dropped. A few months later he was charged with annoying a woman and was fined two dollars. In 1928 he was again arrested on a charge of felonious assault, this time in an event involving shots fired from a moving car. That charge, too, had been dismissed.

Roomettes were cramped but luxurious. The railroads did not dare serve liquor, so passengers brought their own—in this instance, in a fine leather case packed with silver cups, bottles of whiskey and brandy, and four bottles of champagne. The railroad would gladly supply ice and mixers—the soda and ginger ale bottles bearing labels reminding passengers that it was unlawful to mix these beverages with any form of alcohol.

A roomette included comfortable seats during the day, folded down to make beds at night. Each roomette adjoined a tiny private bathroom. Large windows afforded a view of the country through which the train passed.

The California Zephyr's run from Chicago to Los Angeles was scheduled so that the train crossed the flat, dull plains at night, passed through spectacular mountain scenery during the day, then crossed the desert at night and ran through lush California valleys during the day. Passengers could not avoid being aware that the huge steam locomotives, careening through the night, pulling cars filled with elegance, even with grandeur, were the subject of wonder to hundreds of people sitting on porches or stopped at crossings, watching thoughtfully as trains like the Zephyr and the Super Chief roared past, carrying who-guessed-whom to who-knew-where: in any case, to a life that those watchers could hardly imagine.

Imagine— Actually they didn't have to rely on imagination. They could see that envied, glamorous life on the screen—or a version of it, whatever Hollywood chose to portray and sell as real.

Hollywood. Jack had telephoned ahead, and some people were expecting him: Louis B. Mayer, Samuel Goldwyn, Cecil B. DeMille, Adolph Zukor. And, of course, because of Meyer Lansky's call, he was expected by Big Dick DiCalabria.

Wires were delivered on the train:

EXPECT TO DINE WITH ME, TOUR
STUDIOS, AND SO FORTH STOP AS YOU MAY
WISH STOP
           C. B. DEMILLE

The trip was fast. Having left New York not long before noon on Monday, Jack and Charlotte arrived at the Los Angeles station an hour before noon on Thursday.

One's first impression stepping off the train and onto the platform in Los Angeles was similar to the impression one had landing on an airplane flight from Athens to Cairo: an onrush of humid heat, heavy with the sweet odors of tropical vegetation. It was at first overpowering, and one wondered if it would not become enervatingly oppressive. Los Angeles was not tropical, exactly, but it was to a man and woman from Boston. Jack had felt the same way getting off a train in Miami: seized by an impulse to get back aboard the train and retreat.

They stood for a moment on the platform, orienting themselves, conscious of the fact that their clothes were not suitable for the climate. Jack was wearing a gray double-breasted suit, with a gray homburg hat, and he carried a walking stick. Charlotte wore a pink silk dress, a conical pink hat with a bit of veil, and a white fur neckpiece. Fortunately they had lighter clothes in their trunks.

"Are you Mr. and Mrs. Endicott, by any chance?"

They turned to face a swarthy, compact man dressed in a black suit.

"Yes. Yes, I am John Lowell Endicott."

"My name is Ruggiero. I work for Mr. DiCalabria. Mr. DiCalabria sent his car to take you to your hotel. He'd like to see you on his beach this afternoon. I'll drive you there after you've checked in at the hotel. If you'll just come this way— If you'll give me your luggage tickets, I'll see to it that everything is delivered."

Mr. DiCalabria's car was a long, low-slung dark-blue Packard, driven by a uniformed chauffeur. Ruggiero sat in front with the chauffeur.

A small man in a dark suit and white hat went into a telephone booth. He dialed a number.

"Hey. Sonny. Okay, Roosevelt's man is here. He got off the train with a broad. But guess who met him. Ruggiero. Yeah. Right. Hell no, I'm not gonna follow 'em. Wha'd ya want me to do, try to tail Big Dick's car? A sure damned way to get killed. Well . . . What the hell else can I do? Yeah, I'm sure it was him. Big guy, with a little mustache. And get this—carryin' a walking stick. So . . . Roosevelt's trouble-shooter is in town. An' I mean shooter. Let's don't forget what happened to Fine Louie."

The big blue Packard delivered Jack and Charlotte to their hotel, the Ambassador, on Wilshire Boulevard. Their suite was not one of the rooms in the main building but was one of the garden apartments, on the ground floor of a two-story building, where their windows overlooked a lush, constantly watered lawn and, beyond some shrubbery, a big swimming pool. The suite was air-conditioned, and they felt comfortable for the first time since getting off the train. But they couldn't stay long there. Ruggiero was waiting to take them to DiCalabria's beach house. The invitation had the character of a summons.

Arriving at DiCalabria's beachfront house—a villa, actually—in Santa Monica, Jack and Charlotte were led immediately to a second-floor bedroom and invited to change into swimsuits. Mr. DiCalabria and his family were on the beach, the butler said. They should ring when they were ready to go down, and he would come and conduct them.

"I don't see where we have much choice in the matter," Jack said to Charlotte when the door was closed.

Swimsuits in assorted sizes, men's and women's, were on the bed. Many more were visible through the open double doors of a closet. The variations were of size, not style. Nearly all were the standard swimsuit that had been worn for several years now almost as a uniform on the beaches and around the pools—white wool vests and blue wool trunks with white web belts. The only difference between men's and women's suits was that the women's vests were more fully cut. Jack and Charlotte chose suits and beach coats.

On the beach, their host sat under a big yellow-and-white umbrella, smoking a cigar and reading a newspaper.

Big Dick DiCalabria was a trim man with the musculature of an athlete. Apart from a broken nose that had healed leaving the tip of his nose slightly off center, he was handsome. There was a certain voluptuous quality to his face, showing in seductive dark eyes, thick brows, and full lips.

It was impossible to ignore the source of his nickname. The bulge in the crotch of his trunks was enormous.

He flipped his cigar some distance away, into the sand, and rose to extend his hand. "Mr. Endicott," he said. "Mrs. Wendell. I'm pleased to meet you. Welcome to Los Angeles."

"Thank you for your hospitality," said Jack. "Sending your car to the station and—"

"My pleasure. And I figured the only way eastern people could endure their first afternoon in Southern California in August is to go in the ocean. You do swim? I'll join you."

As they walked toward the water's edge, a young blond woman stared at them apprehensively. DiCalabria gestured to her to come toward him, and she trotted up the beach. He introduced her as his wife, Angela. Swinging his arm toward the children scampering in the surf, he said they were his, from his first marriage.

He put an arm fondly around his wife's waist and led her into the water.

Knowing from the FBI sheet that the couple had been married for eight years, Jack guessed Angela had married Antonio DiCalabria when she was seventeen years old, maybe only sixteen. Her attraction was easy to see. She was beautiful in a bland, conventional style, as if she had gone to a cosmetician with a composite picture of half a dozen blond movie stars—say, Jean Harlow, Marion Davies, Joan Crawford, Constance Bennett, Joan Blondell, and Ginger Rogers—and said, Here, make me like that, sacrificing the individuality of each in pursuit of the style.

Jack was a strong swimmer and quickly swam beyond the breakers. Charlotte was bold but not confident of herself as a swimmer and stayed inside the breakers, bouncing up and down on them. So did the two DiCalabrias. The water was cold. It was refreshing.

Back at the umbrella table after a few minutes, DiCalabria suggested to his wife that he had business to discuss with these two people. She trotted back to the surf, to where the children were playing.

"Mr. Endicott—"

"Call me Jack. And this is Charlotte."

"Thank you both," said DiCalabria. "I have a nickname you've probably heard. It doesn't make me mad, the way Bugsy Siegel's nickname makes him mad, but—"

"I wondered about that," said Charlotte with mock innocence.

DiCalabria did not smile. Nor did he scowl. He only nodded and said, "I'd just as soon you call me Tony—and when you speak to other people about me, call me Tony."

"Tony. I know you had a telephone call from Meyer."

"Yes, I did. And any friend of Meyer Lansky is a friend of mine. I won't tell you I wasn't surprised when I heard that a Boston banker is a friend of his—though, to tell the truth, why should I be surprised? What did surprise me was to hear you are a friend of Charlie Lucky also. What is it that makes strange bedfellows? Must be something besides politics."

Jack saw that Tony DiCalabria would be a difficult man to judge. That he hadn't smiled at Charlotte's little joke apparently didn't mean he hadn't liked it. He was, quite simply, an obsessively poker-faced man.

DiCalabria went on. "Champagne? I'm having some. Won't you join me?"

Jack nodded. As the man talked, Jack was gathering impressions. He and Charlotte had observed as they were driven into the DiCalabria villa that it was not just a house—though house it hardly seemed to be, being larger than many hotels—but something of a fortress. A high stucco-covered brick wall faced the street, as did the broad doors of two garages at the north and south ends of the complex of buildings. The dark-blue Packard had swung up to one of those big garage doors, and two men had lifted it from inside. They had been driven in, and they had left the car under the cold and careful scrutiny of the two men. Leaving the garage, they had entered a large grassy court-yard with a fountain in the center, where three ominous-looking men in suits had been chipping golf balls on the lawn. The main house was on the beach side of the property.

Sitting here in the sand, ten yards from the house, Jack guessed that DiCalabria owned a hundred yards of beach-front. His boundaries were marked by men in shirtsleeves but wearing hats: obviously guards. DiCalabria lived within a zone of security.

An ice bucket with champagne was brought to the table. DiCalabria poured. *"Cin-cin!"* he said as he raised his glass.

"You have a beautiful home here, Tony," said Charlotte.

"It's comfortable," he said, and once again it was impossi-ble to tell how he meant the reply to be taken.

"Have you lived in California long?" she asked conversationally, though of course she knew he had not been arrested in New York since 1922 but had been arrested in Los Angeles in 1925.

"Almost ten years," said DiCalabria. "I moved out here right after my first wife died. Land of opportunity, y'know. California. The kids love it, too. I brought Angela out from New York. She'd been the kids' baby-sitter. Well . . . I've been out here long enough to know the ins and outs."

"Which brings us to the reason Charlotte and I came out here," said Jack. "I suppose Meyer explained a little about the problem."

"Yes. Your first problem is this charge that Elliott Roosevelt has got a little girl pregnant."

"Right. We're having dinner with Elliott tonight, to hear his side of the story."

"He won't have any side," said DiCalabria. "He'll be mystified about what's going on. I've met the boy. He's a nice fellow: handsome, nice personality. But— How'm I gonna say this? Elliott is a smart-enough boy. He's no dummy. But he's not . . . shrewd. Put it another way. He's too damn honest. Too trusting."

"Who's accusing him?" Jack asked. "Do you know the girl's name?"

"After I got the word from Meyer, I asked around. The girl is named Norma Jean Chandler. She's sixteen years old, and she's four months pregnant. She was a student at Pershing High School. They expelled her when they found out she's pregnant."

"Is there any reason to think Elliott Roosevelt has ever even met her?" asked Charlotte.

DiCalabria shrugged. "Who could tell? Where would he have met her? I don't know. But it's not impossible."

"Assuming Elliott didn't make her pregnant—which I think is a reasonable assumption—" said Jack, "then it seems unlikely the girl has invented this story. Who's behind her?"

"Start with her mother," said DiCalabria. "Her name is Edna Bascombe. She was divorced from Chandler, the girl's father, then married a man named Bascombe, who doesn't live with her anymore. Edna gets child-support payments from Chandler but otherwise supports herself and the kid as a waitress."

"The story has been kept private so far, as I understand," said Jack.

"Which puts the lie to it," said DiCalabria. "If this was an honest outraged mother, she'd have gone to the juvenile authorities."

"Maybe she's afraid to," said Charlotte. "After all, she's the mother of a sixteen-year-old daughter who is pregnant. There may be a question she doesn't want to have to answer."

"If Elliott is not the father, who is?" asked Jack.

"That's the question," said Charlotte. "That's what the juvenile authorities will demand to know."

"There's somethin' more behind this deal," said DiCalabria. "Suppose Edna's just a greedy woman who's got a pregnant daughter and is looking around for a sucker to take for some money. Why Elliott Roosevelt? There's a thousand guys in this town got more money than he has."

"It's political," said Jack grimly.

"Well . . . sort of," said DiCalabria. "Truth is, some guys don't want any interference with a sweet racket they've got goin'. A 'labor bill of rights'—a 'national labor relations act'—could hurt them bad. There'll never be anything like that out of the Republicans."

"Can you name names?" Jack asked.

"Some," said DiCalabria. "Let's start with the Brotherhood of Set Builders and Painters. When the movie moguls started moving out here, they set a pattern from the first of really abusing the people that worked for them. Hell, they abuse the stars. Imagine what they do to the guys tht build sets. Wages were bad. Hours were bad. But the worst part was that they made the men build flimsy sets, that could fall down. In 1923 they had a disaster. They built this big set, supposed to be a city in ancient Egypt, I think. Maybe Rome. It had big columns, big statues, all that kind of stuff—but of course it was all plaster on chicken wire, held up by rickety bracing behind. So. One day they had to stop shooting because a big temple or something had started to sway. The moguls ordered the carpenters to climb up fast and pound nails. Hurry, hurry! All the cast and extras and cameramen and everybody else were standing around waiting. Suddenly a gust of wind hit, and the whole set collapsed. Two of the carpenters were killed, half a dozen were badly injured, and even some of the extras and people standing around were hurt. Quick, quick! Build it over again. The picture is only half finished. The set builders and painters said no. They wouldn't build unless they could build sets strong enough not to be dangerous. The studio fired them all and tried to hire others. Only a few guys showed up. What's more, the ones who came didn't really know how to build sets. Meantime, the fired guys met and formed a union. They let the studio know they wouldn't come back and build the set unless they could build it their way. What's more, while they were on the subject, they wanted better pay and shorter hours."

"They got what they wanted, too," said Jack. "I remember reading about the whole business at the time."

"They got what they wanted," DiCalabria agreed. "And then they got what they didn't want. By 1927 or 1928 the union was controlled by guys who'd never pounded a nail or slapped on paint in their lives."

"How did they get control?" Charlotte asked.

"They *took* control. The guys I'm talkin' about have their ways. They broke some legs."

"So who are these guys?" asked Jack.

"The president of the Brotherhood is a guy named William Blake. He's a carpenter. He's a straight guy. He's a figurehead. The real head of the union is Carlo Marfeo. He's what's called a wiseguy. He's a member of another brotherhood, if you know what I mean."

"The Friends of Friends," said Jack.

"That's what it's called in Sicily. But you got the idea."

Jack finished his glass of champagne, and DiCalabria poured him another.

"Now," DiCalabria went on. "Some of the studios would rather not have to deal with a guy like Carlo Marfeo. But they have to compete with studios that do. So, the contracts between the major studios and the Brotherhood of Set Builders and Painters are what Marfeo says they're gonna be. And the Brotherhood is not the only union run that way."

"Does Marfeo break the legs of producers?" Jack asked.

"He hasn't had to. The first studio that made a deal with him is an outfit called Birdsong Productions. The head guy is Benjamin Vogel. Vogel means 'bird' in German, and ev-

erything he owns has *bird* in the name. He even looks for
ways to use *bird* in his movie titles. *The Bird Flies. Bluebird.
A Nest of Birds.* He's a little bit nutty, on that subject and
some others."

"*All* the studios have made these contracts?"

"I can't say that. I guess there are some exceptions. But
Lawrence Brothers is in. And some others. Biggies. It puts
pressure on everybody."

"How does this thing work?" Charlotte asked. "Where's
the money?"

"Suppose you're a studio that hires four hundred set
builders and painters," said DiCalabria. "Suppose you're
paying them an average of forty-five dollars a week. That's
one hundred and eighty dollars a month apiece, which is
seventy-two thousand dollars for the four hundred guys,
which is eight hundred and sixty-four thousand dollars a
year."

"And?"

"Suppose your union guys say they want seven-fifty a
week more. That's three thousand dollars a week more on
your weekly payroll, one hundred and fifty-six thousand on
your yearly payroll. You sit down with Marfeo, and he says,
'Give my guys two dollars more a week.' That costs you
forty-one thousand six hundred on your yearly payroll. And
give me fifteen thousand. Costs you fifty-six thousand six
hundred instead of one hundred and fifty-six thousand and
everybody's happy."

Jack watched DiCalabria doing what Meyer Lansky was
reputed to be able to do: make numerical calculations in his
head, without paper. It was what a professional gambler had
to be able to do, quick and creating no incriminating paper.

"Except the set builders and painters," said Jack.

"There'll be some malcontents," said DiCalabria. "He doesn't break legs much anymore. But he breaks noses."

"But he only gets fifteen thousand dollars a year out of the deal," Charlotte objected. "Doesn't seem like much."

"Oh, but that's not all he gets," said DiCalabria. "The original contract, with the eight-hundred-sixty-four-thousand-dollar payroll was a Marfeo deal, too. To hold it down to that level, and to moderate the members' demands about safer scaffolds and so on, he's probably collecting fifty thousand a year. Plus, remember, this is only one studio we're talking about."

"And a 'labor bill of rights' would drive him out of business," said Jack. "If union members could elect their officers in honest, secret elections—"

DiCalabria nodded. "It could run Marfeo out of business. Of course, Carlo Marfeo is not the only guy in this line. You've got lots of unions in the studios, for all the different kinds of workers. We're talking about millions being scraped off the tables of the people who make movies. And not just the movie unions, either. There are plenty of other unions run by wiseguys and legbreakers."

"Have you mentioned Marfeo because you think he's the one most likely to be behind Edna Bascombe?"

"I wouldn't assume, Jack, that the problem comes from the union side. One of the moguls could just as well be involved. They pay Marfeo because Marfeo saves them big money. They don't want a 'national labor relations act,' either."

"So Edna Bascombe could be—"

"Working with any one of a hundred guys. But your first big question, my friend, is different. Your first big question has got to be, Who got the little girl pregnant?"

*   *   *

"I swear to you, Jack, I've never seen or met that girl, much less ever touched her!"

Elliott Roosevelt was a husky, strong-faced young man, in many ways a typical Roosevelt, in others not so typical. Like his father and mother, he was taller than average. Because Governor Roosevelt sat most of the time in a wheelchair, few people realized he was well above six feet tall, as for that matter was Mrs. Roosevelt. The Roosevelt family were big people. In his face and in the unique Roosevelt voice, Elliott resembled his father. But he had declined—no, *refused*—to go to college. He enjoyed outdoor life, even physical labor, and adventure. Maybe he had inherited this from his maternal grandfather, for whom he was named. Or maybe not, since his father had enjoyed these things, too, until polio made them impossible.

Jack was not meeting Elliott for the first time. They had in fact been together a few days earlier this summer, before the Chicago convention, when Elliott had flown the Governor to Cape Cod from Albany in a private plane. Elliott was a skilled pilot. He had done at least his share of the work of sailing *Marietta* up the outer edge of the Cape, running ahead of a powerful storm, working to get the ketch around the tip of the Cape and into anchorage at Provincetown before the storm broke over them.

Charlotte was meeting him for the first time. She was pleased but unsubtly curious.

"Describe all the contacts you've had from these people," said Jack.

They were sitting over dinner in the dining room of the

Ambassador Hotel, at a candlelit table. Jack and Elliott wore black tie. Charlotte wore a wine-colored gown.

"I've had two telephone calls," said Elliott. "The first was from the girl's mother. The second was from the girl. Yesterday I received a package of six photographs of her. They show her in the nude."

"From which you know you've never seen her before, nude or otherwise."

"I have *never* seen her."

"Where are the photographs?"

"Here. I brought them. I thought they might send the police, and I'd be found with nude photographs of this girl. Who'd believe I got them in the mail?"

"Did your wife see them?"

"Thank God, no. She knows nothing of this."

"Can we see the pictures?"

"Of course. I want you to see them, then probably destroy them."

Elliott reached into his inside jacket pocket and withdrew a brown envelope. Inside were what he had described: six snapshot-size photographs of a naked teenage girl. The pictures were not entirely clear, and it was not possible to form a good judgment of her. She looked young and small, as was to be expected. Her breasts were small. Her belly was flat. Her pubic hair was sparse. The hair on her head was light, but that in her crotch was dark.

"She looks miserable," said Charlotte. "As if she did not want to pose for these."

"I imagine she didn't," said Jack. "She's a victim—though not in the way somebody wants us to believe."

"This girl wasn't pregnant when these were taken," said Charlotte.

"Maybe a month or two," said Jack.

"She's a child," said Elliott sadly. "I had nothing to do with her getting pregnant, but what will it do to Father's campaign if—"

"Did they ask for money?"

"No. That's something else. They haven't asked for anything. First, the mother called. She said her daughter was pregnant and I was the father. I said that was impossible, that I'd never met her daughter. Then the girl called. She was crying and asked me why I denied her. Then today the pictures came, without a note. I can't respond to them. I don't know who they are and where to find them."

Jack turned the pictures over and over. "I wonder who developed these," he said. "No camera store, I'd think. You wouldn't want to risk handing over film with this on it to a commercial photo processor—unless it was one you knew very well."

"What they are going to do next, is the problem," said Elliott.

"We know who they are, Elliott," said Jack. "At least we know what names they use."

"You work fast."

"They suppose we don't have any idea who they are," said Jack. "So they have to contact you again. We have to expect that's what they'll do."

"Do you want to tell me who they are?"

"Her name is Norma Jean Chandler. Her mother's name is Edna Bascombe. Do the names mean anything to you?"

Elliott shook his head firmly. "I swear I've never heard either name in my life."

"Well, it's interesting to note that Antonio 'Big Dick'

DiCalabria knows who they are. The word is around in a certain element of Los Angeles society."

"DiCalabria!"

"You've met him?"

Elliott nodded. "You put down a bet in Los Angeles, you've met him, indirectly. You buy the services of a prostitute, you've met him. I've met him more formally. No business relationship. Just met him. What's he got to do with this?"

"He's a friend of ours," said Jack dryly, faintly smiling. "Charlotte's and mine."

Elliott shook his head. "Jack, you are indescribable! My father has always said you are. I breathe easier, knowing you're here. DiCalabria!"

"All right. Now, there's something I want you to do, Elliott," said Jack. "These people are likely to contact you again. If the girl calls, call her Norma. If her mother phones, call her Mrs. Bascombe. If somebody else calls, say you wonder what the hell Mrs. Bascombe is trying to pull. When they understand you've identified them, that ought to shake them a little. They think they're dealing with a naïve young man who's going to send a message to his father. They figure you're defenseless. But don't go any further. Whatever you do, don't mention DiCalabria. Just use the names. I'm counting on that giving them a little scare."

V

On Friday morning, the day after their arrival, they ate breakfast in their air-conditioned suite. With the venetian blinds open, they could see people already splashing about in the pool. The lawns lay under sheets of spray from the sprinkling system. Their apartment and the irrigated gardens of the Ambassador Hotel were a refuge, a refuge Charlotte quickly decided she needed.

Southern California was stifling hot and humid. Los Angeles itself sat at the bottom of a deep three-quarters bowl, bounded on one side by the Pacific Ocean and on the other three sides by mountains. Ocean mists rolling in off the water were trapped in the bowl and sometimes hung over the city half the day or more. Not only that—lately, people had begun to complain that the mist was often intermixed with the fumes from automobile exhausts and from industry, occasionally making the atmosphere irritating to the eyes and nose. Someone had coined a word for the phenomenon. They said it should be called *smog*.

When finally the sun broke through, it impressed Charlotte, who had never been in California before, as blinding in its white intensity. Soon, on a summer day, waves of heat rose from the pavements. "God knows I like sunshine, but enough is enough!"

She said this as she and Jack were on their way to Paramount Studios, where Cecil B. DeMille worked, even though his was an independent production company. He had sent a Cadillac limousine to pick them up. They sat in the spacious rear seat, cooled by two small, rubber-bladed electric fans. Two red roses stood in crystal vases mounted just behind the doors. A bar folded down from the wall separating passengers from the driver: a bar offering ice, Coca-Cola, ginger ale, seltzer water, and plain water. People who wanted to break the Prohibition law had to supply their own liquor.

Gates were hurriedly pushed aside to admit the DeMille limousine to the studio, and the driver sped across the lot to a soundstage. A young man came to the car and asked Jack and Charlotte to sit and wait for a few minutes, since Mr. DeMille was shooting. They waited that few minutes, until Cecil B. DeMille came out.

"Mr. Endicott, it is a pleasure to see you again!" he said, extending his hand.

Jack introduced Charlotte, and DeMille kissed her hand.

Cecil B. DeMille was a man of medium height, whose curly brown hair remained intact only along the sides and across the back of his head. He had intense brown eyes and a wide, mobile, expressive mouth. Though he was smiling now, they would soon see his face turn intensely thoughtful as he worked. He was wearing a white shirt, open at the neck, and a pair of khaki trousers—not the boots and breeches that were an element of his highly contrived persona.

"We've met before, of course," he said to Jack. "I was one of the men who applied to First Boston Provident Trust for some financing when we were making *The Ten Commandments.*"

"I remember," said Jack. "I'm afraid our bank, my uncle Henry in particular, is a little too conservative to lend money for motion-picture production."

"You'd have made a profit if you had invested in that picture," said DeMille.

"Well, you didn't ask me to invest personally," said Jack. "You asked the bank. Investing our personal funds and investing our depositors' funds are very different things."

"Would you have invested if we had applied to you personally?" asked DeMille with a sly smile.

"No," said Jack with a broader smile. "I don't know enough about the industry."

DeMille laughed. "If you'd like to see us shoot the next scene, come on in," he said. "It's not entirely coincidence that you've arrived to see us do an interesting little sequence. I invited you this morning so you can see this."

They were shooting a sound picture. Nearly all pictures were made with sound now. DeMille explained that once shooting began, everyone but the actors must be absolutely silent, since the microphones would pick up every word or noise anyone made.

In fact, the microphones would pick up the whirring of the camera; and for this reason, the camera was enclosed in a heavily padded soundproof booth, with only the lens protruding—and it through a tight, padded sleeve.

"It gets very warm inside the camera booth," DeMille

explained. "The cameraman is drenched with sweat after only a few minutes, so we have to let him go offstage and shower while another man works the camera for a while. We *must* have sound. Audiences demand it now. But it places some painful limitations on the medium."

Charlotte and Jack were most interested in the set. It was a sunken marble bathtub, set in a marble alcove. A modern bathtub, not a bath for Cleopatra, it was equipped with fixtures that looked like gold and with marble shelves where an array of bottles and jars offered scents and unguents to the bather.

On the screen the alcove would look like a refuge of luxurious privacy. On the set it faced the camera and was open to the view of forty or fifty people.

"Let me introduce our beautiful star who'll be appearing in this shot," said DeMille.

He nodded toward a young woman who came toward them. She was dressed in a robe with fur at the neck, wrists, and ankles. As she walked across the soundstage, she crushed a cigarette in an ashtray offered her by a young man. She was typical of the young Hollywood actress. Her hair was bleached and stiff. Her eyebrows were plucked, and her eyes were accentuated with dark makeup. It was in fact her eyes that gave her whatever individuality she possessed. They were blue, round, and wide. Her mouth helped, too. It was small and somewhat puckered, as if she did not entirely approve of what she saw around her.

"Mr. Endicott, Mrs. Wendell, let me introduce the star of this picture—a coming young actress named Bette Davis."

Bette Davis tipped her head to one side as she nodded. "Thank you. My pleasure," she said in precise diction, accented to suggest an English background, yet really too American to be English.

"Ready to take a bath, Bette?" DeMille asked.

She nodded at DeMille and spoke to Jack and Charlotte. "My lines in this scene are terribly difficult to memorize, as you will see," she said.

DeMille led his two guests to a point at the side of the scene, well to the right of the camera, where they sat down in wood-and-canvas chairs. He drew a small silver police whistle from his pocket and blew a short, peremptory blast. "Quiet!" he yelled.

He did not yell things like "Lights! Camera! Action!" He pointed upward, and the electrician switched on the dozen or so powerful floodlights, carefully situated to fill the bath alcove with shadowy light. He pointed at the camera booth, and a man standing beside it pounded on the wall. He snapped his fingers, and a man with the slapstick stepped forward, showed the camera the chalked numbers of the scene and take, and slapped the stick down with a resounding snap.

Two young actresses dressed as maids walked onto the set and turned to gaze expectantly to a point just to the left of the camera, where Bette Davis waited. She walked forward, affecting an air of easy arrogance, the demeanor of a woman expecting service and comfortable with it.

The two maids stepped to either side of her, unfastened the robe, and slowly removed it. From the camera's angle, only the bare shoulders and back of Bette Davis were captured for the audiences who would see the picture. From the perspective of DeMille, Jack, and Charlotte, the actress was nude and she stepped down three steps and submerged herself in the tub.

"Cut!"

The water had been colored with a dye, so that the naked body of Bette Davis was faintly obscured. Doubtless on black-and-white film it would be even more shadowy. Audiences would be left with no doubt, though, that she was really naked under the water, not covered with some sort of flesh-colored swimsuit. It was a DeMille trademark. He managed to work a bathtub scene into nearly every one of his pictures.

An attendant hurried forward to offer Bette Davis a hand towel. She had begun to perspire.

"Too damned hot, C.B.!"

"We aim to please. Another time you said too cold."

"I'll turn red like a lobster."

"The story is that we'll be shooting color film in another five years or so. When that time comes, we'll worry about actresses who turn red or blue."

"You sadist."

She remained in the water while the camera booth was moved forward and positioned to take a closeup shot of her.

The process was repeated, and another quarter of a minute of film was shot. Then the lights were switched off, the cameraman emerged from the booth, and a crew began rolling the booth to an adjoining set. The fur-trimmed robe had been carried off to the wardrobe, apparently, and one attendant came forward to hand Bette Davis a terry-cloth robe as she climbed out of the water. Anyone interested had a momentary look at her nakedness.

"Someone offer me a cigarette," she said.

DeMille dragged two wood-and-canvas directors chairs close to his and gestured a suggestion that Jack and Charlotte sit down. He told an assistant to let the crew break for lunch.

"You'll be at the Goldwyns' house for dinner?" he asked Jack.

"Yes. Very kind of you."

"Well, I suggested he invite you, but he wanted to do it anyway. The only question was what evening."

"Very kind in any event," said Jack.

DeMille watched as Bette Davis walked off the soundstage and left them without anyone in earshot. "I understand your visit to Los Angeles is not a matter of tourism," he said.

"Word gets around," said Jack.

"Los Angeles was a town when we first came here," said DeMille. "Now it's a city. Hollywood is a town. Better said, Hollywood is a small town, a tight-knit little community. No one has any secrets that amount to anything."

Jack glanced around. "What can you tell me about Carlo Marfeo?" he asked.

"I will if you'll tell me where you got the name."

"From Antonio DiCalabria."

DeMille smiled. "When you hit a town, you move fast," he said. "And you've just demonstrated what I was saying, that this is a tight-knit little community. Big Dick DiCalabria is my bootlegger."

"Really?"

"As a favor. He's a bigger man than that."

"We swam on his beach yesterday afternoon," said Jack.

"And he told you something about Carlo Marfeo?" asked DeMille incredulously.

"I'll give you another name," said Jack. "Benjamin Vogel."

"I don't for a moment doubt your word, but it's not like Big Dick to talk that much."

"One more name. Norma Jean Chandler."

DeMille shook his head. "I have no idea who that one might be."

"Okay. Let's get back to Carlo Marfeo."

"He's the contract agent for the Brotherhood of Set Builders and Painters."

"Makes *your* contracts?"

"What can I do? DeMille Productions can't pay more for set building than Birdsong or Lawrence Brothers or half a dozen others. This is a competitive business."

"Besides," said Jack, "he might break legs if you tried to do business without him."

"I've never tested that theory," said DeMille.

"What do you think of the idea of a 'labor bill of rights'?"

"It could ruin the motion-picture industry," said DeMille bleakly. "I mean that literally, Mr. Endicott. It could ruin the industry."

"Let me correct you about that," said Jack. "I'm a banker. I know almost nothing about your industry. You've just said it's competitive. It won't hurt you, then, if *all* the studios have to pay a fair wage. What could hurt is *you* paying a fair wage while Birdsong pays less."

"It would increase overall costs," said DeMille.

"So the theaters have to raise ticket prices a nickel. I think the American people won't object to adding a nickel to the price of a movie ticket if it results in fair wages and safer working conditions for the men and women in the industry."

Cecil B. DeMille smiled thoughtfully. "It appears you are an idealist, Mr. Endicott. That's not what I took you for when we met in Boston. A Democrat idealist."

"A hardheaded Republican banker," said Jack.

DeMille squeezed his chin between his thumb and index finger. "What can I do for you, Mr. Endicott?"

"To start with, you can call me Jack. Mrs. Wendell would rather be called Charlotte."

"My friends call me C.B.," said DeMille. "So what can I do for you, Jack?"

"There are rumors in circulation—more than just rumors, in fact—that some men like Carlo Marfeo may try to put pressure on Governor Roosevelt to withdraw from the presidential campaign. Failing that, they might try to create a scandal and discredit him. I need to know everything I can learn about that."

"In Hollywood vernacular," said DeMille, "you want to 'head 'em off at the pass.' "

"That is exactly correct," said Jack.

"Well, give me a little time to do a little digging," said DeMille. "Between you and me, and in confidence, though I'm no friend of Governor Roosevelt and find his idea of a 'labor bill of rights' a little frightening, I'm more frightened of something else. *In confidence,* Jack—in confidence—some of us have been watching a criminal element moving in on Hollywood. It's because there's money here. Where there's meat lying on the ground, shortly there'll be maggots. Where there's loose money, shortly there'll be mobsters. You'll be at the Goldwyns' for dinner this evening, right? I'll be there. We may be able to give you some more specifics."

DeMille had taken the lunch break to suit his convenience, and it was still before noon when his limousine left Paramount to take Jack and Charlotte back to the Ambassador Hotel.

"Driver." Jack spoke to the driver with the small microphone that hung within reach from the rear seat. "Do you know where Pershing High School is?"

"Yes, sir."

"Well, take us there first. I want to visit there for a few minutes."

Pershing was a large urban high school, ten blocks or so from Pershing Square. It was a brick building, three stories high, with a set of playing fields behind.

"I'm going to ask you to wait in the car," Jack said to Charlotte. "I have a bit of a role to play here."

Inside, he found the halls quiet. The summer session attracted only 10 or 15 percent of the enrollment, and classes were in session. He had no difficulty finding the school office and walked in to confront a gray-haired receptionist.

"Good morning," he said.

The woman stared at him, conspicuously surprised to find at her desk a tall, handsome gentleman with a mustache, dressed in an obviously expensive suit, holding his hat and cane in one hand and offering his card with the other. She looked at the card.

JOHN LOWELL ENDICOTT
Vice President
First Boston Provident Trust

"What, uh . . . What can we do for you, sir?" she asked in a clipped voice, neither hostile nor cordial.

"I should like to see the headmaster," said Jack, modulating his voice to convey a Boston-Harvard accent. "Or the principal. The officer in charge."

"Do you expect to enroll a child here for the fall semester?" she asked.

"Oh, no. No," he said, faintly smiling, and offered no further information.

"Well, I suppose who you want to see is the principal, Mr. George Rosenbusch. I'll take your card to him."

A moment later the principal of Pershing High School came out of his office and extended his hand. He led Jack into his office and offered him a chair.

George Rosenbusch was a tall, spare man, maybe fifty-five years old, gray, wearing his hair clipped short. He had high cheekbones and a long face. His office was inadequately cooled by an oscillating electric fan, and it was apparent that he had just tightened his necktie and put back on the jacket of a gray-blue suit that was slightly too small for him.

"It's not often that I meet the vice president of a Boston bank," he said deferentially. "Is there something I can do for you?"

Jack nodded. "In confidence, Mr. Rosenbusch," he said. "I want to speak with you in complete confidence. You have my word, my absolute assurance, that I will do nothing to discommode or embarrass you if you see fit to give me some information I am looking for. In fact, if the information turns out to be important to me, I will conceal absolutely the source where I got it."

Rosenbusch tried to frown and smile at the same time. "This sounds ominous and mysterious, Mr. Endicott." He flicked a speck of dust off his jacket pocket, where a thick orange-and-black fountain pen was clipped. "Are you asking for confidential information from the school files?"

"It would be confidential," said Jack. "It would be, except for the fact that the subject of the information is trying to use it in a public way to embarrass someone."

Rosenbusch sighed. He was uncomfortable. "I suppose we had better move to specifics," he said quietly.

"Yes, I agree. Not long ago you expelled from this school a girl by the name of Norma Jean Chandler. You expelled her because she was pregnant."

Rosenbusch nodded vigorously. "Yess. Yess. Absolutely. What kind of example would it set for others if we allowed a sixteen-year-old girl to go about the halls pregnant?"

"A bad example, Mr. Rosenbusch," said Jack sympathetically. "A very bad example. Oh, I'm sure you did the right thing when you expelled her."

"Then what is your question?"

"Well, I'm curious about one thing," said Jack. "She couldn't have been more than two months pregnant when you expelled her. So how did you know she was pregnant? Was she showing it already?"

The principal shook his head. "No. She told it. She told it around the school."

Jack had cut the face from one of the nude pictures of Norma Jean Chandler. He handed the bit of photograph to Rosenbusch. "Is that her?"

Rosenbusch nodded.

"What kind of student was she, Mr. Rosenbusch?"

The principal shrugged. "Below average. No disciplinary problem."

"Do you know who the father is?"

"She didn't say. We didn't ask. Well . . . Actually, we did ask if it was a student here, and she said no."

"Do you have any sense of her family background and so on?"

"Mr. Endicott, a school administrator gets to know something about two kinds of pupils: the unusually bright ones whom you hand awards to, plus the ones who make trouble. Norma Jean was not very bright; and, until she told it around the school that she was pregnant, she was no trouble."

Jack drew a deep breath. "Odd question," he asked, "but are you sure she *was* pregnant?"

"Oh, yes. The school nurse examined her."

Jack stood and extended his hand again. "Mr. Rosenbusch, you've been extraordinarily helpful. I'm grateful."

"Could you answer a question for me, sir?" the principal asked.

Jack nodded.

"I wonder why the vice president of a Boston bank comes to make this inquiry? Is that an odd question?"

"Not at all, and the answer is that Norma Jean and her mother have suggested that a friend of mine is the father of the child. I am not sure why."

"You suspect blackmail?"

"It's possible."

Charlotte could not conceal her annoyance. "I'm sitting out here sweating . . . frying . . . and— Well, did you find out anything?"

"Something very curious," said Jack. "The principal says

they knew Norma Jean was pregnant because she told it around the school that she was. He had her examined by the school nurse, and the nurse confirmed it. I—"

"Who is this nurse? I still wonder if the girl really is pregnant."

"Well, I wonder something else," said Jack. "If Pershing High School expelled a sixteen-year-old girl because she was pregnant, why didn't Mr. Principal Rosenbusch or his nurse report that fact to the juvenile authorities of the County of Los Angeles?"

In his office, George Rosenbusch picked up his telephone and nervously dialed a number.

"Hello. Rosenbusch here. Yes, I'll wait."

While he waited he tapped a pencil on his desk. Through his window he could see Endicott getting into a Cadillac limousine. A woman had waited in the car. My God . . .

"Yes, uh . . . Rosenbusch. A man just left here, a man from Boston by the name of Endicott. He came to ask about Norma Jean. Well . . . what could I do? I couldn't deny she was a pupil here. I didn't tell him anything much. He seemed to know it all, anyway. How could he know her name and that she had been a pupil in this school? He suggested she's being used for blackmail. Yes. Yes. Of course. I will. You can be sure of it."

Back at the Ambassador Hotel, Jack and Charlotte took the time to swim in the pool for half an hour. While they were there, a bellboy brought a message.

It was a handwritten invitation on an engraved card:

San Simeon

I would be very pleased if you could spend the week-end at my home here. If this is acceptable to you, please so indicate, and I will arrange to have a car and driver call for you tomorrow morning. As you may know, we are very informal here, though I do try to do black tie at dinner. Sincerely hoping to see you, if not this weekend then as soon as possible.

William Randolph Hearst

A messenger was waiting for the reply. Jack sent word that he and Charlotte would be ready at ten in the morning.

Samuel Goldwyn was known for many things.

Shallowly, he was known for his malaprops. "Include me out," he was supposed to have said. "A verbal contract is not worth the paper it's written on." "I'll tell you in two words—im-possible." "We can always get more Indians off the reservoir."

Originally his name was something unpronounceable by Americans. An immigration officer changed it to Goldfish. The story was told that when he and Edgar Selwyn formed a movie production company they decided the company name should be a combination of each of their names—so coming up with the name Selfish Productions. Shortly they saw the error and changed it to Goldwyn. Then Samuel Goldfish went to court and changed his name to Goldwyn.

He was a flint-hard businessman who was devoting his whole life to making the best motion pictures that could possibly be produced, and even those who laughed at some of his vagaries held him in high regard.

The Goldwyn home on Laurel Lane was modest and comfortable—as the homes of movie moguls went. It was not one-tenth as lavish and pretentious as the DiCalabria villa Jack and Charlotte had visited the day before. Though it had the swimming pool and projection room that producers' homes had to have, these were inviting and tasteful, anything but ostentatious.

Samuel Goldwyn met Jack and Charlotte at the door and ushered them warmly into the house. He introduced them to his wife, Frances, and led them back to the veranda overlooking the swimming pool.

The dinner party was for a few guests only. Besides Cecil B. DeMille, Jack recognized only Erich von Stroheim and Jean Harlow.

They were served champagne, and Jack and Charlotte were introduced to all the guests.

Erich von Stroheim, who by reputation at least had been an officer in the Austrian Imperial Guard, earned his living as a director and as an actor portraying ramrod-stiff Prussian army officers—known as "the man you love to hate." As a director he was a recognized genius. His films, though, had proved far too expensive to produce and far too realistic for American tastes.

Jean Harlow was the most bleached of all bleached blondes. With the coming of sound, her brassy voice had contributed to her success. Her detractors said she owed her success to a small trick she played in her dressing room before each appearance on camera. She rubbed her nipples with ice cubes, they said, so whatever she wore, short of wool, displayed two dramatic budlike protuberances.

After fifteen or twenty minutes, Goldwyn stepped up beside Jack and said, "I understand there is something you and I should be talking about."

Jack nodded noncommittally.

"Well, C.B. said there is."

"All right. Yes, there is."

Samuel Goldwyn was taller than the average man. He was bald, but his great black eyebrows were intimidating. His eyes were small and deep-set. His chin was strong. He had a reputation for being an overpowering man; but here, at home with guests, he was affable and warm.

DeMille saw Jack and Goldwyn in conversation manifestly more intense than sociability required, and he joined them. They walked out to the far end of the pool and sat down around a wrought-iron table.

"I think," said Goldwyn immediately and bluntly, "we should know what we are talking about."

Jack nodded. "I am a personal friend of Governor Roosevelt," he said. "There is reason to believe someone in Los Angeles has launched a conspiracy to try to cause the Governor to withdraw from the presidential campaign. Failing that, they may try to create a scandal that will so embarrass him that he might feel compelled to withdraw. And there may be more than that involved."

"Specifically?" asked Goldwyn.

"The Governor's son Elliott has been privately accused of causing the pregnancy of a sixteen-year-old girl."

"Which he didn't do?"

"I feel sure he didn't. Apart from my confidence in the young man, there are anomalies in the case. For example, no one has reported the pregnancy of a sixteen-year-old girl to the juvenile authorities—not her mother and not the principal who expelled her from high school."

Goldwyn glanced at DeMille. "That does seem odd, doesn't it?"

Sam Goldwyn nodded. "C.B. tells me you talked to Big Dick DiCalabria, who gave you the name Carlo Marfeo. Marfeo is a disgusting thug. I pay set builders and painters Brotherhood wages, but I won't sign a contract with the Brotherhood. I won't pay a nickel to Marfeo. The last time he sent a hoodlum, I had the man thrown into the street."

"What about getting a leg broken?" asked Jack.

"He breaks one of mine, I'll break two of his," said Goldwyn. "I'm not afraid of him. Bullies are cowards. In the Warsaw ghetto, it was true. Here, it is no less true."

"Sam doesn't fool around," said DeMille respectfully.

"If Marfeo comes near me again, I'll report him to the Infernal Revenue Department."

"Well, what do you think of Vogel, who goes along with him?"

"Vogel's a schlemiel," said Goldwyn.

"Marfeo's not the only one in this game, I imagine," said Jack.

"This is my cue to tell you who else? There's lots of who-elses. The business agent for the Wiring and Lighting Workers Union is a thug named Sean Flynn. He uses the same tactics as Marfeo."

"Is there any connection between Marfeo and Flynn?"

"Not that I know of. If you're looking for one great big conspiracy, it's not there. What we've got is a bunch of petty crooks skimming money off the picture business."

"Mr. Goldwyn, have you ever heard the name Norma Jean Chandler?"

Goldwyn turned down the corners of his mouth and shook his head.

"Edna Bascombe?"

"No. This your sixteen-year-old girl?"

"And her mother."

"Take a word of advice, Mr. Endicott. Look for a way for your friend to settle this thing. If it takes some money, pay it. An accusation of this kind is the worst thing that can happen to a man. Accused of another crime, a man gets a fair trial. They have to prove him guilty. This is the only crime where a man is expected to prove he's *not* guilty."

"I'm afraid you're right," said Jack.

"Careers have been destroyed in Hollywood," said De-Mille. "Still more will be. It's the most unfair thing in the world, but there it is. Let a little girl make this accusation, it will be believed."

The three men rejoined the other guests. In a little while the group sat down over a quiet, elegant dinner. Later, they sat down in Samuel Goldwyn's home theater and watched an advance showing of *Grand Hotel*.

VI
—

San Simeon was more than two hundred miles north of Los Angeles. It was more than halfway to San Francisco, in fact. For this reason, someone had telephoned the hotel and offered the suggestion that Mr. Endicott and Mrs. Wendell be ready to leave at seven rather than at ten. It was also suggested that breakfast could be taken in the car. A basket would be packed.

The car was a Rolls-Royce. The coastal scenery was some of the most beautiful in the world. The picnic breakfast was superb: lox and bagels, chilled melon, with champagne, then pastries, coffee and tea, and an after-coffee brandy if they wanted it.

Although William Randolph Hearst maintained several opulent homes, the one identified with his name was the castle he built at San Simeon, on the Pacific coast. Variously called La Casa Grande and La Cuesta Encantada, it sat on

350,000 acres of Hearst property, and the drive from the boundary of the Hearst estate to the castle was seventeen miles.

As the Rolls-Royce passed through a gate, the driver spoke into a microphone and said, "We are on Mr. Hearst's property from this point."

The acreage was fenced because it was an open zoo. It was divided into zones, with fences that separated categories of species. The deer, goats, eland, and ostriches, for example, were confined to different acreage from that where lions and tigers roamed wild.

As the Rolls-Royce made its way up the road toward the castle, the car stopped from time to time to allow animals like giraffes and moose to cross the road. Signs advised that the animals had the right of way.

Finally, as the car came around a curve, they had their first view of the house, through a break in the foliage. No one ever failed to be impressed.

The castle itself was huge, built in a pseudo–Spanish/Moorish style—built actually in the Hearst style, which was more grandiose than grand and yet not vulgar.

Jack and Charlotte had read that, inside and out, the estate was a collection. Floors, walls, ceilings, pools, staircases, fireplaces—besides the art and furniture—had been purchased, disassembled, crated, and shipped here. Hearst was an avid collector—some said looter—who had accumulated an eclectic agglomeration of furniture and art, ranging from a marble floor recently excavated at Pompeii to the choir stalls from medieval churches, from vapid white marble nymphs of uncertain provenance to fine Renaissance madonnas, from the mosaic pool of an Italian villa to the beamed ceiling of a German monastery, from chased armor to illuminated manuscripts.

If two words could have described San Simeon, they might have been *big* and *much*. Visitors could, the story went, spend a day wandering through and admiring the collections, just as they might spend a day in the Louvre or in the British Museum. Much of what Hearst collected was not distinguished art. But he had good taste, and much of it was. San Simeon was his monument to himself, and he had lavished thought as well as money on it.

The castle was a complex of buildings, culminating in the towered alcazar at the crest of the hill. Besides the castle itself, several distinguished European houses had been disassembled and shipped here, where they were reassembled on the slopes of the hill and served as guest houses. The one assigned to Jack and Charlotte was a small English manor house, complete with nineteenth-century English furnishings and English servants.

"Mr. Hearst will be at the tennis courts this afternoon, sir," said the butler. "If you would care to join him, appropriate dress might be tennis whites, if you have them. If you have not, I can, I believe, supply. For the lady as well, sir."

"A bite of lunch would be appropriate, too," said Jack.

"Yes, sir. We anticipated you would require lunch. It will be laid on the terrace in fifteen minutes, sir."

Jack had anticipated the tennis whites and had brought some. Charlotte had not and wore what the house supplied when she went with him to the terrace. She wore a pleated skirt that ended halfway between her hips and knees and a cotton knit shirt.

Marion Davies was waiting on the terrace. She, not Mrs. Hearst, was the hostess at San Simeon. An undeniably beautiful blond movie actress, she had been the mistress of William Randolph Hearst for more than a dozen years. Whether or not she was a talented actress was problematical, since the Hearst newspapers uniformly pronounced her every performance brilliant, which engendered resentment in other papers and caused them to pan her more than they otherwise might have. She was thirty-five years old, a onetime tap dancer and chorus girl in the *Ziegfeld Follies,* then actress in many and various movies.

"I hope you've been received properly," she said. "If anything's lacking, just speak up."

Marion Davies was not wearing tennis whites but a dark-blue sailor suit with bell-bottom trousers. She had in her hand a Scotch and soda.

"Better have a drink," she said. "It's W.R.'s one idiosyncracy. He serves two cocktails before dinner and sherry with. Nothing more. The servants are instructed to remove from guests' luggage anything they bring of their own. Of course, they never do." She laughed. "I guess he's had too many people get drunk around here. I hate to say it, but he's of another generation, you know."

Jack swept his arm up, toward the towers of the palace. "I'd heard of this place," he said. "I'd seen pictures. But I had no idea how magnificent it is."

Marion Davies nodded. "Tell W.R.," she said. "For him, you can't say anything too good about Casa Grande. He dotes on praise for it. He calls it 'the ranch,' incidentally—Rancho Casa Grande."

" 'The ranch,' " said Charlotte. "Some ranch."

Marion Davies smiled warmly. She was an engaging woman, comfortable in her controversial role. She knew that William Randolph Hearst was one of the most-respected, yet most-hated men in America, for the way he used his newspapers.

Jack knew that Hearst laid claim to having swung the Democratic convention to Roosevelt by persuading Speaker Garner to withdraw and throw the Texas delegation to the New York Governor. He also knew it wasn't true. He suspected that Hearst knew of the connection between him and the Governor—and that was why he was a guest at San Simeon this weekend. Hearst had large political ambitions of his own. He might want to use Jack as a messenger to Roosevelt, to demand a cabinet post. He might want to be governor of California, or senator—offices that might lead to the presidency, an ambition he seemed never to have given up, although he was almost seventy years old.

Marion Davies chatted amiably while Jack and Charlotte ate their lunch. She told him that there were fewer guests in residence this weekend than was usual. Gary Cooper and Clark Gable were there, she said—and Bing Crosby. Gloria Swanson and Clara Bow had arrived together a short time ago.

"Sometimes W.R. invites sixty or seventy people. God knows, you can lose that many in this place. Do you play tennis?"

"I do," said Jack. "I can't claim to be very good at it, but I play."

"W.R. never plays anymore. He'll be happy if you play croquet with him."

"Croquet it will be," said Jack.

The butler's suggestion that tennis whites would be appropriate proved accurate. Only Clark Gable and Bing Crosby were on the court, not really playing a game but lackadaisically hitting a ball back and forth. Clara Bow was in the nearby swimming pool, paddling around the fountain in the center. A naked marble naiad poured a stream of water from a jar into the pool. Gloria Swanson, wet and obviously just out of the pool, sat with Gary Cooper at an umbrella table, talking with their host, William Randolph Hearst.

Hearst rose and came toward Jack and Charlotte, hand extended. "Welcome to the ranch," he said. "Everything been taken care of?"

"Beautifully," said Jack. "And I— Well, I'd heard of this place, seen pictures of it, but I'm astounded anyway. It is magnificent."

Marion Davies had been right in saying Hearst would receive praise for his castle the way a dog receives a pat on the head. His pleasure with the compliment was innocently conspicuous.

William Randolph Hearst was sixty-nine years old and moved a little ponderously, but he was vigorous and alert. His face, familiar to every American, was strong and square and eloquent of his moods. His eyes were large and round and fastened in a sticky gaze on the eyes of whoever was before him. His ears were big. His gray hair was thick and fell over the left side of his forehead. He was not wearing tennis whites but rather a beige single-breasted summer-weight suit with white shirt and a colorful red-white-and-green necktie. He wore white shoes.

"Join me," he said, pointing to the table where he sat with Gary Cooper.

The tall actor rose and gravely shook hands with Jack and Charlotte. It was apparent that his offscreen persona did not vary much from what was seen onscreen. "Sure is a nice day to be here, isn't it?" he said.

"Mr. Endicott is a good friend of Governor Roosevelt," said Hearst. "I hope he'll join me in trying to persuade him not to go socialist."

"I'm sure he's not thinking in those terms," said Jack.

"Well, what is this 'labor bill of rights,' this 'national labor relations act'?" Hearst asked.

"The mobsters, racketeers, have muscled their way into control of many labor unions," said Jack. "That's one of the things the Governor wants to stop."

"That's, of course, fine," said Hearst. "But what about interfering with the rights of workers to contract with employers?"

"We're not talking about interfering with honest contracts, Mr. Hearst," Jack said. "Unhappily, some dishonest employers pay bribes to mobster union agents. The employer gets cheap labor, the mob gets a handsome payoff, and the working people get stiffed."

"I'll have to see evidence of that, Mr. Endicott."

Jack nodded. "Maybe you will. I know you'll cover it in your newspapers, once you've seen the evidence."

Hearst nodded phlegmatically. "I will," he agreed. "Of course I will."

"Oh, W.R., we were going to play croquet!" Marion Davies protested.

"Yes, I did promise to do that," said Hearst. He lifted himself heavily. "Will you join us?"

Hearst and Marion played partners, as did Jack and Charlotte, Cooper and Swanson. The course was laid out over a vast expanse of lawn, trimmed like a putting green, and it took a while for people not accustomed to that and to the oversized balls and mallets to learn how far a ball would travel. Their host and his partner won the first game easily, though Jack observed William Randolph Hearst pausing often to reach behind himself and rub his back. Jack and Charlotte won the second game. Gary Cooper and Gloria Swanson seemed unwilling to risk offending Hearst by really competing, and they lagged behind in both games.

When all sat down at the table again, Hearst seemed winded. He received a note from a servant, scribbled on it, and accepted a glass of iced tea from another servant.

"We'll be joined in a moment by another guest," said Hearst. "Benjamin Vogel has just arrived. Birdsong Productions. He may have some opinions on your 'labor bill of rights,' Mr. Endicott."

Marion Davies seemed to take a clue. "This is going to get heavy," she said. "C'mon, Coop, Gloria. Charlotte and I challenge you to another game."

Charlotte was reluctant to leave the table, but she had little choice.

"Ben's an important producer," said Hearst. "He's never done a picture starring Marion, but I'm hoping he will."

Jack understood that the appearance of Vogel this weekend was no coincidence. "I've heard his name," he said.

"He's made some good films," said Hearst. "I suppose he's underfinanced. That's an easy thing to be in the last few years. I've dabbled in motion-picture production myself in a small way. The business hemorrhages money. Just hemorrhages it. On the other hand, with a success the money accumulates the way the old song has it—'My God, how the money rolls in.' Y' know?"

"Yes. My bank does not lend money for stage or screen productions."

Benjamin Vogel arrived, bustling across the lawn in a white summer suit and white shoes, a yellow straw boater on his head, round horn-rimmed spectacles on his nose. At a distance, he bore a resemblance to Harold Lloyd. Closer, his features were Lloyd's but crammed down from top to bottom, as if he had been squeezed by a vise. His chin was weaker, his nose was shorter and thicker, the whole face was coarser.

"W.R.! Good of you to invite me! I apologize for arriving so late. I missed the morning train and . . . Well, I chartered a plane and flew up. And this must be Mr. Endicott! Ben Vogel, and it's a real pleasure to meet you."

"Your reputation precedes you, Mr. Endicott," said Hearst.

"You race a Bugatti," said Vogel as he sat down and put his hat aside on another chair.

"Occasionally," said Jack.

"Enough to be known for it," said Vogel. "You fly. You sail. Play polo—"

"Only a little, many years ago," said Jack.

"And bridge, with many master's points."

"I am a playboy and a wastrel," said Jack.

"And a shrewd manager of money," said Hearst. "My business editors tell me you are worth several times what you inherited and have continued to make money even through the Depression."

"My uncle Henry is my business adviser," said Jack insouciantly.

"My editors think differently," said Hearst. "They say you have distinctly outstripped your uncle, in terms of wealth. They tell me you are by far the wealthiest Endicott."

"Well, I married some money."

"And divorced some," Hearst persisted. "No, I hear you are a very shrewd businessman."

"Mr. Endicott, I suspect," said Vogel, "is one of those Easterners so habituated to great wealth that he finds it déclassé to talk about it."

"Not at all, Mr. Vogel," said Jack. "I never mind talking about love or money."

Hearst's great face split into a hearty laugh.

Vogel smiled weakly as he accepted a glass of iced tea from a servant.

Two young women in bathing suits and white tennis shoes went out on the court and began to hit a ball, with much more force than Bing Crosby and Clark Gable had been using. Hearst turned to watch. After a minute or so, Crosby and Gable split into doubles teams with the two young women, and they began to play tennis in earnest.

"We were talking about Governor Roosevelt's idea of a bill of rights for labor," Hearst said to Vogel.

Vogel frowned. "A thing like that could ruin our industry," he said.

"I'll be hard to convince of that," said Jack.

"It could run our labor costs so high that we'd be driven out of business," said Vogel.

"By whom?" Jack asked. "I hear you're a competitive industry. If everyone's labor costs go up, who benefits? Who loses?"

"The moviegoing public," said Vogel. "We couldn't make as many pictures. The small businessman in the industry."

"Carlo Marfeo," suggested Jack. "Sean Flynn."

Vogel shook his head. "Who are they?"

"The business agent for the Brotherhood of Set Builders

and Painters," said Jack. "The business agent for the Wiring and Lighting Workers Union."

"Oh, yes. I've heard of Marfeo. Yes. Agent for the BSBP. Well . . . You have to have set builders. You have to have electricians. They can cost you a fortune on every picture."

"Not if you can make a good deal with Marfeo," said Jack. "Not if you can make a good deal with Flynn."

"One of my partners takes care of that sort of thing," said Vogel in a tone obviously meant to dismiss the subject. "I don't know how he works it out."

"A 'labor bill of rights' would make it a great deal easier to work out," said Jack. "By eliminating the mobsters who skim a percentage off the whole thing."

Vogel shook his head firmly. "I wouldn't know," he said. "You call these union agents 'mobsters'? The only name that comes to my mind when the word *mobster* is used is a New Yorker who came out here some years ago, named Big Dick DiCalabria. He is reputed to be the kingpin of crime and vice in Los Angeles. He runs the bootlegging, the prostitution, the bookmaking. By reputation, he destroys anyone who invades his territory. I'd be surprised if there are other mobsters operating in Los Angeles."

"I'm afraid that's a little naïve, Ben," said Hearst. "Crime's a big business. It's competitive, too."

Vogel's nod to Hearst was a short bow. "Well, as a journalist, you are privy to a lot of information that never comes to me," he said. "I've only spoken of what I've heard."

"And you hear that Governor Roosevelt's possible 'labor bill of rights' would be damaging to your business," said Jack.

"That's what I hear," said Vogel. "Maybe I'm wrong, but that's what I hear."

*   *   *

Dinner would be served at seven. Guests were expected to appear in the Great Hall no later than twenty minutes before seven. It was only then that drinks were served, no more than two per guest. William Randolph Hearst would appear promptly at a quarter till seven, and he expected to greet all his guests when he arrived.

The Great Hall was baronial. A foursome could have sat around a table and played bridge in the fireplace, which had been brought to California from a real baronial hall some-where in Europe. A fire burned in it even on an August evening. The tons of stone that surrounded people in the castle never lost their damp and chill, Marion Davies complained. Suits of armor stood in niches around the room. Knightly banners displaying a score of armorial bearings hung high above. There was not a table that a man could lift. It would have strained most men to lift one of the chairs. Dimly lighted paintings on the wall were by Renaissance, some even by pre-Renaissance, artists. Oriental rugs covered part of the dark floor.

Jack and Charlotte arrived about 6:30 and were promptly served Scotches—doubles, since the staff were under instructions from Marion Davies not to skimp. W.R., she had explained over lunch, was not opposed to drinking and would have two drinks himself—which would not be doubles—but was disgusted by drunkenness and did not want to risk it. As she had also said, not many guests were there this weekend. Gable, Cooper, and Crosby appeared in black tie, as did Vogel. The two young women who had played tennis that afternoon appeared in satin gowns. Jack meant to learn their names but hadn't yet.

A huge jigsaw puzzle was affixed to a wall. It was less than half worked, and hundreds of pieces with adhesive backing lay in faience bowls. The guests stirred pieces and looked for one that fit. It would please their host to find that they'd made progress while they waited for him, and the two tennis girls in particular made a real effort to find pieces.

At twenty before seven, Marion Davies appeared, with Gloria Swanson and Clara Bow. They were dressed in light-opera uniforms: Ruritanian army officers. The uniforms were white with red collars, gold fourragères and epaulets, gold and silver medals, some with jewels. Marion, who apparently was meant to hold the highest rank, wore a maroon-and-gold ribbon over her shoulder and across her breast, bearing more medals. The white trousers were skintight. The boots were gleaming black.

"It's an idiosyncracy with W.R.," Gable muttered in Jack's ear. "He loves to see Marion in pants, particularly in military uniform with pants. He's dressed the others that way, too, so she won't be too conspicuous."

The mistress hurried to the great sideboard that served as a bar and grabbed a drink. She tossed that one down quickly and grabbed another. Another element of her reputation was that, while she was by no means an alcoholic, she drank like a man.

She came across the room to Jack and Charlotte. "Get another drink before W.R. gets here," she said conspiratorially. "He'll think it's your first, and then you can have a third one. That is, if you want it."

"I like your uniform," said Charlotte.

Marion Davies smiled. "My situation has its advantages and disadvantages," she said.

"I'm only sorry you didn't have one for me," said Charlotte.

"You just got yourself an invitation to another weekend," said Marion. "I'll tell him, and he'll want to see you in an outfit like this." She smiled at Jack. "We like dress-up parties. Plan on wearing—Well . . . something. We'll provide. I'm gonna suggest you'd make a great Chinese mandarin."

The Baron of San Simeon arrived. Beaming with pleasure and pride, he shook the hand of each man, kissed the hand of each woman, and only then accepted a glass of sherry from a butler.

He spent a minute or two talking with the two young women who played tennis, then broke away and came to Jack and Charlotte.

"You understand, of course, that Brother Vogel is not here this weekend by coincidence," he said to them. "He genuinely believes that Governor Roosevelt could damage his industry. I'm not so sure myself."

"Driving the mobsters out of any industry can only benefit that industry," said Jack.

"I made some telephone calls since we spoke this afternoon," said Hearst. "This man Marfeo that you mentioned—he's dangerous. He's from Philadelphia. They have as dangerous mobsters there as they have in Chicago. He has a criminal record. He has been in prison for violent crimes."

"Vogel says he doesn't know him," said Jack. "But Vogel does know him."

"I wouldn't be surprised."

"I appreciate your checking into his background," said Jack.

"Be careful, my newfound friend," said Hearst.

They went in to dinner. The table was set with place

cards, and Jack found himself sitting between Gloria Swanson and Bing Crosby. Charlotte was between Gary Cooper and Clara Bow.

"I like your uniform," Jack said to Gloria Swanson.

To his surprise, she blushed. She was not the vain, pretentious, haughty woman she wanted people to think she was. He knew she was the mistress of Joseph Kennedy, the Boston Irish businessman who had invested in movies. She turned out to be smaller than he had expected, and more vulnerable.

"I feel like an idiot," she whispered.

"You look charming. It goes with the setting. Don't be embarrassed."

To his further surprise, she reached for his hand under the table, took it, and squeezed it. Her hand was cold.

William Randolph Hearst presided over his table like a medieval baron, bestowing his paternal glance on each guest in turn, repeatedly. He said little. He ate sparingly.

Each guest was served by an individual attendant who stood behind the chair. He kept the guest's water glass full. He poured two glasses of dry sherry and after that no more. These attendants wore dark-green livery. Half a dozen young maids carried dishes to and from the kitchen. They wore dark-green also: bodices and short skirts flounced with crinoline, with white caps and aprons.

The food matched the setting. Jack and Charlotte could have wished only for red wine instead of the sherry. It was their host's only idiosyncracy that proved an inconvenience.

Gloria Swanson touched Jack's hand from time to time. She was thirty-five years old and a successful businesswoman as well as Hollywood figure, but she wanted reassurance. He squeezed her hand, and she drew his hand over so that it rested on her leg. He realized that if Charlotte had not been with him, he could have cuckolded Joe Kennedy. The idea amused him, but realistically he was glad Charlotte was there.

They had undressed for bed when they heard a rap on the door of the English manor house. Jack drew on a robe and went to the door. Marion Davies was there, carrying a bottle of Scotch, wearing white silk pajamas.

"I need a nightcap," she said. "And not alone. W.R.'s asleep. You two are the only *couple* here. If he finds out I sneaked out to visit *you*, it's okay."

Charlotte came out in a white peignoir over a silk night-gown, and the three of them sat down in the living room, before a dark, cold fireplace. They sipped Scotch straight, from wine glasses.

"Did you see the buffalo?" she asked. "I don't know how many we've got, but you know keeping a herd of buffalo is doing something for America. There aren't many left, but the ones who live here are safe. If somebody doesn't keep some of them alive, pretty soon there won't be any. W.R. loves animals. Guess how many dogs he's got. I have only one. I love that one. W.R. loves them all. Except for a monkey we had. Kelly, we called him. He took strong likes and dislikes to people, for no reason you could imagine. When he didn't like somebody, he'd poop and throw it at them. He's in a zoo now. W.R. wouldn't put up with that. He's a very straight guy, W.R. Doesn't like off-color jokes. Doesn't like what's going on under his roof tonight. I mean, God knows who's sleeping with who. When we've got fifty guests, it gets absolutely confusing. When I do the place cards, who'm I supposed to seat next to who? A couple who slept together last night, or not? Can you imagine how much time I spend trying to answer questions like that?"

She was tipsy, not drunk. She stayed half an hour, left the bottle of Scotch, and slipped away toward Casa Grande and the suite she shared with Hearst.

She had been gone no more than three minutes when there came another knock at the door.

Benjamin Vogel.

Still dressed in black tie, he came in and sat down where Marion Davies had been. "I waited for her to leave," he said. "I need to talk with you." He glanced toward Charlotte.

"She knows everything I know," said Jack.

"I'm a messenger," said Vogel.

"I'm not surprised," said Jack.

"Sure I know Marfeo," said Vogel. "He's only one. The story about you, Mr. Endicott, is that you blocked Dutch Schultz and Bo Weinberg when they meant to assassinate Governor Roosevelt. That story's around about you. The story is that you shot a couple of guys. So the story also is that you're not on the inside of the law, exactly."

Jack paused to light a Herbert Tareyton. "Just what do you mean by that?" he asked.

"You're not holier than me, that's all," said Vogel.

"I interpret that to mean you acknowledge *you* are operating outside the law."

"Whose car met you at the railroad station?" Vogel asked.

"Obviously you know."

"That's a hell of an alliance," said Vogel. "The Governor of New York and Big Dick DiCalabria. I wonder if Mr. Hearst knows about it."

"Governor Roosevelt doesn't know about it," said Jack.

Charlotte poured herself a splash of Scotch. She didn't offer one to Vogel.

"What I can't understand," said Vogel, "is why a man of your stature would come to California, ally himself with a man like DiCalabria, and start to nib in our business."

"Just what is 'our business,' Mr. Vogel? Just how am I starting to 'nib in'?"

"Do you want to talk about the little girl?"

"What little girl?" Jack asked.

"The one you inquired about at Pershing High School yesterday afternoon."

Jack turned to Charlotte and laughed. "All questions answered," he said. "Including ones we didn't ask. Now we know why Mr. Rosenbusch didn't report Norma Jean's pregnancy to the juvenile authorities. Now we know why the school nurse didn't. Or was she really examined by a nurse, Vogel?"

"If you want to suggest she's not pregnant, she'll be examined by any doctor you want to appoint," said Vogel.

"I don't doubt the poor child is pregnant," Jack said. "That's not the question."

"You want to deny the Governor's son is the daddy. She'll testify under oath about that."

"That would be a very risky thing to do," said Jack. "If she testifies, she'll have to tell when and where she was with Elliott. What if he has plenty of evidence that he was in Texas that whole week? Or in Albany?"

Vogel shrugged. "We would hope it doesn't come down to a proceeding at law . . . testimony and all that."

"You say 'we would hope.' Who's 'we'?"

"Mr. Endicott, you've already named us. You have a

marked talent for moving very fast. Within two days after arriving in California, you've identified Norma Jean Chandler and her mother, plus me, plus Carlo Marfeo and Sean Flynn. There are others. I suppose you'll identify them, too. We hope you don't decide to shoot one of us."

"Why would that be necessary?" asked Jack calmly as he tapped his cigarette on an ashtray.

"Let's get back to Norma Jean," said Vogel. "The little girl is pregnant. No question. If she makes a public statement, the newspapers are gonna eat it up. No question about that, either. If that happens, it's not gonna make much difference whether or not Mr. Elliott Roosevelt can be *proved* to be the culprit. By the time the case is proved or disproved, the election will be long past."

"And the damage will have been done, you suppose."

Vogel nodded. "It will have been done."

"Well, obviously you want something out of this. What is it?"

"Governor Roosevelt is known to be a man in poor health. Let's suppose he announces the strain of the presidential campaign has proved too much for him. Let's suppose he withdraws. Then—"

"Then what?"

"Then the next President of the United States will either be Herbert Hoover or John Nance Garner. Businessmen like me much prefer Hoover. But we can live with Cactus Jack Garner. Neither of those two is going to try to promote some sort of 'labor bill of rights.' Neither one of them is going to make it harder for a businessman to earn a profit."

Jack stood up and walked to the sideboard, where Marion had left the Scotch. He poured himself a drink and didn't offer one to Vogel. "It's utterly amazing to me how naïve some 'businessmen'—as you'd like to be styled—can be. Dutch Schultz is a 'businessman' within your definition. He figured the death of Governor Roosevelt would stop the movement to repeal Prohibition. Well, let me tell you something, Vogel. Prohibition will be repealed within the next two years, Roosevelt or no Roosevelt. And the next Congress, or the one after that, is going to pass a 'national labor relations act,' whether Governor Roosevelt is President of the United States or not. Even if this blackmail scheme of yours stops the Roosevelt candidacy, Garner will be elected President; and, though Cactus Jack might not sponsor a labor bill, he won't veto one. Hoover might veto one, and he'd be overridden."

"I told you I'm only a messenger," said Vogel. "Would you want to tell my associates the same thing? Would you want to meet with my associates?"

"Will they meet with mine?"

"Yours . . . ?"

"Meyer Lansky for one. Lucky Luciano for another."

"You travel in, uh . . . odd circles, my friend."

"Politics makes strange bedfellows," said Jack.

VII

Hearst sent a private train, just two cars this weekend, from San Luis Obispo back to Los Angeles. Jack and Charlotte returned on the train with the Hollywood people. Released from the drinking restrictions of San Simeon, most of them relaxed thoroughly on the way back. The train arrived a little before midnight Sunday, and they took cabs.

In their garden apartment at the Ambassador Hotel, Jack and Charlotte found messages waiting for them.

DINNER? WHICH EVENING? DICALABRIA.

CALL WHEN CONVENIENT. MEYER L.

E R ON TELEPHONE THIS EVENING STOP
TERRIBLY UPSET STOP PLEASE SEE HIM AND
ADVISE STOP FDR

There was a hand-scribbled message from Elliott himself, who had stopped by the hotel, written it, and left it in the box. It read:

Please telephone as soon as you can, even if it is after midnight tonight (Sunday). Something has come up.
                                                              Elliott

Jack put the call through, and Elliott answered. He asked Jack to receive him yet tonight.

Three-quarters of an hour later, Elliott Roosevelt was in the garden apartment.

"To start with," he said, "look at these."

He handed Jack an envelope. Inside were the negatives of the nudes of Norma Jean Chandler.

"How'd you get these?" Jack asked.

"I found them," said Elliott. "And thank God I did!"

"You're excited. Need a drink?" Charlotte asked.

Elliott shook his head. He paused, though, for a moment distracted by the sometimes-exotic beauty of this extraordinary woman. Then he went on, a little more slowly, to explain: "Did you ever wake up in the night with an odd, irrational sense that something wasn't right? I mean, don't you sometimes get this sense that you've wakened because something has been just enough to come through to you in your sleep? I don't know. I sometimes have a sense that tiny sounds I wouldn't notice when I was awake are enough just the same to get through to me when I'm asleep. I'll tell you something. When I wake up in the night, it's almost always at seven minutes after the hour. Seven minutes after one, seven after three, and so on. I wonder if there's not some kind of burr on a gear in my alarm clock that makes some sharp little sound at seven after. I—"

"Anyway, you woke at seven after—"

"No, it wasn't seven after. That's another point. But I woke up and had this sense there was someone in the house. I sat up. I listened. My wife Betty was with me. It didn't wake her. I didn't wake her. But I keep a pistol in the nightstand by the bed, and I took it out and slipped downstairs. It was quiet. I checked the doors, the windows. Everything was okay. It *seemed* like it was okay. But I couldn't shake this idea that someone was in the house. Or had been in the house. I checked all over. Nothing. Then I saw it."

"Saw what?" Charlotte asked impatiently.

"There's a little desk in the living room. With an ordinary little chair. The living room is carpeted. You know how a piece of furniture makes little indentations in carpet? I sit on that chair, and when I get up I see four little marks on the carpet, where the legs and my weight have squashed the fibers down. I've sometimes wondered if there isn't any way to prevent that. When I get up from that chair—I don't know . . . The dents annoy me, and I make a point of leaving the chair sitting in its dents, so they won't be visible. Anyway, the chair was sitting out of its dents. The legs were sitting on top of the fiber."

"Betty could have moved the chair," said Charlotte.

"Yes, possibly. But she knows I like to leave the chair sitting in its dents. Anyway, the dents made me wonder if the chair hadn't been moved. That's what made me open the drawers. To open the drawers, conveniently, you'd have to move the chair back. You wouldn't *have* to move it. But to open the drawers conveniently, you'd want to move the chair."

"So . . . ?"

"I looked into the drawers. And there it was—this envelope with the negatives in it."

"Planted," said Jack.

"Planted," Elliott agreed. "For the vice-squad detectives
who arrived at eight in the morning. They came to the door.
They told me someone had suggested I had some obscene
pictures and would I mind if they looked? I said, 'Help
yourselves.' They went straight to the desk, opened the
center drawer, shrugged and apologized, and left."

"A setup," said Charlotte glumly.

"What had you done with the negatives?" Jack asked.

"I thought about burning them," said Elliott. "Then I
thought . . . not the world's greatest idea. I dressed and left
the house. Betty slept through all of this. I took the envelope
to a cemetery four blocks from the house. I folded the envelope and tucked it down into a vase on an old grave, down
in the rue of flowers left maybe on Memorial Day. I picked
the envelope out of there on my way here just now."

"Did Betty sleep through the visit of the vice squad?"
Jack asked.

"Thank God, yes."

Jack stepped behind the young man and slapped him on
the shoulder. "You've done well so far, Elliott," he said. "I
think I'd better get your father on the phone, if I can."

"Yes. Tell him I'm leaving in the morning. I'm flying to
Chicago, leaving before noon tomorrow. Father is making a
campaign swing through the West next week. I'm meeting
his train in Chicago and will be traveling with him. Tell him
Betty is not coming after all. She really doesn't like to fly.
Gee, I wish this mess could be straightened out before Father
gets here."

*   *   *

The night-duty officer at the governor's mansion in Albany
was reluctant to ring the Governor at this hour, but he did.
Missy answered. She woke the Governor, and Jack gave him
a full report.

He put the negatives in Charlotte's jewel case, took it over
to the hotel desk, and asked the night clerk to lock the jewels
in the safe.

Elliott had waited in the garden apartment. "You did the
right thing," Jack told him. "Exactly the right thing. But
don't try to do anything more. If there's another contact,
call me. Don't do anything else. Just call me."

On Monday morning, Norma Jean Chandler and her mother
Edna Bascombe sat on the wooden porch of a small run-
down house on Santa Catalina Island. Both wore flowered
cotton dresses cinched at the waist with patent-leather belts,
and both sat with their skirts pulled well up around their
hips to let the breeze blow over their legs. Both smoked
cigarettes.

Norma Jean was chubby. At sixteen she had the breasts
and hips of a woman, but her belly showed no sign of pregnancy. Her mousy light-brown hair was uncombed and un-
washed. Her eyes were puffy and bloodshot. She had been
crying.

Her mother was tall and stringy. Her complexion was
coarse, probably from years of excessive smoking. Her lower
teeth were yellow, and two were missing. She wore an upper
plate and constantly pushed at it with her tongue to keep it
in place.

"Ferry's in," said Norma Jean. "Ferry's come to Devil's Island. Man come to visit the prisoners."

"Them men'll be comin' up here. Don't you talk back to 'em ag'in. They're not the kind you mess around with."

The girl snorted contemptuously. "I already messed around with one of 'em."

"You know what I mean. This is the best deal you'll ever have, baby, so don't screw it up."

"Yeah, well . . . I'm scared, just the same."

A few minutes later three men arrived in a rattling island taxicab. They were dressed similarly in gray or blue suits with gray snap-brim hats. As they mounted the steps to the porch, the girl and the women pulled down their skirts.

"Edna . . . Norma Jean . . ." one of them said.

"Mr. Marfeo," said Edna.

Carlo Marfeo was distinguished by a flattened nose that had apparently been broken, maybe more than once. In fact, his whole face had the look of a man who had fought in the ring—or, more likely, on the street. His lower lip was thick. His lids were heavy, making him look sleepy, and his right eyebrow was split in two by a white scar. He wore a conspicuously expensive gray suit with white pinstripes.

He sat down in the one vacant chair on the porch, and the other two men leaned against the rail.

For a long moment Carlo Marfeo stared at Norma Jean. Then he said, "Look at you. Looka you, f' Christ's sake! Listen, girlie. You get in the goddamned house right now and take a bath! Wash your hair! And do it every day, you hear me? Put on some of them clothes I bought you. You may be a whore, but I don't want you lookin' like one. You get me? An' somethin' else. If I ever again catch you smokin' a cigarette out where anybody can see you, I'll slap you into next week."

He turned on her mother. "I'm buyin' a poor innocent little girl that got knocked up by a lecher. Plus an aggrieved mother. Not a pair of . . ." He looked up at one of the men leaning on the rail. "What's the word I want?"

"Slatterns," said the man.

"Thank y', Chickie. Yeah. That's what I don't want. No slatterns. Neither one of you. Next time I come out here, I may be bringin' somebody to meet you. I find you lookin' like this . . . Well, just make sure I don't find you lookin' like this."

Norma Jean rose and went toward the door, on her way in to take the bath he had ordered.

"Wait a minute. We may have to go into town, sometime soon. Just you alone. Mama stays here. You be ready, all the time. Lookin' good. Now, beat it. Take that bath."

When the girl was inside the house, Marfeo handed her mother a twenty-dollar bill. "You got your orders," he said coldly.

Jack left his taxi and walked into the United California Bank. Wearing a banker's suit, complete with homburg hat, and carrying his stick, he presented his card and asked to see the president of the bank. Two minutes later he was in the office of Charles Harold McIntyre.

"I am pleased and honored to meet you, Mr. Endicott," said McIntyre, who was the epitome of a traditional bank president, the kind of man who struck fear and trembling into the hearts of loan applicants. With nothing but a fringe of white hair around his bald dome, he wore a great white mustache in the middle of his ruddy face and regarded every visitor with the same wide-open, skeptical eyes. "I have of course heard of First Boston Provident Trust. I hope I can be of service to you."

"You can, Mr. McIntyre," said Jack. "I should like to rent a safety-deposit box for a week or so."

" 'Rent.' Not at all! We will place one at your disposal, compliments of the bank."

"The matter is a little out of the ordinary," said Jack. "I should like to have the box under an assumed name. I assure you I am doing nothing illegal. It's not a matter of tax evasion or anything of that nature. Traveling with me is a woman, the widow of an old friend. I have discovered, to my amazement and rather to my chagrin as well, that she is carrying with her in her luggage an exceptionally large quantity of jewelry. It seems that the family of her late husband has laid claim to much of it, contending it is family property. You understand the kind of dispute."

"Oh, yes."

"She fears that they might employ agents to steal it from her room at the Ambassador Hotel. More realistically, I fear they might attempt a legal seizure through the processes of California law. The matter is before the Massachusetts courts, but they might try to—"

"I fully understand."

"When we go back to Boston, they won't dare touch the property. Its ownership is being decided by a judge there. But here . . . Well, she might have to litigate the question all over again."

McIntyre smiled. "And you should like to hide it where they can't find it. That will be no problem. Under what name would you like the box?"

"John Adams," said Jack, grinning broadly.

McIntyre laughed. "Yes, yes! John Adams it is. You've the jewelry with you?"

"In my briefcase."

"Well, sir. It's done. And you and the lady are in Los Angeles for . . . ?"

"Vacation, mostly," said Jack. "No banking business, in any event. Perhaps a little personal business. Do you mind if I ask you if you know a couple of names?"

"Not at all. Let me order us coffee. We California bankers somehow feel we are out of the business mainstream, as you may imagine. It is a pleasure to talk with a Boston banker."

Jack paused while the banker spoke into his intercom and ordered coffee, then said, "Actually, I wonder if the day won't come when we in the East look to California for leadership in business."

"We lead in a few ways now," said McIntyre. "When I came to Los Angeles in 1919, it was a *village*. There are two necessities for this city to survive and succeed. One is water. The other is air conditioning. Anyway, who did you want to ask me about?"

"Let's start with Benjamin Vogel."

"I hope you haven't invested in Birdsong Productions."

"I haven't. But tell me why I shouldn't."

"Between us, as businessmen . . . Right? Vogel is Viennese. He was an actor briefly, then a director, and finally a producer in the Viennese theater before the War. He came to the States in 1912 or '13, skipping out on a lot of debts, apparently. He came to Los Angeles about ten years ago. His story was that he was a refugee from Austrian anti-Semitism—which is an interesting point, because he's not a Jew."

"How do we know that?"

"He's notorious for his, uh . . . 'casting couch,' if you know what I mean. Several young actresses have testified that he's not a Jew."

Jack smiled. "Someone told me there are no secrets in Hollywood."

"There are if you make an effort to keep them," said McIntyre. "Of course, no one in the motion-picture industry wants to keep secrets. The business thrives on gossip."

"Anyway, Vogel . . . ?"

"Abuses young women. Abuses his partners. Abuses his employees. And lately has acquired a reputation for an affiliation with gangsters."

"And speaking of gangsters, what about Antonio DiCalabria?"

"I hope you're not investing in any of *his* ventures. The word *gangster* applies to DiCalabria, just as you've suggested. Vogel is slime. DiCalabria is dangerous."

"Carlo Marfeo."

McIntyre's brows rose. "My God, Mr. Endicott! Surely you don't know these men!"

"Vogel for certain and Marfeo probably are involved in a plot to blackmail a friend of mine. DiCalabria has offered to help me, in a limited way."

"Why on earth would he do that?"

"A mutual friend asked him to."

The banker drew in a deep breath, then sighed loudly. "Mr. Endicott, I deal with a security agency here in Los Angeles. Let me put you in touch with them. You may need their services."

"I appreciate that, Mr. McIntyre, but for the moment I'd rather handle the matter myself. For one reason, I couldn't involve a detective agency and not tell them the name of my friend. I want to keep that secret."

"Not the kind of thing bankers usually do," McIntyre observed. "Do you play golf, Mr. Endicott?"

"I have been known to," said Jack. "I am not good at it. I like to fly. I sail. I race cars."

"I've got a sloop in the water down at Long Beach," said McIntyre. "If you're going to be in town long enough, maybe we can spend a day sailing."

"I would enjoy that."

Half an hour later the photographs and negatives of Norma Jean Chandler were locked up in the John Adams deposit box.

Jack had telephoned Meyer Lansky early in the morning. Lansky had been out. Now, about noon California time, he called him again and reached him.

"I just wanted you to know," said Lansky, "that Benny is coming to L.A. He's got an idea about opening a place like Piping Rock, not in the city but out in the desert somewhere. He wants to talk to DiCalabria about it. He's on his way now. He'll look you up when he gets there."

"Fine . . ." said Jack uncertainly.

"Listen," said Lansky. "No man ever had a better friend than Benny Siegel. You can trust him. I'd trust him with my balls. The only thing is, he's got a hot temper. And he believes in direct methods, if you know what I mean."

"I understand."

"How is DiCalabria treating you?"

"Friendly and helpful."

"He owes me. But what Benny's going to ask him for may even us out. So be careful."

"Meyer, I'm grateful to you. The DiCalabria connection got me off to a good start out here."

"Be careful about the identification," said Lansky. "It also wins you some bitter enemies."

"Ever hear of a man named Carlo Marfeo?"

"Never. Must be small peanuts."

"Sean Flynn?"

"Beware of the Irish, Jack."

Sean Flynn, contract agent for the Wiring and Lighting Workers Union, sat in his office in downtown Los Angeles and looked out over the Pacific. If Carlo Marfeo looked like a man whose face had been damaged in the boxing ring, Flynn was a man who'd definitely had that experience. A former middleweight fighter, he had become a legbreaker when his ring career floundered. His nose, his ears, his eyes, his cheekbones, his chin—all showed signs of mauling and breaking. His hair was sandy-red, his sunburned face was freckled; his eyes were light blue.

"I know the son of a bitch," he said to his brother Jimmy. "*You* know the son of a bitch. Know *of* him. Brahmin bastard. First Boston Provident Trust. Looks down his nose at every Mick ever born."

"Like to bust his nose," said Jimmy.

Jimmy still thought of himself as a welterweight, and he bounced around the office, sparring with the air. He was Sean's brother, no question, but Sean had to wonder whether there hadn't been a different father somewhere in the picture. Jimmy was slender, taller than Sean, with delicate features that had never been smashed in the ring. He'd never been in the ring much, but he'd demonstrated a talent for avoiding punches. If he could have delivered any of his own, he might have been successful. His hair was brown, his complexion olive, as if Daddy had been Italian. But he was Jimmy Flynn, just the same.

"Jimmy . . ." said Sean with mock patience. "Suppose the handlers climbed up to the corner before the bell. Suppose you turned your back on the guy you were fighting to go over and shoot a punch at one of the handlers? What'd happen?"

"What?"

"The guy you were fighting would cream ya. That's what would happen."

"So."

"So forget busting the nose of this asshole Endicott. He's nothing but a handler. Think about the guy in the ring. He's the guy that's gonna bust *your* nose. Roosevelt's the guy that's gonna bust ours."

"Unless he has an accident," said Jimmy.

"Now what could ever make you think that a careful man like Governor Roosevelt could have an accident?"

"Happens sometimes," said Jimmy.

"If it doesn't, we're gonna lose a sweet business," said Sean. "That is why we have to use brains. Gotta get the right guys together. Gotta use brains."

"Governor's coming to California next week."

Sean nodded. "Wonder what could happen?"

"What about that guy that claims he's a son of Annie Oakley? He claims he can light matches with a rifle at fifty feet."

"He's a nut," said Sean.

"Guys with that kind of talent sometimes are. Suppose we got him to try it for us. Suppose he didn't know who he was working for, really. Suppose he got caught and couldn't tell who'd hired him."

"You got it all worked out, little brother?"

Jimmy shrugged. "I got an *idea*," he said. "You got a better one?"

Jack and Charlotte sat on Antonio DiCalabria's stone terrace and watched the sun set into the Pacific. DiCalabria had suggested on the telephone that they not dress for dinner. He himself had, in fact, removed his jacket and tie and sat in a white dress shirt open at the collar. Jack did not take off the jacket of his light blue Palm Beach suit. He was cool enough.

DiCalabria had asked his wife to show Charlotte around the house. Charlotte would rather have stayed on the terrace to hear what the two men had to say to each other, but she could not without being rude refuse Angela DiCalabria's ingenuous invitation.

"I tried to find out something for you, and I haven't had any success. Norma Jean and her mother are missing. Gone. Left their house. Edna quit her job. Whoever's behind her is hiding her someplace."

Jack told him about the negatives. He did not say where he had put them.

"You can bet they kept other sets of prints," said DiCalabria. "Probably more negatives, too. You can also figure those two vice-squad guys are on somebody's payroll. Incidentally, where's Elliott Roosevelt?"

"Halfway to Chicago by now," said Jack. "He left on a flight this morning. He's meeting a westbound train there.

The Governor's making a campaign swing this way. He'll be in Los Angeles next Monday—a week from today."

"Uh-oh. You have to figure they'll try to give him a warm welcome. They'd love to splash the scandal on the front pages next Monday."

"The next move is up to them, I guess," said Jack. "I don't see what I can do to stop them."

DiCalabria got up and walked to the French doors, where he could peer into the house. "Before your lady comes back, I want to give you something," he said. He returned to the table and reached under it for a leather case Jack had noticed.

"What's this?" Jack asked as DiCalabria pulled from the case something wrapped in a leather belt.

"It's a Browning automatic," said DiCalabria. "In a shoulder holster. Take off your coat and let me help you get the thing on and get it adjusted before the ladies come back."

"Tony . . . I'm not sure—"

"*I'm* sure. I know what you're up against, and I'm sure."

It was better not to offend the man, so Jack took off his jacket and allowed DiCalabria to strap the holster under his left arm, where the pistol would hang out of sight but readily available to his right hand.

"I know you understand how to use it," said DiCalabria. "Don't unless you have to. But you might have to."

Jack shrugged the harness into a more secure and comfortable position. He reached in and drew the automatic. It was a Browning Model 1910, a 9mm six-shot pistol. He had seen several like it in France in 1917 and '18. Belgian officers carried them. So did some of the French. It was small enough not to make a bulge under his jacket, yet it fired a heavy bullet and would drop a man in an instant. DiCalabria handed him an extra clip, loaded with six more cartridges.

"Do you call this a 'biscuit'?" Jack asked as he hefted the revolver and sighted it on a gull down the beach.

DiCalabria laughed. "Not me. That's what some of the guys back east would call it."

The night he had to shoot Louis Feinman—"Fine Louie"—he had been carrying his father's old .38 Smith & Wesson revolver. He expected this Browning would be far more accurate.

"It's a fine pistol," he said. "I appreciate the loan and will return it. Anyway, I hope I will. The last pistol I carried wound up at the bottom of the Chicago Sanitary Canal."

"*We* dump 'em out to sea," said DiCalabria blandly.

Jack shoved the Browning into its holster. Charlotte would of course see it later, and he would have to explain it.

"Well . . . let's pop some champagne," said DiCalabria. "I'm expecting another guy, incidentally."

"Are you aware that Benny Siegel is coming to Los Angeles?" Jack asked. He felt certain that DiCalabria did know, but confiding the fact to him might seem like a favor.

"I know. When I was a kid back home, Irish and Italian guys could beat up on Meyer and get away with it. You tried to beat up on Benny Siegel, he'd kill himself trying to kill you. You know him well enough not to call him Bugsy?"

"I've met him only once, but Meyer told me never to call him Bugsy."

"Right. Meyer is all brains. Benny is all muscle—including his head."

"What about Sean Flynn?" Jack asked.

"Someday I'm going to kill him," said DiCalabria.

"Because . . . ?"

"Because there's no limit to his greed and ambition. Where'd you get his name?"

"From Samuel Goldwyn."

"There's a gutsy guy," said DiCalabria. "But he'd better be careful about Flynn. Flynn's as nutty as Benny Siegel. It's guys like him that give a lot of other guys a bad name."

Angela DiCalabria led Charlotte back onto the terrace. The butler had just brought the champagne her husband had mentioned, and shortly they lifted their four glasses.

"Jack, this house is lovely," said Charlotte.

He could tell from her voice that she was not just paying a shallow, proforma compliment. "What I've seen certainly is," he said.

"Tony and I couldn't have done it ourselves," said Angela. "We hired people."

DiCalabria grinned with innocent pleasure. "Kid from Italy. Kid from Poland . . . Well, her parents, actually. We've learned to tell the difference between what's pretty and what's not."

The sunset light faded as they sat and sipped champagne. The butler came, leaned close to DiCalabria, and said something quietly. DiCalabria nodded.

"Our other friend has arrived," he said. "Do I tell you who he is, or do you want to guess after you see him?"

"Oh, let's guess!" said Charlotte.

"Tony . . ." said Angela unhappily, for the first time showing herself disagreeing with her husband. "Do you have to?"

"He's fun," said DiCalabria.

The butler brought the new guest to the terrace, carrying with him a bottle of gin and a glass on a tray.

The guest was a man in his late sixties, maybe his seventies: bulky and awkward, a little unsteady on his feet. He had a broad middle-American face, with a big red nose, big ears, teary ill-focused eyes. His barber had run clippers well above his ears, leaving a stubble of hair on the sides of his head but oiled-down strands on top. He wore a shiny black suit, a wrinkled shirt with a loosened necktie, and spats on his shoes.

Jack recognized him. He was Billy Sunday, the thundering tent-show evangelist.

"How kind of you to invite me," he said to DiCalabria. "And who might these fine people be?"

"Billy," said DiCalabria. "Meet John Lowell Endicott, a banker from Boston. And this is his friend, Mrs. Charlotte Wendell."

"Charmed," said Billy Sunday with a deep and clumsy bow. He sat down, snatched up the bottle of gin, and poured himself a glass. "I used to be a baseball player. Did you know that, Mr. Endicott?"

"I did indeed, Reverend Sunday," said Jack.

Charlotte started. She had not, until Jack used the name, realized who the man was.

"Baseball is a very . . . *Christian* game, you know," said Sunday as he sipped gin. "Did you ever think of that? It is. The contest between the pitcher and the batsman can be likened to the contrast between Satan and Christ."

"But which is which?" asked Charlotte.

"It makes no difference," said Sunday. "The point is the unending contest. The struggle. It's edifying to watch. It preaches a moral lesson. I've had two careers: ball player and preacher. For the second, I've drawn strength from the first."

"Mr. Sunday is going to convert Angela and me," said DiCalabria.

"Into what?" asked Charlotte contemptuously.

VIII

On Tuesday morning, Jack visited the office of the Los Angeles Superintendent of Schools. He had a simple question, he said. All he wanted was the name of the school nurse for Pershing High School. An hour later he knocked on the door of a woman named Myra Logan.

He handed her his card.

"Do we know each other?" she asked skeptically. "I guess I'm entitled to believe a man with an engraved card saying he's a Boston banker is not an insurance salesman."

"We haven't met, Miss Logan, and I assure you I'm not here to sell insurance or anything else. I have a quick and simple question I'd like to ask; and, if you will do me the favor of answering it, I will be gone in half a minute."

"If it's about anything that comes up in the course of my work, that's all confidential," she said. She was an exceptionally tall woman, rail-thin, wearing round steel-rimmed eyeglasses, with her graying black hair tied back tightly. "Professional ethics, you understand."

"I do understand. Maybe my question is one you *can* answer. You visit Pershing High School on a regular basis, do you not?"

"Yes, I do."

"Did you, during the spring semester, examine a sixteen-year-old girl at Pershing High School to determine if she were pregnant?"

Miss Logan's chin jerked up. "Good heavens, no!"

"The girl was expelled from Pershing. Mr. Rosenbusch says she was examined by the school nurse, who found her pregnant. Could it have been another school nurse?"

"*I* am the school nurse for Pershing High School, Mr. Endicott."

"Yes. Miss Logan, if there were some sort of certificate in the school records, saying this girl was expelled because you found her pregnant—"

"That would be a falsehood, sir!"

"If your signature was on some sort of medical record—"

"It would be a forgery!"

"Yes. Would you be sufficiently interested to check? And if you do, and find a falsehood or forgery, would you be kind enough to let me know?"

"Just what is your interest?"

"There is a possibility someone is trying to commit extortion."

"Using *my name?*"

"I'm afraid so. Maybe not. But maybe."

* * *

In the Santa Monica Mountains, a few miles north of the beaches of Santa Monica, Scotty Oakley lived in a ramshackle wooden house he grandly called his ranch house. He insisted he was the illegitimate son of the famed American sharpshooter Annie Oakley. He said he had inherited her skill with a rifle and could equal most of her sharpshooting tricks. From time to time he traveled with western shows; and whether or not he was as good as Annie Oakley, he was good enough to impress audiences with his marksmanship. He had a problem, of course. He drank. He never stayed with a show long enough to earn much money.

"Hi, Scotty," said Jimmy Flynn. "I brought you somethin'."

Scotty was sitting on an old automobile seat he had dragged up on his porch and made the settee from which he sat and watched his domain: an expanse of dusty land littered with junk between his porch and a small stream of clear water that rushed past on its way to the Pacific, beyond that a wooded slope that rose to the edge of the valley.

"Yeah? What'd you bring me?"

Jimmy opened a duffel bag he had carried to the house and poured its contents out on the weathered boards of the porch floor. He had brought Scotty half a dozen bottles of bourbon and a dozen boxes of .30-30 cartridges. "Thutty-thutties," they were called—rifle ammunition.

"Well . . . That's nice of ye. Afraid I disremember yer name."

"Bob Wallace," said Jimmy. "Remember the show you did in Bakersfield."

"Ahh . . ." said Scotty uncertainly. "Right. Right. Remember ye well."

"You're one hell of a shot, Scotty. You have to be as good as your mother, though I never did see her."

"No, I ain't as good. Never claimed to be. But I inherited somethin' from her. I got a sharp eye and a steady hand." He nodded for emphasis. "Yessir. Sharp eye and steady hand."

Scotty Oakley was in his forties, Jimmy guessed—though he might have been taken for sixty by anyone who hadn't seen him demonstrate that he did in fact have a sharp eye and a steady hand. He hadn't shaved for a week. In fact, he was probably one of those men who had himself shaved once a week, by a barber. His vividly blue eyes peered out from a tangle of deep wrinkles. His hair was black. He wore bib overalls with a blue work shirt, a crushed felt hat, and obviously expensive black cowboy boots.

If he meant to pretend abject rural poverty, the boots gave him away, as did the collection of expensive guns lying about: two Winchester lever-action rifles, a Savage lever-action mounted with a telescopic sight, a pump-action Remington shotgun, a Colt .44 revolver, and a German 9mm parabellum Luger—all these guns oiled and wiped free of dust.

"See that there squirrel acrost the crick?" Scotty asked. He pointed, and Jimmy did see: a red fox squirrel in a pine tree fifty yards or more away. "See that there pine cone right above his head?"

Scotty picked up one of the rifles and, taking aim for no more than three seconds, fired. The pine cone shattered, and the squirrel fled in terror.

"N' point in killin' the squirrel," said Scotty. "Scairt 'im bad 'nough."

Scotty unscrewed the cap off one of the bottles of bourbon and took a tug.

Jimmy sat in silence for a long moment. He had a sense of timing. Finally he asked, "You ever shoot a man, Scotty?"

"You ain't the first man ever come out here and ast me to do it."

"I didn't ask you."

"No. You just come out to bring me whiskey and ca'-tridges. I ain't never done no show in Bakersfield, by the way."

Jimmy waited. Then he asked, "You want me to go away?"

"Not till I hear yer proposition."

Jimmy grinned. "Okay. What do you think of communism, Scotty?"

"Evil thing. Evil thing. You want me to go over to Russia and shoot that fella Stalin?"

"No."

"Then you got it in mind to kill Governor Roosevelt when he's in town next week."

Jimmy Flynn shook his head. "I'm not sure I want to do business with you. You're too smart."

"Lemme think, now. How'd you figger? You figgered you'd get a dumb ol' coot back in the hills to take a shot at the man. You figured th' ol' coot'd prob'ly kill him. You also figgered th' ol' coot'd like as not get caught. But he's so damn dumb, he'd think he'd been hired by Bob Wallace—whoever that wuz. Don't work that way, cousin. Don't work that way at all."

"Then how does it work?"

"Hand me five hundred dollars cash, and I'll tell you how it works."

"I don't have five hundred on me."

"Come back when ye do."

In 1932 presidential candidates did not have Secret Service protection. By telegram, Louis Howe asked the chief of police of Los Angeles to regard John Lowell Endicott as a representative of the Roosevelt campaign, for the purpose of discussing the arrangements to protect Governor Roosevelt during his visit. On Tuesday afternoon, Jack went to police headquarters to meet with the chief.

"I may as well be frank with you, Mr. Endicott," said Chief Bryan Jackson. "We will do everything we can to protect Governor Roosevelt when he is in Los Angeles. But when a man elects to ride in an open car through the streets of a city, if someone wants to attack him, someone will attack him, and there's not much we can do about it. We will give him a motorcycle escort to clear the way. We will put men on the running board of his car—though politicians don't like that; it blocks people's view of the candidate. If some anarchist wants to throw a bomb into an open car, he'll do it, just the same. Franz Ferdinand was assassinated at Sarajevo . . ."

"A rifleman on a roof," said Jack.

"If I had my way, the Governor would ride in a closed car," said the chief. "Then he's going to speak in Pershing Park. Outdoors."

"As I understand the schedule," said Jack, "he arrives at Union Station, rides in a motorcade to Pershing Park, speaks, then rides in a motorcade to the Ambassador Hotel for a private luncheon with . . . With—"

"Fat cats," said the chief.

"So there's exposure in the two motorcades and in the park. Obviously he's safe once he's inside the Ambassador Hotel."

The chief nodded.

"Is there any such thing as identifying potential assassins in advance?"

"Sure. Known anarchists. Known Reds."

"Known sharpshooters?"

Chief Jackson shrugged. "There are some employed by the movie studios. They're the only ones I'd know about."

"What do they do for the movie studios?" Jack asked.

"You ever see a picture called *Little Caesar*? You remember the scene where Edward G. Robinson as the gangster is shot? He was supposed to have taken just one bullet, in the arm, but a whole lot of others broke glass and chipped bricks a foot or two from him. Well, that was studio sharpshooters. They really fired those shots. They knew exactly where Robinson would be standing, and they placed their bullets damned close to him—but they never hit him. It's a specialty."

"I thought they were little powder charges, popped by electricity."

"Sometimes. More often, real shots, fired by sharpshooters."

"Well, Chief, I appreciate your time. I'm sure the Governor will be as safe in Los Angeles as he will be in any city in the United States."

"That's as much as I can promise you, Mr. Endicott."

"I'm going to name two names that are of particular

concern to me," said Jack. "Carlo Marfeo and Sean Flynn."

"Bad actors," said the chief. "I wish I could just lock them up while the Governor is in town. But that wouldn't do any good. Neither one of them would move against him personally. They'd hire somebody. And I'm surprised you mention only those two. There's a worse one. Big Dick DiCalabria. I'd give anything to get *him* into San Quentin."

Chickie had been watching Elliott Roosevelt's small house for five hours. He was ready to swear nobody was at home. To be sure, he went across the street and rang the doorbell. Nobody answered. He was sure. He went to a telephone in a gas station four blocks away and called Carlo Marfeo.

An hour later a black Chrysler pulled to the curb behind Chickie's Chevrolet.

"This has gotta go fast," said Marfeo. "We got no time for clownin' around. In and out, gone."

"Right," said Chickie.

"You got the door open?"

"Waited for you."

"Well, go do it, fer Christ's sake!"

Chickie walked across the street and to the door of the house, trying to look casual. He put a small tool in the keyhole of the simple lock. He'd checked that when he came to ring the bell. The lock was simple. Why people thought they protected their homes with five-dollar, three-tumbler locks he would never understand. A practiced burglar, he took no more time to open the lock than he would have taken with a key. He glanced at the Chrysler and walked into the house.

Carlo didn't come across the street. Chickie had figured

that. No, Carlo stayed in the car and behind the wheel, in case anything went wrong. He sent Joe Coyne.

With the girl. Coyne hurried across the street with the girl and the camera.

"Get in here! Hurry up!"

"I don' wanna do this!" Norma Jean wailed tearfully.

"Wanna don't count," snarled Coyne. "Clothes off, kid, and make it snappy. C'mon! *Hurry!* We can't stay in here!"

The frightened girl took most of a minute to strip herself naked.

Coyne looked around the room, spotted in an ashtray three cigarette butts with lipstick on them, and said, "Hey! The guy does have broads here."

"The guy is married, dummy," said Chickie. "Wonder why there's *only* butts with lipstick. Where's his . . . ?"

"Do I hafta?" wailed the naked Norma Jean.

"Hafta," said Chickie. "Straighten your face up. Smile! Siddown on the couch."

The girl sat down, leaning forward to hide her breasts and crotch.

"Sit up! And, smile, goddammit! Legs apart! Smile! Make like you're havin' a great time!"

Coyne aimed a Kodak folding camera at Norma Jean. She obeyed. He stepped back from her and focused. He wanted the girl clearly in the center of the picture, but he wanted enough of the room to identify it clearly. Let the Roosevelt boy claim he'd never seen her when he faced naked pictures of her taken in his own living room!

"Awright. Spread wider. Smile. *Smile, goddammit, smile!*"

* * *

"You know," said Jack to Charlotte, "there's a company here in Los Angeles that will rent you an automobile. *Rent* it to you, by golly. Well, I've rented one, so tonight we're nobody's guest for dinner; we're going out on our own."

"The Cocoanut Grove is right here in the hotel," she said. "I'd like to visit that one night while we're here."

"We will. But I got this car. It's a Ford, would you believe it? The rental company delivered it. We can drive it all we want to, for so much a day plus so much for mileage. I want to try one or two places I've heard about."

Charlotte shrugged. "I imagine we're going to do what you want."

They had spent three-quarters of an hour in the swimming pool, had come in and showered, and now were relaxed on the bed, nude, sipping at Scotches. It was plain to both of them that feelings gradually building could not much longer be subdued and that they would shortly couple. At forty-eight, Jack enjoyed sex more, though less quickly and less often, then he had ten years before—a great deal less quickly and less often than he had twenty years before. He had learned to bring to it a restraint that resulted in deeper, more memorable pleasure than he had ever known from it before—especially with a woman like Charlotte.

Almost ten years younger than he was, she was unwilling just to be a receptor of whatever stimuli he might imagine; she wanted to be an inventor as well. She was an erotic woman. Even when she was fully and formally dressed, her slanted narrow eyes were full of suggestion. Now, as she lay on her back on the bed, with her breasts lying flattened and spread, and her belly lying concave inside her pelvis, she was losing interest in talk—as was he. Their eyes met, and anticipation replaced every other interest.

* * *

The blind on the bedroom window did not touch the sill. The gap of four or five inches was of no consequence because thick subtropical shrubs grew to a height halfway up the window.

The same shrubbery shielded from view the men who crouched between the shrubs and the wall. One of them was Chickie. The other was Coyne, the man who had taken the pictures of Norma Jean in Elliott Roosevelt's living room. Chickie knelt, his attention fixed on a broken-open twelve-gauge double-barreled shotgun. It had been cut down, leaving no more than eighteen inches of barrel, not that much of the stock. Chickie was shoving two big shells into the chamber.

"Are they in the bedroom?" he asked Coyne.

"And how! Looka this! Looka this!"

Chickie put his face closer to the window and looked in. "Jesus!"

"Whatcha call *doin' it!*"

"You don't have that damned camera with you?"

"Man, do I wish I did!"

Forgetting the shotgun for the moment, Chickie stared openmouthed.

He wore rubber surgical gloves. The shotgun was free of fingerprints and would be left under the window. The thunderous blasts of both barrels would cause panic. He and Coyne would crawl along the wall, behind the shrubbery, and turn the corner of the garden-apartment building. Then they would emerge and calmly walk to the parking lot. They had pistols, but they didn't expect to have to use them.

"Camera . . . Hell, I wish I had a movie camera."

"Too bad the broad's gonna get it, too," said Chickie. "She's worth something."

"Well—"

"Not till they're finished. What the hell? Doing it now would spoil their fun and ours."

They crouched and stared until their knees began to hurt and they had to change positions.

"Chickie . . ."

Coyne touched Chickie's arm. He pressed his finger to his mouth and nodded toward the lawn beyond the shrubbery.

Chickie peered out. A dozen people, some in swimsuits, others in white, had congregated on the lawn. They carried croquet mallets and balls, and two men began to drive the end stakes for the court, others to pace off the distances and set the arches.

"Jesus!"

Others came, bringing tables and chairs. In a minute there would be as many as twenty people on the lawn.

Chickie broke open the gun and dropped the ejected shells in his jacket pocket. He shoved the barrel of the sawed-off shotgun into a rope loop under his jacket. It made a bulge but was not immoderately conspicuous. He and Coyne scurried toward the corner of the building, pushed their way through the hedge, and walked away—leaving three elderly guests mystified as to what those men had been doing behind the hedge.

Jack and Charlotte left the Ambassador a little after seven, amused to be driving a little Ford but glad for the independence that came with the novelty of renting a car. Jack had brought a white dinner jacket in his trunk, and Charlotte had urged him to wear it. She herself wore a short white silk dress, very simple line, almost like a slip. It did not cover her shoulders or her knees and displayed deep cleavage, but it was covered by a sheer blue organdy overdress that blurred the lines of her cleavage and of her legs from knee to midcalf. She wore shoes with rhinestone buckles, and the Lanier Emerald hung in her décolletage.

The Browning automatic hung in its soft-leather holster under Jack's left shoulder. Charlotte had stared at it solemnly but had raised no objection to his carrying it. They had talked about it when he first returned to the hotel with it, after DiCalabria gave it to him; and she had agreed that if DiCalabria thought he should carry it, probably he should.

"I haven't carried a firearm since 1918," he had said. "Until this year—"

"It's your association with Governor Roosevelt. It's not your fault. Or his."

Before they left Saratoga Springs, Meyer Lansky had given Jack the name and address of a place in Malibu. It was worth visiting, he had said. DiCalabria had confirmed that and had telephoned the proprietors to say that Mr. Endicott should be received as his guest. Called La Casa Pacifica, it was a nightclub casino.

It was, in terminology Lansky had explained, a carpet joint. A sawdust joint was a raw gambling operation, often in the locked back room of a pool hall. Originally, that a place was a carpet joint meant that it had carpet on the floor, as opposed to concrete and sawdust, where gamblers spit tobacco on the floor. Carpet meant elegance. By 1930 many of the carpet joints were elegant indeed, none more so than Lansky's Piping Rock at Saratoga. They paid high prices to hire entertainers.

Jack and Charlotte were welcomed and led to a stageside table.

The comedian playing La Casa Pacifica that week was Joe E. Lewis. Lewis had started out as a singer, but in 1927 in Chicago certain mob types, furious because he had left one job to take another, had beaten him senseless and slashed his throat. After that he would not sing. He insisted to the police, just the same, that he had no idea who might have attacked him or why. After that, Joe E. Lewis was never without work, even though he sometimes missed shows: too drunk to appear. He moved from one carpet joint to another, always well paid but always gambling and often losing most of his salary to the house. He was a heavy drinker and a chain-smoker, and it was his style to wander among the tables, followed by a spotlight, carrying a tumbler full of whiskey and dragging on a cigarette. Most of his comedy was one-liners.

"They say nothin's more fun that sleeping with a chorus girl. Wrong. It's more fun to sleep with *two* chorus girls."

"You show me a man without money, I'll show you a bum."

"Doc tells me I've gotta stop drinkin' or I'll never see my old age. Yeah? Well, whatta ya see more of: old drunks or old doctors?"

"Maybe I *do* gotta stop drinkin'. I'm beginnin' to see the handwriting on the floor."

The people in the club seemed to appreciate all this, and he got laughs and applause.

After they had eaten a dinner of filet of sole served with white wine, Jack and Charlotte went into the gaming room, and Jack took a seat at a blackjack table. Charlotte didn't play. She stood behind Jack while he played for an hour and demonstrated why he was called Blackjack Endicott. When he gathered up his chips and cashed them in, he had won a little more than a thousand dollars.

Even so the owner of the club came out to the foyer as they were leaving, thanked them for coming, and asked them to come again.

The hour was a little after eleven, and fog coming in off the Pacific hid the ocean from view. It even blurred the lines of the cars in the parking lot. Jack handed his ticket to a boy, who ran off toward the lot to find the Ford.

"They were gentlemen about your taking them for a thousand," said Charlotte.

"They have to be," Jack said. "Actually, it's good for the house to have the other gamblers see a man taking the house for a thousand once in a while. If nobody ever won, it would raise certain suspicions."

The boy returned with the Ford, Jack tipped him, and they drove off, onto the Pacific Coast Highway and east and south toward Santa Monica, Wilshire Boulevard, and the Ambassador Hotel.

With the fog thickening, Jack kept his speed down to about thirty-five miles an hour. His own car had powerful fog lights, but the little Ford had only its modest headlights. Fortunately, there was no traffic. The single car in sight behind did not overtake them. Jack could see its headlights in the rearview mirror: two blurry points of light.

Charlotte lit a cigarette. "You're a fun man to travel with," she said. "Poor Bob was a worrier."

"I'm very glad you're with me, Charlotte."

"Someone must have said to you that bringing a woman with you to Los Angeles is like carrying coals to Newcastle.

You'd have been swamped with starlets if I weren't around."

"I'm glad you're with me," he repeated.

"I decided not to fall in love with you. It's not an easy resolution to keep."

He reached over with his right hand and stroked her leg.

She laughed: a small, melodious laugh. "I even resolved not to go to bed with you."

"I resolved not to press you to do it," said Jack. "I didn't want to—"

"You waited for me to *jump* in your bed. Well, you didn't have long to wait, did you?"

"Regrets?"

"Oh no. I've just been wondering a little what future we have." She turned and slipped her half-smoked cigarette out the window. "Don't answer. I don't want to hear right now."

"I don't have an answer," he said.

"*Jack . . .*" The tone of her voice had changed abruptly. "The car behind us is—"

He checked in the mirror. The car behind—it was a larger car than the Ford, maybe a Chrysler, anyway a coupe—had pulled out into the left lane and was edging slowly up alongside the Ford. The driver did not seem to want to pass, only to pull up and run parallel.

Jack eased off on the accelerator to let the car pass. The coupe—it was a black Chrysler—slowed down, too.

"*Charlotte!* Get down. Somebody is going to fire a shot at us."

Jack gripped the wheel with his left hand and with his right drew the Browning and flipped off the safety. His guess had been right. As the Chrysler moved directly alongside, he saw the barrels of a sawed-off shotgun thrust through the window.

He did not hesitate. He fired. The distance was short, no more than five feet, and the slug struck the gunman in the Chrysler on the left cheekbone and tore through his head.

Jack caught a glimpse of the terrified, gore-splattered face of the man driving the Chrysler. He took aim at him, but the man had already jammed the accelerator to the floor, and the Chrysler surged forward and outran the Ford.

IX

They had been back in their hotel room no more than fifteen minutes when the telephone rang. The hotel operator asked if Mr. Endicott would take a call from a Mr. Antonio DiCalabria. He took it.

"Was that you?" asked DiCalabria.

"Yes."

"The dead man was Salvatore Ciccenza, known as Chickie."

"I won a thousand dollars at the blackjack table," said Jack.

"Would I have sent you to a joint that'd try to kill you for winning? C'mon! Chickie worked for Marfeo. So now we know how serious they are."

"Dead serious."

"You all right? Charlotte all right?"

"We're all right. Sitting here drinking more Scotch than we ought to."

"Glad I lent you the 'biscuit'?"

"Yes. I'm grateful to you, Tony."

"Okay. Now look. The driver's a guy named Joe Coyne. The Santa Monica police have him. He was driving seventy miles an hour with a bloody stiff in his car. He's explained that somebody shot his friend, for no reason at all and he was driving so fast because he was scared."

"How did he explain the sawed-off shotgun?"

"Is *that* what they had? He must have tossed it. Anyway, Marfeo's lawyers are at the station, and they'll have Joe Coyne out of there within the hour. He won't talk. You can count on that. So you won't be identified, and you won't have to answer any questions."

"You're sure he won't talk?"

DiCalabria was silent for a moment. "He won't talk. One way or another, he won't talk. Count on it."

"They'll try again, won't they?"

"Right. Be careful. But Marfeo doesn't have a big organization. He'll have to hire somebody. That'll take him a day or two. I'll try to find out who he hires."

"I'm hugely indebted to you," Jack said somberly.

"I'll present my bill to President Roosevelt."

Jimmy Flynn didn't have much time. On Wednesday morning he was out in the Santa Monica Mountains again, this time carrying five hundred dollars in cash.

"Y' bring me any more presents?" asked Scotty Oakley.

Jimmy handed over two more bottles of whiskey.

"Th' five hundred is for tellin' y' *how*, y' understand. The doin' of it is worth a whole lot more."

"I didn't suppose it would be any other way."

Scotty nodded. "You talkin' about changin' the course of history," he said. " 'Cause, what I hear on th' raddio tells me this man Roosevelt is gonna be elected next President of the United States."

"We know that," said Jimmy.

"What do ye figger would have been the right fee for Gavrilo Prinzip, if he'd escaped to collect his fee?"

"Who?"

"Ye don't read yer history, like Scotty does. Prinzip was the man that shot the Austrian archduke at Sarajevo in 1914. Changed the course of history. I been thinkin' about this since you was here yestiddy. Changin' the course of history has gotta be worth an awful lot of money."

"Not worth more than somebody's *got*," said Jimmy Flynn.

"Well . . . It's an awful risky proposition. You wouldn't be thinkin' about it just because you don't like the face of this man Roosevelt. It's got to be worth a lotta money."

"I'm giving you five hundred dollars to tell me how you'd do it," said Jimmy.

Scotty Oakley fell silent. He stared at the littered ground in front of his house, at the rushing stream, at the brush and trees beyond, up at the mountain. Eventually he sighed. "That there Savage," he said, "is what they call a varmint rifle. It fires a small bullet, but it fires it at an awful velocity. You can load the ca'tridges with silver-point bullets, with hollow tips. Awful accurate. Don't make a big noise. But when that bullet hits, it spreads out and breaks up and goes through, makin' a terrible wound. I've kilt deer with it. That bullet flies so fast that yer movin' target don't move far whilst the bullet's comin'. That's the gun I'd use if I'd made a deal to kill a man."

"Have you ever killed a man?"

"Have *you?* That kind of question ain't perlite."

"Our man will be moving in an open car through the streets of Los Angeles. He'll make a speech on Pershing Square. Then he'll go to the Ambassador Hotel in an open car. I suppose the best place to get him would be while he's getting into or out of a car. He has to be lifted, you know. That means he'll be all but standing still. He—"

"No."

"No?"

"There'll be folks all around him then, leanin' over him, all like that. It's while he's in the car, that's where you get him. Politician, he'll be wavin' at the crowd. He'll want his bodyguards out of the way so's people can see him. If people can see him, *I* can see him."

"Where will you be?"

"Nobody's gonna know. Includin' you."

"Including—"

"Stop figgerin' Scotty for a dummy, my lad. I shoot Governor Roosevelt, you best shoot me. Isn't that right? Leave no witness. Maybe even get your money back. That's why I work alone, and that's why you pay me in advance."

"That's crazy!"

"You gotta be crazy to wanta try it. I gotta be crazy to do it. But them's m' terms. You kin git somebody else easy 'nough, I figger. Haven't y' tried?"

Jimmy Flynn stared thoughtfully at this wild man. "How much money are you talking about?" he asked.

"Fifty thousand dollars, cash," said Scotty blandly.

Jimmy gasped. "My God, man!"

"Scotty's got to go to South America, or somewheres, and live th' rest of m' life. Don't seem like too much. You think about it. Governor Roosevelt will be in town on Monday. Lemme know Friday or Sattiday. I'll have to make some arrangements, load some special ca'tridges.''

Jack and Charlotte were wakened by a telephone call.

"Mr. Endicott, I'm Harry Draper, city editor of the Los Angeles *Examiner*. Mr. Hearst has directed me to call you this morning and ask you to come to the office and see some photographs we've received."

"Pictures of a girl, I imagine," Jack said dryly.

"Yessir. That's what they are."

"All right. When?"

"Mr. Hearst is coming down from San Simeon and is expected here about eleven. Could you be with us then?"

"I'll be there," Jack said.

By coincidence he encountered William Randolph Hearst in the lobby of the building, and they went up on Hearst's private elevator together. They exchanged pleasantries but said nothing about the reason for their meeting. They did not want the elevator girl to overhear any conversation about the photographs.

They went to a large walnut-paneled conference room— blessedly air-conditioned—on the top floor of the twenty-five-story building. The city editor, Draper, was waiting for them there, as was the editor-in-chief of the *Examiner*, David Bright. Their formidable publisher took his place in a thronelike leather chair at the head of the table and gestured to Jack to take the chair to his right.

"All right," said Hearst. "Let's see these pictures."

Draper and Bright exchanged a glance. Draper spoke.

"The photographs are quite disgusting, Mr. Hearst." Bright added, "Lewd."

With a peremptory sweep of his hand, Hearst ordered the pictures put before him.

Jack recognized Norma Jean Chandler. In one of the pictures she leaned back on a couch, quite naked, with her heels planted on the front of the cushions, her legs spread wide. In another she stood in front of a small desk, with one foot up on the chair in front of the desk. Jack was certain that was the desk and chair Elliott Roosevelt had mentioned.

"There's a letter," said Bright.

The letter was typewritten. It read:

These pictures were taken by E. Roosevelt and are of a sixteen years old girl named Norma Jean Chandler. The place is Roosevelt's front room. You can check that by going and looking at the house. He's been fooling around with that little girl, and these pictures prove it. You want to interview her, it can be arranged. Will be in touch by phone.

Citizen

"You speak for the Governor," Hearst said to Jack. "What do you think?"

"It's obvious, isn't it? Extortion."

"Yet I think we have to know," said Bright, "if these pictures were indeed taken in Elliott Roosevelt's living room."

"Suppose they were," said Jack. "That doesn't prove Elliott took them."

"It goes a long way toward proving it," said Bright. He was a small chubby man, bald, who wore a pince-nez on a black ribbon. "We have to expect, Mr. Hearst, that these photographs have been sent to other newspapers. They'll scoop us. What is more, since it is known that we editorially support Governor Roosevelt, we will be accused of suppressing the story for his advantage."

Jack squinted over the photograph of the girl standing at the desk. "Do you have a large magnifying glass handy? I mean a powerful magnifying glass."

Hearst produced the magnifying glass from a drawer in the table. Jack used it to study the picture more closely.

"Look at something, gentlemen," he said. "Look at the newspaper lying on that little desk. Even with the magnifying glass you can't read anything. But look at the style. That's the *Examiner*. See your little American flag up in the corner? You can count the number of letters in the last word of the logo. Eight. *E-X-A-M-I-N-E-R*. It's not the *Herald*. It's not the *Times.*"

"We're pleased to know that Mr. Roosevelt reads the *Examiner*," said Bright. "But what does it prove?"

"Maybe nothing," said Jack. "But maybe something. We can't read the date. That's much too small. But we can compare the layout of columns, the general pattern of the front page. Do you have recent *Examiner*s handy?"

Hearst pointed to a stack of newspapers spread out on a smaller table. "There are the last two or three weeks," he said.

Draper brought the papers to the table. "Here's yesterday's," he said. "Then Monday's and so on."

Jack looked back and forth between the tiny image of the folded newspaper on the desk and the actual *Examiner*s. "Better than I thought," he said. "Gentlemen, these pictures were taken yesterday."

"Really?"

"Look at yesterday's front page. An eight-column banner headline. A five-column picture, set to the left so there are two columns of type to the right of the picture and one to the left. Under the picture you have two two-column heads and one one-column head. You can't read a word, even of the banner headline in this little photograph, but you can see the same layout of the newspaper."

"I see something else," said Hearst. "That picture is of the North Fork Dam. You can't see it in the little picture, but the configuration is identical. Don't you agree, David?"

David Bright fixed his pince-nez on his nose and squinted at the photograph of Norma Jean Chandler with the newspaper behind her on the desk. "Yes . . ." he said. "I think it's clear enough that this is yesterday's paper."

"Then I will ask you gentlemen to do me a favor. Will you check your wire services? There should be a story about Governor Roosevelt arriving in Chicago. Yesterday."

Harry Draper used a telephone to order sheets torn from the Teletype machines in the newsroom downstairs. While they waited, the three men stared at the photographs.

"Who is she?" Bright asked.

"She was a student at Pershing High School," said Jack. "She's pregnant, according to the principal there, who expelled her. He says the school nurse examined her and found her pregnant. The school nurse says she didn't. In any case, the matter was not reported to the juvenile authorities."

"How do you know?" asked Hearst.

"I inquired here and there," said Jack blandly.

Draper grinned. "Have you ever considered working as a newspaper reporter?" he asked.

The sheets from the wire-service Teletypes were delivered promptly. They pored over them.

"You've made your point," said Hearst suddenly. "Here. Story from International News Service, Chicago, August 23, 1932."

> Governor Franklin D. Roosevelt arrived in the city this morning, on a train from Albany, New York. He will address a meeting of businessmen at Merchandise Mart at noon, and in the afternoon the campaign will leave Chicago for points west. The Democratic candidate for President will speak from the rear platform of his train in several cities during the next few days and will make major appearances in Omaha and Denver as the train makes its way to Los Angeles, where it is expected to arrive on Monday, August 29.
>
> Governor Roosevelt is accompanied on his westward campaign swing by his campaign manager, James Farley, and by his personal adviser, Louis Howe. Mrs. Eleanor Roosevelt is not accompanying the Governor on his trip. The Governor is usually accompanied by one of his sons, and for this trip the son with him is Elliott Roosevelt. Elliott, 22 years old, lives in California and flew to Chicago by airline.
>
> Interviewed at the airport, young Mr. Roosevelt expressed his enthusiasm for airline travel, calling it fast, safe, and convenient.

"So Elliott was in Chicago yesterday when these pictures were taken," said Jack. "I said extortion. It is extortion."

"A crude attempt to damage the Roosevelt candidacy," said Hearst.

"I believe I should telephone every other editor in town," said David Bright.

"Please do," said Hearst. "Start now."

Jack reached for the letter that had come with the photographs. "Read the last words again. 'Citizen' will call and would like to arrange an interview for the girl."

"You're thinking of trapping him?" asked Hearst.

"Why not?"

"What a story!" exclaimed Draper.

"If it becomes a story, we defeat the purpose," said Jack solemnly.

"A point well taken," said Hearst. "Let's reserve judgment on that. Harry, if 'Citizen' calls, try to arrange the meeting he suggests."

Except that Antonio DiCalabria claimed and sporadically enforced suzerainty over all liquor traffic, gambling, and prostitution in Los Angeles, Ventura, and Orange counties, the metropolitan area was not divided as Chicago and New York were. Even so, Sean Flynn regarded the southern part of the city as his territory, and Carlo Marfeo regarded the northern part as his. Since their chief revenues came from their dominance over labor unions, territory was not important to them. Each had better sense than to try to move in on the other's unions, and they did not compete or clash.

The Flynn brothers liked to meet for lunch at a restaurant on a dock in Hermosa Beach, called Captain Frank's. At one time Captain Frank's had been favored because, situated as it was at the end of a wooden dock standing on piers, approaching Prohibition agents would be seen and identified long before they reached the door, giving everyone inside a chance to pitch illegal drinks out the windows and into the

Pacific. That was no longer a problem. Essentially, the agents had given up.

The Flynns monopolized a large round table in a corner. At smaller tables forming a crescent around their table, their toughs sat, making sure that no one unwanted approached the brothers. Sean and Jimmy were both there that day. With them was Jacob Fisher, business agent of the Union of Bit Players and Extras.

"It is a lot of money," said Fisher. He was a wizened man, bald, with a liver-spotted face. He nodded for emphasis. "A very great deal of money to place at risk." He spoke with a faint accent and with the studied care of a man to whom English was not his native language. "We would be placing a great deal of trust in a man of whom we know little."

"Divided among three of us, maybe four, it's not so great," said Jimmy.

"I was speaking of my share," said Jacob Fisher gravely.

"Well," said Sean Flynn, raising a glass of whiskey. "Your health, Jacob. Let's wait and see what Carlo says."

"Carlo suffered a serious misfortune last night," said Fisher.

"We heard about that," said Sean. "Chickie was a good boy."

"Carlo is imprudent too often," said Fisher.

"Well . . . We have no control over Carlo. Which is okay by me, because the only alternative is to make some guy head man over all of us. And that's not going to be one of us. It would be a guy like Big Dick, and I sure as hell don't want to find myself working for him."

"That's the way it's going," said Fisher. "In the East, the Sicilians have decided to put an end to the independent businessmen and rule everything through a committee of bosses."

"If we don't solve this problem of a 'national labor relations act,' " said Jimmy Flynn, "we won't be independent businessmen anymore."

"Let's leave that till Carlo is here," said Sean. "There is no point in covering the same ground twice."

Marfeo arrived a few minutes later. He came into the restaurant with two bodyguards, who glanced around and checked every patron of the place before they sat down at one of the tables circling the corner table.

"Our sympathy, Carlo," said Sean. "I suppose you know who did it."

"I know," said Marfeo darkly. "And I'll get the son of a bitch. You can bet on it."

"I wouldn't want to be him," said Jimmy.

"The fish here is good," said Sean. "I'm hungry. Let's order before we talk business."

They didn't have to order drinks. Bottles of whiskey and gin sat in the middle of the table, with a bucket of ice and bottles of mixer. Bottles of white wine sat in buckets around the table. Marfeo poured himself a glass of gin over ice and told Sean to order for him. Sean told the waiter to bring them a tray of fish, whatever was best today, with potatoes and salads and bread. They would serve themselves from the tray.

"Jimmy has a proposition," said Sean to Marfeo.

"I'll be quick," said Jimmy. "We can talk the details later. Roosevelt will be in town Monday. I've got a rifleman who can kill him. He's good. He can do it from a long distance, like from a roof, with a rifle that doesn't make much noise. Problem is his fee. He wants fifty thousand."

"Cheap at twice the price," said Marfeo, "but it won't be necessary."

"Why not?"

Marfeo ran his hand down across his flattened nose, then flicked a bit of lint off the lapel of his costly double-breasted gray suit. "The Governor's son has a sixteen-year-old girl pregnant. When that story breaks, Governor Roosevelt will withdraw."

"How's it gonna break?" asked Sean.

"It's already broke. I broke it this morning."

"I believe it would be well if you spoke specifically," said Jacob Fisher.

Marfeo glanced into the eyes of the other men. "I sent the newspapers overnight a set of pictures of this girl, nude, with her legs spread and all like that, taken—get this—*taken in the Roosevelt boy's living room!*"

"Who took these photographs?" asked Jacob Fisher.

Marfeo grinned. "Why Elliott Roosevelt himself. Who else?"

"The newspapers have these pictures *now?*" asked Sean. "You gonna confide in us?"

Marfeo glanced at the others again, this time without his triumphant smile but with a morose mien. "Chickie and Coyne took them," he said quietly. "Chickie— Well, you know. And poor Joe Coyne had a boating accident this morning." He stared out to sea. "He might go floating past anytime."

"Please give us the facts," said Jacob Fisher. "I would like to know the facts about this young woman and Governor Roosevelt's son."

"The girl is real," said Marfeo. "She's really pregnant. By Chickie, if you wanta know. Sometimes you can give a man a real fun assignment, as a reward. Chickie was a good boy, and he deserved his fun. Of course, the Roosevelt boy never saw her. The first time we tried to do a job on him, he didn't fall. This guy Endicott, from Boston, fouled things up, I figure. He's who killed Chickie, too, incidentally. I owe that son of a bitch one, and he's gonna get it. But the girl is smart, and we've got her one hundred percent under control. I'm gonna let some newspaper guys interview her, with her mother. When the story breaks—"

"But sooner or later the truth will come out," said Jacob Fisher. "This is an ill-conceived proposal, in my opinion."

"By the time the truth comes out, Governor Roosevelt will have been forced to withdraw. The Democrats will run Garner, and he's got no ideas about a 'labor bill of rights.' By the time the truth comes out—and only a little of it will ever come out—the little girl and her mother will be living in Mexico. Or Cuba. Or—"

"I don't want to hear about it," said Jacob Fisher.

"Well, there's always the other possibility," said Marfeo, taking a swallow of whiskey.

"Okay," said Jimmy. "You're saying the newspapers ought to break the story today, tomorrow at the latest. If it's good enough, Roosevelt withdraws. We've got five days. If the story doesn't do what we want it to, then—"

"Then let's hear about your rifleman," said Marfeo.

When Jack returned to the garden apartment at the Ambassador Hotel, Charlotte was sitting in the living room with a visitor. It was Myra Logan, the school nurse. She sat primly, but she was sipping Scotch.

"I came to see you, Mr. Endicott, to tell you I examined

the Chandler girl's record in the superintendent's office. She was expelled from Pershing High School as you said. The expulsion was reported by the principal, Mr. Rosenbusch, on a form prescribed for that purpose. He has access to the files for his school, and he seems just to have brought the expulsion in and filed it himself. Anyway, it was brought to no one's attention. I endorsed it. That is to say, I purportedly endorsed it. The truth is, my signature is a forgery."

"Surely that would come out in the course of the investigation that's surely going to happen," said Charlotte.

"By the time the investigators got to those details, the damage would have been done," said Jack.

"May I be allowed to understand what's going on?" the nurse asked.

"Norma Jean Chandler is involved in an extortion plot," Jack said. "I think she really is pregnant. They hoped not to have to allow her to be interviewed or examined, and her expulsion from high school, apparently after examination by the school nurse, would have been evidence enough to justify news stories about what she is supposed to claim happened."

"Who?" asked the nurse.

"I'd like to keep that confidential," said Jack.

"Mr. Rosenbusch is certainly involved," said Charlotte. "Wouldn't ordinary procedure be to report the pregnancy of a sixteen-year-old to the juvenile authorities?"

"It is required," said the nurse. "And it has been done now. I did it yesterday. The juvenile court issued an order for Norma Jean Chandler to be taken into custody. However . . . the girl cannot be found. She and her mother have moved out of their house. Her mother quit her job. Your accusation is supported by some very peculiar circumstances. What is more, this morning Mr. Rosenbusch was subjected to some very severe interrogation. I don't know what was learned, but I understand he has been suspended as principal."

Jack grinned. "The scheme is beginning to fall apart."

When Myra Logan had left, Jack telephoned Benjamin Vogel.

"I thought you might be interested to know that Principal Rosenbusch has been suspended," Jack said to him. "The nurse's signature on the expulsion report turns out to be a forgery. There's a warrant out for Edna Bascombe and an order for the detention of Norma Jean Chandler."

"I have no idea what you're talking about," said Vogel coldly.

"Maybe you ought to give this information to your buddies. Your little conspiracy is falling apart. You've still got time to drop it, forget the whole thing. That'd be the easy way."

Five minutes later Vogel was on the phone with Carlo Marfeo.

"Listen, they've rung in the law! The juvenile authorities are looking for Norma Jean and her mother. That boob Rosenbusch fouled us up."

"Who says?"

"Endicott says."

"You wanta take his word?"

"Why would he say a thing like that if it's not true?"

"Makes no difference, anyway," said Marfeo. "Tomorrow the story will be on the front page of every newspaper in Los

Angeles. And that ends the whole thing. No need for any rifleman."

"Rifleman?"

"You heard me, Vogel. Rifleman."

"I never associated myself with any—"

"If it some way comes to hiring the rifleman, I want ten thousand dollars from you. Your share of an expensive deal."

"Carlo, for God's sake!"

"Ten thousand, Ben. But don't worry about it. Little Norma Jean is gonna solve our problem."

Late in the afternoon, Jack returned to the conference room of the Los Angeles *Examiner*. Hearst had returned to San Simeon, but Bright and Draper were there.

"We had a call from 'Citizen.' He'll make his little girl available for an interview."

"What did you tell him?"

"We said we'd send a reporter. He asked for a photographer, too."

"Where and when?"

"It's interesting," said Bright. "Tomorrow morning. Our reporter is to be aboard a sailboat in the channel between the coast and Catalina. Our boat will be approached by a powerboat. If there's any other powerboat in sight, they won't come near. We can interview the girl from the deck of our sailboat. When it's over, the powerboat will speed away, leaving us too slow to follow. Any ideas?"

"A few," said Jack.

* * *

Charles Harold McIntyre had offered Jack a sail on his sloop. He was surprised when Jack telephoned and asked him to make that sailing date an early start Thursday morning. He was more surprised yet when Jack explained to him what they would be doing. The idea appealed to his sense of adventure, though, and he agreed enthusiastically.

They waited at the dock for some clearing in the morning fog, then set out into the San Pedro Channel on moderate wind and a gentle swell. Aboard were McIntyre, Jack, Harry Draper, a reporter, and a cameraman, also two crewmen to work the sails. The white sloop, named *Alice*, flew three signal flags—N J C.

Following instructions, they sailed halfway to Catalina and then turned south into the Santa Catalina Gulf.

They were an hour out when they spotted a speedboat approaching from the west. As it came nearer, they could see men watching them through binoculars. Through their own, they could see three men on the speedboat—and two women.

Before the speedboat came too close, Jack, stripped to black swimming trunks, slipped over the east side of *Alice* and into the water. He took a grip on a rope handed down to him by one of the crewmen and allowed himself to be dragged along.

When the speedboat was a hundred yards away, one of the men aboard waved a yellow-and-black flag on a pole. It was the signal to stop. McIntyre ordered the sails taken in. Shortly he ordered an anchor dropped. Within a few minutes, *Alice* was stopped and sat rising and falling on the swell.

The speedboat cut its engine to idling speed and approached.

A crewman leaned over and helped Jack to drape a coil of thick rope around his shoulders.

One of the men on the powerboat tossed a rope up to the deck of *Alice*. A crewman carried it aft and attached it to a cleat near the stern. That was Jack's instruction: to tie the speedboat near the stern of the schooner. Another crewman tossed fenders over the side, then caught a second line and bound it to a cleat.

"All right! Who's aboard?"

Harry Draper spoke. "I am the city editor of the *Examiner*," he said. "I have a shorthand reporter and a cameraman with me. We are ready to interview the girl."

"Who's from the other papers?"

"We are the only paper represented."

"You call 'em?"

"We called them."

Two of the men on the speedboat wore suits and hats and looked likely to be armed. A man in shirtsleeves ran the boat. Norma Jean Chandler sat on a seat in the stern, looking forlorn. Her mother sat beside her, smoking a cigarette.

"Well . . . Other papers were supposed to—"

"What could I do? I couldn't force them to come."

"But just one paper . . ."

"You want something bigger than a Hearst newspaper?"

"Awright. We'll stand up front. The girl will stand back here. You can take pictures of her, not of us. No foolin' around."

"No fooling around," Draper agreed.

The two men walked forward, and Norma Jean stood and stepped to the rail of the motorboat. Wearing a white cotton dress with little flowers for a pattern, she stood hunched, looking miserable. The photographer peered down into the hood of his Graflex camera and began to focus on her.

"My name is Norma Jean Chandler," she said in a weak, teary voice. "I'm gonna have a baby. The father of my baby is Mr. Elliott Roosevelt, the son of the man who's runnin' for President. He promised to marry me. I didn't know he was already married."

"When did this happen?" asked Draper.

"I started seeing him a little after Christmas, a little after New Year's."

"Did you have sex with him?"

"Sure. How else would I get pregnant?"

"Did he take pictures of you?"

"Dirty pictures," she said, nodding. "At his house. At mine, when my mother was working."

"Where are you living now, Norma Jean?"

"I don't wanna say."

"Why not?"

" 'Cause I'm ashamed. I'm gonna go away and have my baby and I guess put it up for adoption. I don't want nobody botherin' me."

Jack clung to the rudder of *Alice*. He drew deep breaths. Then abruptly he submerged and swam underwater, under the stern of the sloop and to the stern of the speedboat. He had heard the men say they would be forward. Edna Bascombe would be focused on her daughter and the reporter and cameraman. He risked rising for a breath, just under the stern of the motorboat. Underwater again, he looped his rope over the propeller shaft, just ahead of the propeller, and knotted it tight. He let the rest of it—fifty or sixty feet of heavy rope—trail away in the water, sinking from the weight of a small lead sinker he had earlier fastened to the other end. Finally he swam back under the stern of the sailboat and surfaced, gasping.

"Why are you telling us this, Norma Jean?"

"I don't want that man to get away with the dirty things he done to me. If I let him get away with it, he'll do it to some other girl."

"Okay, thanks," said Draper. He nodded to McIntyre.

The crewmen unhitched the lines and tossed them back to the powerboat. The two boats quickly drifted apart. The crewmen raised anchor and began to raise sail. Jack climbed aboard on the far side.

The man at the wheel of the speedboat started the engine. It rumbled authoritatively.

Wind filled the sails of the sloop, and soon it was fifty yards from the powerboat.

The man at the wheel of the powerboat engaged his clutch and advanced his throttle. The water churned at the rear for a moment, then suddenly the engine stopped. The propeller and shaft were fouled with fifty feet of rope.

Half an hour later, while the men on the speedboat were still struggling to cut away the rope, two Coast Guard cutters arrived. Norma Jean Chandler and her mother were taken into custody. The men on board were arrested and handcuffed.

X

Cecil B. DeMille lived in Los Angeles—not in Beverly Hills or Santa Monica but in Los Angeles. His house sat on a low, wooded hill in the very center of the burgeoning city. As before, he had sent a car to pick up Jack and Charlotte at the Ambassador, and it turned off a busy city street, through a gate, and into DeMille's private acreage. The drive wound around the hill until at last it reached the summit and the one-story, rambling, idiosyncratic house.

DeMille, Jack had been told, rarely attended Hollywood functions and rarely entertained at home. When he did, the group was likely to be small.

Mrs. DeMille, a gracious lady, came out to greet them, and she led them into the house.

It was not grand but cozy and cluttered. She took them through hallways and interconnecting rooms and at last into a parlor, where Cecil B. DeMille sat chatting with two men.

"Ah," he said. "I'm glad to see you. Sam Goldwyn's party was nice, but I wanted to have you to dinner here. Let me introduce you to James Cagney and Edward G. Robinson."

The two actors had risen—the short, saturnine Robinson, he of the squashed-down round face and the heavy, expressive lips, and the husky, happy-faced, sandy-haired Irish Cagney. They shook hands with Jack and Charlotte—a little shyly, Jack thought, considering that they were motion-picture tough guys.

"You asked me on the phone about sharpshooters," said DeMille. "I thought I'd invite a couple of men who've had experience with them."

A maid entered, wheeling a cart newly replenished with iced champagne, Scotch, bourbon, and gin, with a bucket of ice, glasses, and mixers.

"I hope we won't be having grapefruit with our dinner," said Charlotte to Cagney. His most famous movie scene to date had been the one in which he shoved half a grapefruit into the face of the actress Mae Clarke. "Would I be safe, Mr. Cagney?"

"Y' talked to me the way that dame did, you'd get grapefruit right in the kisser," snarled Cagney, mimicking his own screen persona.

Charlotte laughed. "I understand the way the scene was originally written, you were supposed to shove an omelet in her face."

"Too messy," said Cagney.

"And Mr. Robinson," she said. "Let me see . . . In *Little Caesar,* your name was . . . Rico?"

"My name is Emmanuel Goldenberg," said Robinson in his characteristic flat, dry voice.

Charlotte grinned mischievously. "And what is your real name, Mr. Cagney?"

"Jimmy," said Cagney.

"Eddy shouldn't confess so readily," said DeMille.

"What he won't tell you about himself," said Cagney, "is that the real Eddy is nothing at all like Little Caesar or any of the other tough guys. Me, I'm a roughneck, but Eddy's a gentleman. He's an art collector."

"Really, Mr. Robinson? What do you favor?"

"Mostly what I can't afford," said Robinson with a little smile. "I collect in a small way. I have a few rather nice things. A Modigliani, for example."

"You have sophisticated taste," said Charlotte. "No one without it would choose a Modigliani."

"Actually, I only know what I like."

DeMille did not invite his guests out to a terrace or a pool. If he had, they would have had a view through the trees of the busy city. The size of his estate would not have isolated them entirely from the sounds of the city. One of the earliest moviemakers to arrive in California, he had created for himself a small enclave in the middle of what had then been a small city, and the city had since surrounded him. He lived comfortably inside his house, in the midst of an eclectic agglomeration of things he liked.

This parlor, for example, would not have impressed anyone as the center of the most successful entrepreneur of the film industry. The six—DeMille and Mrs. DeMille, Robinson and Cagney, Jack, and Charlotte—sat about in soft chairs upholstered in English prints, sipped their drinks, nibbled on crackers and cheese, and genuinely relaxed. DeMille had said no dinner jackets, and the men wore light suits.

"What film do you have in production now, Mr. De-Mille?" Charlotte asked.

"A Biblical production called *The Sign of the Cross*," said DeMille. "The bathtub scene with Bette Davis was not, incidentally, a scene from that picture. Next year, I hope to do a film based on the history of Caesar and Cleopatra."

"Have you cast a Cleopatra?"

"I'm thinking of a young French actress named Claudette Colbert."

"I'm afraid I haven't heard of her."

"You will. But now— We were going to talk about sharp-shooters. I've hardly ever had an occasion to hire one, which is why I asked Jimmy and Eddy to come and tell you their experiences."

"Bad experiences," said Robinson.

"Well . . . The technicians are working on a new idea," said DeMille. "They'll plant little charges where bullets are supposed to hit and set them off with electricity."

"In the meanwhile," said Cagney, "we get shot at. And it can be dangerous."

"We remember the scene where you were shot at as Little Caesar," Charlotte said to Robinson.

"Machine gun," said Robinson. "The man learned to handle a machine gun during the war, and he's an expert with it. I'll tell you, though, you don't have to act to look frightened when he opens fire. That set was chopped to pieces. If I'd been eighteen inches to my left, I'd have been chopped to pieces."

"I can top your story, Eddy," said Cagney. "We were shooting the picture called *Taxi*. I was in the car, and I was supposed to pop up, fire two pistol shots, then duck down just before the machine gun opened fire and shattered the glass in the car windows. Everything was okay. The fella's aim was perfect. But there was a barricade of heavy lumber behind the car, supposed to catch and stop all the slugs. One of those bullets hit the head of a nail and ricocheted. It went all around the soundstage and could have killed someone. It went through the camera booth, hit some props, and finally dropped into one fella's coat pocket."

"Do you know any of these men personally?" Jack asked.

"I make it a point to get to know 'em," said Cagney. "I figure they'll be more careful shooting at a friend than at a stranger."

"There is one named Bailey," said Robinson. "He's the machine-gun expert, probably the one that fired at you in the car, Jimmy. I trust him, but I'll tell you, I once examined a brick wall he'd shot at. The tiniest mistake—" He shook his head.

"There's not enough money in the game for those fellas to make a living at it," said Cagney. "They come in when they're called. All of them do something else for a living."

"One of them is a gunsmith," said Robinson. "He has a shop somewhere downtown. Another one I've seen around the sets is an extra. He works on a lot of films. Puts on makeup and feathers and plays Indians."

"Westerns make money for them," said DeMille. "Those plus the gangster films."

"How many would you guess there are?" Jack asked.

"Not many," said Cagney. "Not more than twenty, I'd say; and of those, about ten make most of the money."

"If you were looking for one of them who might use his marksmanship to kill somebody for money, which one, or ones, would you suspect?"

Edward G. Robinson turned down the corners of his

mouth and shook his head. "I can't say I know any of them who'd do that. They're a pretty clean-cut, straightforward bunch of fellows."

"Of course, there's Oakley," said Cagney.

"Well . . . He's just eccentric."

"Tell us more," said Jack.

Robinson nodded. "Scotty Oakley claims he's the illegitimate son of Annie Oakley. He shoots in Wild West shows. A fine shot with a rifle. He doesn't get as much work as he might because he's eccentric and obviously drinks heavily. He seems to bear a grudge against the world because his mother—that is, the woman he claims was his mother—denied her relationship to him. He's harmless, though, I'm sure."

"Yeah, I don't suppose he'd hurt anybody," said Cagney.

"You never can tell," said Mrs. DeMille thoughtfully.

"Does anybody know you're here?" Sean Flynn demanded of Carlo Marfeo. "You shouldn't've come here. We don't know you anymore."

"I brought my share of the rifleman money," said Marfeo. "What you asked for."

"Fifteen thousand?"

"Seventeen."

Hearing that Marfeo was coming out the dock, the Flynns and Jacob Fisher had moved quickly to an upstairs room, where casual diners in Captain Frank's would not see the wanted man at their table. The upstairs room had windows overlooking the Pacific, but it was smaller and was uncomfortably warm. The windows were open, letting in a breeze

off the sea but also letting in moths that fluttered around the
ceiling light.

The men had taken off their jackets, revealing the pistols
they carried in shoulder holsters. Sean Flynn had a revolver.
Jimmy didn't. Neither did Jacob Fisher. A fourth man had
a big Colt automatic under his left arm. He was a handsome
man, almost to the point of effeminacy in the cast of his eyes;
but he had an iron jaw and a look of menace around the
mouth.

"Incidentally," said Flynn, "I guess you haven't met
Benny Siegel."

"No. Benny's from New York. I'm from Philly. Good to
meet you, Benny."

Siegel nodded but did not offer his hand.

"The cops are lookin' for you," said Sean.

"The girl talked," said Marfeo. "I figure."

"Yeah. Which makes you hot."

"It's no big deal," said Marfeo. "The heat'll die down. It's
bound to die down, soon as they see what a cheap little slut
the girl is."

"You believe this?" asked Jacob Fisher. "I don't."

"Well . . . Maybe I'll have to run down to Mexico for a
while. I thought maybe you guys would help me out. You
know, this deal has left me with just about no organization
left."

"You've screwed up, Carlo," said Sean. "I want the
straight answer to a straight question. Is the seventeen thousand all yours, or did you get some from Vogel?"

"I got some from Vogel," Marfeo admitted.

"So Vogel knows about the rifleman."

"No problem. He's in my pocket. Hey, the deal about

usin' the girl was Vogel's idea. He thought we oughta try doin' somethin' smart, instead of— You know . . ."

Sean nodded, then grunted, "All right. Let's see the cash."

Marfeo took parts of the money out of each of four pockets. Jimmy Flynn counted it.

"I don't want you comin' around here again, Carlo. You said Mexico. You make it Mexico. While you're away, I'll take over your union. When it's safe for you to come home, I'll give it back to you."

" 'Kay," Marfeo muttered skeptically. "You'll get a good piece of money out of that in a year. S'pose you could hand me some of it now, for expenses?"

Sean shoved the seventeen thousand across the table at Marfeo. "Take that there," he said. "Now, how you gonna get down to Mexico? Drive?"

"Figure I have to."

"They're lookin' for your car. Can I hope you haven't got it parked right outside?"

"I—"

"Keys. It's gotta be moved. One of us guys'll drive you to Mexico. You can't cross at Tijuana. They'll be lookin' for you there. Better get over to Arizona somewheres, then down and across the border. You can catch a train then. My idea is, you should go to Cuba. Lot more fun than Mexico."

"I'll drive Carlo down to Mexico," said Siegel. "I like the mountains and the desert. Don't get to see 'em often enough."

"Deal, Carlo?"

"Deal," said Marfeo without enthusiasm.

Sean Flynn watched Carlo Marfeo rise from the table and

go to the window to look out to sea. Then he winked at Bugsy Siegel.

The next morning, Friday, Jack arrived at Birdsong Productions about ten o'clock. He sent in his card, and within minutes he was in the office of Benjamin Vogel.

"All right, so how much did I have to do with it?" Vogel asked. "I was a messenger boy, as I told you at San Simeon."

"A great big question," said Jack as he put his hat and stick on a chair and sat down facing Vogel's desk. "Did Norma Jean or her mother know your name? Did Marfeo promise her you'd make her a movie star, for example?"

Vogel shuddered. Literally: he shuddered. "God know what that idiot may have done! I'm sitting here dreading a call from the juvenile officers—or, worse, detectives with a warrant."

"If you haven't got one yet, you may be off the hook," said Jack. "Norma Jean has been in custody almost twenty-four hours. Uh . . . she really is pregnant, isn't she?"

Vogel nodded.

"Who did it?"

"A young man who worked for Marfeo. His name was Salvatore Ciccenza, known as Chickie. It was a completely straightforward deal. The girl and her mother were to get a lot of money—which they were to spend in Cuba. The girl submitted to . . . Chickie, and pretty soon she was examined and was pregnant."

"The money came from you?"

"Some of it."

"You realize that if the girl knows about your part in it and talks, you are in deep, deep trouble."

"What are *you* going to do?"

Jack glanced around the room. One item of furniture was a big leather-covered couch. "Is that a casting couch?" he asked.

"Yes. But—"

"I'm not going to do anything. About you. All I know about you is what you've admitted to me. In court, it would be your word against mine—and maybe Charlotte's for part of it, when you were feeling such hubris. Is it true that young actresses—?"

"Young actresses—*Some* young actresses. *Most* young actresses, I guess I should say . . . Lie down on casting couches. All over town. It's the way this town works. Some young men, in fact—"

"Spare me."

"Hollywood is a state of mind, as much as anything else," said Vogel. "You decided to come out here bringing Charlotte with you. And I congratulate you. She's obviously a marvelous woman. But if you'd been alone, I could have arranged for you to enjoy the most beautiful, luscious girls you could ever hope to see."

"Vogel . . ." said Jack. "I have a sense that the blackmail deal is not everything that's going on. The police are looking for Marfeo, and the charge carries a long sentence. You may have gotten away with this one—or you may have if nobody makes any big effort to connect you with what they did to Norma Jean Chandler. If there's something else going on, you had better tell me."

Vogel shrugged and turned up the palms of his hands.

"Okay. But don't forget something else. You are dealing with some very rough boys. You may be beyond your depth."

* * *

Jack Endicott had heard the name of Sean Flynn, but he had never seen him. Sean and Jimmy Flynn knew the name Blackjack Endicott, but they had never seen him. They passed one another in the hall outside Vogel's office, without recognizing one another.

Vogel knew the Flynns. "I was expecting you," he said. "Did you see the man who just left?"

"The dude with the cute hat and the walking stick?" asked Sean.

"That dude was John Lowell Endicott."

"If I'd know that—"

"If you'd known that and made a move, he'd have killed you," said Vogel.

"He killed Chickie," said Jimmy Flynn.

"Almost killed Bo Weinberg," said Vogel.

"Well, be that as it may," said Sean. He lit a cigarette and sat for a moment, regarding Vogel as if he was renewing his acquaintance and his judgment. "Carlo has left the state. Left the States, in fact. Every cop in L.A. is lookin' for him. He won't be back for a year or so. In the meantime, I'll be the business agent for the Brotherhood of Set Builders and Painters. We'll just continue things the way they've been, and everybody'll be happy."

"Alive and happy," said Jimmy, in case there was any misunderstanding.

Vogel shrugged. "We've got a problem," he said. "Carlo was the one who arranged things with the girl. Except— Except that Chickie arranged one important element. What we don't know for sure is if any of those guys used my name or yours when she could hear. Or to her mother. You can bet the girl and the mother are going to sing every song they know. Both of them are behind bars."

"The deal with the girl wasn't Carlo's idea," said Jimmy. "It was yours. It was a dumb idea, Vogel."

"What's dumb," said Vogel, "is the other idea: the idea of the rifleman."

"What would be dumb," said Jimmy, "would be to lose our businesses cold and go broke—which is what is going to happen if this guy Roosevelt sticks the federal government's nib into labor relations."

"You can't kill the man."

"The hell we can't, and we've got some money of yours invested in the deal."

"Murder—"

"For Christ's sake, Vogel! What do you think happened to Lacey?"

"I didn't—"

"The hell you didn't. Carlo Marfeo paid the gunman with dough you gave him. What was it for, Vogel? If you wanta hide, you gotta hide behind something more substantial than you got between you and the death of Lacey."

"Killing a candidate for President of the United States! It's different."

Jimmy Flynn pinched his chin between thumb and index finger. "Lemme see, now," he said. "If I remember right, three *Presidents*, not just candidates, have been shot. Lincoln . . . Garfield . . . and McKinley. Somebody took a shot at Teddy Roosevelt when he was a candidate. Those guys were nuts. They walked right up and . . . BANG! Our man will shoot from a distance."

"You can't!"

"Wanna bet?"

* * *

David Bright, editor-in-chief of the *Examiner*, had asked Jack to meet him at Juvenile Hall at noon.

"You won't believe how grateful the other editors are," said Bright. "They were ready to fall right into what Marfeo and the girl's mother were selling."

"They believe us, then?"

"Mr. Endicott," said the florid, rotund man with the pince-nez, "you would not *believe* the credibility we have! It may win Governor Roosevelt endorsements he might otherwise not have received."

Juvenile Hall was one of those government buildings newly erected in the 1920s that looked as if it had been put up by a cement contractor. Jack walked with Bright through bleak corridors, looking for an office where they were supposed to meet with a juvenile referee.

The juvenile referee, when finally they found her, was a woman with the appearance and manner of a reformatory matron: her gray hair so tightly bound in a bun that Jack wondered if it did not cause her headaches, wearing rimless octagonal eyeglasses and a gray dress that would have been complete only if it had been adorned by a big ring of keys.

Her name was Mrs. Kinney, and she said, "The girl has given a complete statement. That is to say, I assume it is complete. It is ugly enough, I must say. I thought you might want to review it, to see if you have anything to add. Would you like to see her?"

"No, no . . . that won't be necessary," said Bright.

"Mrs. Kinney," said Jack. "I am a man, uh, with some resources. It's not impossible that I might be able to help this abused girl. I mean, maybe I could find a place for her, back East where nothing of this horrible episode is known. I'd like to see her, for a moment."

Norma Jean Chandler was wearing handcuffs when she was brought to Mrs. Kinney's office. Those were immediately removed. She was dressed in a limp gray dress, thoroughly wrinkled, and black cotton stockings.

"Who're you?" she asked hoarsely of Jack and Bright.

Jack told her. "I'm the man who swam under the boat yesterday morning and looped the rope around the propeller shaft. I'm a friend of Elliott Roosevelt. Mr. Bright is a newspaper editor. We're ready to believe—in fact ready to try to convince Mrs. Kinney—that you're the victim of a lot of people who used you, not yourself a girl who wanted to do wrong."

The girl looked at Jack, skepticism and hostility plain on her face. "You're crazy. I wanted the money."

"What money?" he asked. "How much were you going to get? I mean, how much would have been in *your* hands, not in your mother's?"

Norma Jean Chandler stared at Jack for almost a whole minute. Then she said, "Mom would have taken care of me."

"Like she did when she made you give yourself to Chickie?" he asked coldly. "Sixteen years old . . . Was that taking care of you?"

The girl put her head down on her arms on the table and began to sob.

Mrs. Kinney surprised Jack by putting her hand on the girl's head and patting it gently. "Norma . . ." she whispered. "This is something that happened. It's not the rest of your life."

"It is," the girl wept.

"No. There are all kinds of things that can happen. This man is from New York—"

"Boston."

"Boston. And he says he might be able to help you. Maybe you can go back East, where he's from, and start a new life where nobody will know anything about what's happened here."

"What's going to happen to my mom?"

"She's going to prison. There's no question about that. For what she did to you—"

"She was just trying to take care of me."

"You don't believe that," said Mrs. Kinney. "There are all kinds of ways of taking care of a girl, other than doing what she had you do."

"What you want me to do?"

"If there's anything you haven't told us, tell us now."

"What if . . . What if those guys tried to kill somebody?" asked Norma Jean.

Carlo Marfeo had left Captain Frank's with Benny Siegel last night, carrying seventeen thousand dollars stuffed in his pockets. They had driven away in Jimmy Flynn's car, on their way to the Mexican border. Marfeo had insisted they not drive away from Los Angeles before morning. He knew he couldn't go home and pack a bag, but he declared they must not leave town that night. Siegel guessed why and agreed to hole up in a tourist cabin in Pasadena.

In the morning Marfeo lingered over breakfast in a diner near the tourist court. He ate pancakes, ham and eggs, and drank three cups of coffee. He also bought and scanned three newspapers. None of them said anything about Elliott

Roosevelt. None of them said anything about Norma Jean Chandler. None of them said anything about him, and he wondered if he was as hot as he'd been told.

When at last he was ready to leave, he asked Siegel to drive first to the post office in Long Beach. "I gotta pick up a package."

Benny Siegel was patient. He liked Jimmy's car, a maroon-and-yellow Graham, and he was intrigued by the beaches and the desert and mountains. He was conscious of the glances he drew from girls along the streets. They saw his gray snap-brim hat and his well-tailored tropical-weight light-blue suit. They were interested too in the heavy-lidded but intense eyes that returned their glances.

The girls did not spare a second look for the hunched, glowering Marfeo, not for his equally handsome hat and pinstriped gray suit, certainly not for his flattened nose and scarred face.

"What's the package?" Siegel asked before they reached the post office.

"I mailed myself somethin'," said Marfeo.

Siegel went inside the post office and watched Marfeo collect his package at the counter. It was a small box, wrapped in brown paper and securely closed with both tape and twine. When they returned to the car, Marfeo wanted to lock it in the trunk.

They set out to the south then. It was well after ten o'clock. The sun was high and brutally bright. Marfeo suggested they not drive down the coast highway. That, he said, was the most direct route to San Diego and Tijuana, and if the cops were really looking for him that might be where they'd look. Better, he said, to drive east to Palm Springs, then south from there. Benny would see spectacular scenery that way, Marfeo promised.

Both men took off their jackets and loosened their neckties. Siegel unstrapped his harness and put his shoulder holster in the backseat. He shoved his heavy Colt .45 down in the pocket on the car door.

"Know what?" he said to Marfeo. "I got a friend in New York that's had a radio installed in his car. Imagine that! The batteries go in a crate on the passenger-side floor, which makes it kinda awkward for the feet, but does he get music! I'd like to have a radio in this baby. Gee! That'd be swell, wouldn' it?"

Having no radio, Benny Siegel substituted the best he could by singing. He started with "Bye Bye Blackbird," then sang "Life is Just a Bowl of Cherries" and "Wrap Your Troubles in Dreams," followed by "Brother, Can You Spare a Dime?"

Marfeo stared glumly out the window. The road snaked a way up into the mountains, and Siegel could not drive more than thirty miles an hour most of the time.

"Where's gonna be a good place to stay?" Siegel asked. "I mean, we ain't gonna make the Mexican border today, for sure."

"No," said Marfeo. "There's not much south of Palm Springs. We could wind up in some lady's boarding house. Maybe we oughta stay in Palm Springs tonight and go south early in the morning."

"Nice place, Palm Springs?"

"Oh yeah."

"They need a carpet joint?"

"I don't know. It's hard to do in California. Think about

Nevada. It's the only state in the union where casino gambling is legal."

"A thousand miles from nowhere," said Siegel.

"That's why they made it legal: to attract the business. Union Pacific can get you up there from L.A. in, like, four hours."

"Four hours each way to go to a carpet joint?"

"Gotta make it a hotel," said Marfeo. "A resort hotel. Get guys to come for a week. Set it up with luxury rooms, with air conditioning, plus great eating, the best drinks, the best broads . . . swimming pools, shows . . . the works."

"Yeah?"

"I don't know. Seems like a good idea to me."

For a few miles after that, Siegel was silent. He didn't talk, and he didn't sing.

In a sharp turn on a mountain road, he suddenly pulled the car off into the dust and sand. "Gotta take a leak," he said. "Hey. You better too. 'Kay?"

Marfeo shrugged and opened the door on his side of the car. He glanced both ways on the road and saw no other cars. He walked ten or fifteen feet away from the car and began to unbutton his fly to urinate.

Carlo Marfeo didn't guess what Bugsy Siegel had in mind and stood carelessly with his back toward the New York mobster. Siegel pulled the Colt .45 from the pocket on the door of the car. He rested his hand on the hood of the Graham to steady his aim, and he fired one shot. That was all he needed to fire: one shot, one big, heavy .45 caliber slug, into the back. Marfeo pitched forward, twitched for a few seconds, and lay still. His heart and lungs had exploded.

Siegel opened the trunk and took out the wrapped package Marfeo had mailed to himself at the Long Beach post office. Using a pocketknife, Siegel cut the package open.

It contained what he thought. He closed the trunk and locked it in again, but a quick look at the contents of the package told him Marfeo had mailed himself at least $100,000.

That's what Bugsy had figured. He swung the car around and headed back for Los Angeles, singing "Happy Days Are Here Again."

XI

Returning to the garden apartment at the Ambassador Hotel, after his meeting with Norma Jean Chandler, Jack found an impatient Charlotte had left the apartment and gone to the swimming pool. He found a note asking him to join her. He decided a swim was not a bad idea and changed into a swimsuit.

Charlotte was sitting at an umbrella table, smoking a cigarette and sipping ginger ale. He sat down with her.

"Well, did you see the princess?"

Jack nodded. "Pitiable child."

Charlotte pointed at a man and boy swimming in the pool. "Small world, Jack. Would you believe we'd run into Joe Kennedy out here?"

Jack looked at the sandy-haired man. Sure enough, it was Joseph P. Kennedy. He was from Boston and of course was acquainted with John Lowell Endicott. Jack had never been a man to exclude anyone from his circle of friends just because a person was Irish.

"It's not surprising to see him in Los Angeles, actually."

"That's his son with him. Not the eldest. That's Jack. He's fifteen."

Jack nodded. "It's not easy to keep track of the Kennedys. What's he have, an even dozen children?"

"If he has his son with him, he's not out here to see Gloria Swanson," said Charlotte. "He wouldn't bring the boy with him—"

"Why not? He had Gloria Swanson as a guest at Hyannis. His wife knew all about her. I wouldn't be surprised if the older children knew, too. But I do understand the Kennedy-Swanson affair is over."

"He lost a lot of money on pictures."

"No. He *made* a lot of money on pictures. Gloria Swanson lost money. Not Joe. There may have been a flaming passion, but Joe is Machiavellian about writing his contracts."

Joseph Kennedy and his son climbed out of the pool—two muscular males in blue trunks and white swimming vests. Jack shook hands with both of them, and they sat down together under the umbrella.

"Dumb place to be in the middle of the summer," said Joseph Kennedy. "I understand Frank Roosevelt will be here Monday."

"I'm doing a little advance work for him," said Jack.

"*You?* A big Republican like you?"

"Old college chums," said Jack.

Kennedy reached over and tousled the sandy-red hair of his fifteen-year-old son. "Hear that? That's why you're going to Harvard. Jack'll do what he can to help Governor Roosevelt, even if they're on opposite sides of the political fence. A Harvard man would betray his father if the old man had gone to Yale."

"Rah-rah," said Jack dryly.

The Kennedy boy grinned.

"Will you be here, Joe, when Frank speaks in Pershing Park on Monday?"

"That's why Jack and I are out here," said Kennedy. "I'm one of the sponsors of the luncheon being held here in the Ambassador Hotel, for movie-industry people."

Jack laughed. "Should have known. Young man," he said to Jack Kennedy, "you're going to meet the next President of the United States."

"I've already met the Governor," said the young Kennedy.

Jack turned to Charlotte and smiled as he shook his head. "When I was fifteen years old, the President was William McKinley. My father never introduced me to the President of the United States. Of course, McKinley was from Ohio, and my father considered him infra dig. In fact, my father didn't much care for Presidents, thought them banal on the whole—*un-Bostonian*. He could tolerate Theodore Roosevelt because *he* was a Harvard man—if only he hadn't been so *brash*. Cabots, Lowells, Endicotts, Lodges, Saltonstalls . . . Presidents should have been chosen from among *them*. Since they weren't, my father did not seek their acquaintance and was somewhat surprised when they didn't seek his. So I never met any of them. I met Calvin Coolidge once and do know Herbert Hoover casually, but Frank Roosevelt, if he becomes President, will be my first friend in the White House."

"What are you doing for Frank out here?" Kennedy

asked. "The party organization is not aware you're doing anything."

"Tying up a couple of little loose ends," said Jack.

"Can you tell me what they are?"

"I'm afraid not."

That comment stifled the conversation. Everyone sat uncomfortably, looking around the pool, looking at fifty people dressed in almost-identical suits of blue wool trunks, white web belts, and white wool vests. A moment's glance was enough to see that most of them were violating the National Prohibition Act by pouring liquor into the ginger ale and seltzer bottles bearing labels advising that so doing was against the law.

"Mr. Endicott! Mr. Endicott! Telegram for Mr. Endicott!"

The telegram was from Frank Roosevelt:

MUCH CONCERN ABOUT PROBLEMS YOU ARE WORKING ON IN L A STOP DO YOU HAVE ANY WORD STOP CANNOT OF COURSE BE DISCUSSED BY WIRE STOP MAYBE TELEPHONE DURING DENVER STOP STOP

Jack had hardly finished reading the telegram when a boy arrived with a second wire for him. This one was from Elliott:

WOULD BE MOST USEFUL IF YOU AND FATHER AND I COULD MEET BEFORE MONDAY STOP ARE YOU AWARE THAT UNITED CAN OFFER FLIGHT L A DENVER STOP FLIGHT NOT MUCH MORE THAN SIX HOURS STOP YOU COULD MEET WITH US DENVER AND RETURN L A SAME DAY STOP PLEASE ADVISE STOP

* * *

At 7:00 A.M. Saturday morning, Jack arrived at Los Angeles Flying Field to board a United Air Lines flight with an ultimate destination of New York. Denver would be its second stop. It would land and refuel at Salt Lake City and next at Denver. After Denver it would fly on to Omaha, where it would stop for the night. In the morning, passengers would board for Chicago. After that it would land at Cleveland. From there came a really adventuresome two more legs of the journey, since the airplane would fly on in the dark of night. After Cleveland it would land at Scranton, Pennsylvania and then take off for New York. Arriving in New York just before midnight, its passengers would have completed their journey from Los Angeles in approximately forty-one hours.

Jack was aboard only for the flight to Denver, which would take about seven hours. He expected to meet the Roosevelts in early afternoon. He had made reservations to fly back on a night flight—on which, he was told, he would likely be the only passenger, since few people could be persuaded to fly at night over the huge dark stretches of the American West.

As a pilot himself, and one who had flown at night, he was not afraid. In fact, he told the clerk at the airline counter that if he was the only passenger he would like to sit in the right seat of the airplane, where he could take control in case the pilot became ill.

The airplane was a Ford 4AT Tri-Motor, an all-metal aircraft called the Tin Goose. It had a radial engine on the nose and two more in pods suspended under the high wing. It carried ten passengers, and leaving Los Angeles that morning it took off with a full load.

The cabin was comfortable. Passengers sat in cane-backed

seats—cane-backed because that made them lighter. Each seat had a window, so each passenger had a view of the landscape. From time to time the pilots sent back handwritten notes telling what was below. A thermos of coffee was passed through the cabin early in the flight. During the stop at Salt Lake City, box lunches were brought aboard.

During the flight Jack became acquainted with a woman sitting across the narrow aisle from him. She was flying all the way to New York. He was pleased to meet her. She was Mildred Babe Didrikson. The 1932 Olympic Games had been held in Los Angeles, and she had won gold medals for the eighty-meter hurdles and for the javelin. During the conversation she remarked that she enjoyed playing basketball and golf and would have liked to compete as a boxer.

"Is there anything you *don't* like to play?" he asked her.

"Yeah, with dolls," she said.

The flight arrived on time at Denver, with most of the passengers feeling a little wobbly as the result of brief oxygen deprivation as the plane had climbed to more than ten thousand feet to cross mountain ridges.

Elliott Roosevelt was waiting at the airport with a car. The Governor, he said, had addressed a luncheon and was attending a Democratic Party rally in a Denver park. He drove Jack to a railroad siding where the campaign train waited to pull out and resume its westward journey. The train would move on to Salt Lake City on the tracks of the Denver & Rio Grande and after a speech there switch to the tracks of the Union Pacific for the run to Los Angeles.

On the way in the car, Jack told Elliott the resolution of the Norma Jean Chandler affair, not including the fact that Carlo Marfeo's man Chickie had tried to kill him—and had died in the attempt.

"I'm grateful to you for that," said Elliott. "It takes an awful burden off me, and one off Father, too."

"I'm concerned about something else, though," said Jack. "We've frustrated some people in their effort to drive your father off the Democratic ticket by creating a scandal. That doesn't mean they are going to give up. That we beat them on this thing may drive them to try something more drastic. I'm going to have to tell your father that."

Missy LeHand was in the platform car at the rear of the short train. So was Louis Howe. Howe was, of course, smoking a Sweet Caporal and hacking. Missy poured Jack a Scotch and soda without asking if he wanted one.

"Well, what about the movie moguls?" Howe asked. "I guess you've met most of them?"

"No, just a few of them."

"Where do they stand on the election?"

"They're tough-minded businessmen first of all," said Jack.

"We have to make a point to them," said Howe. "People who haven't got money to buy groceries haven't got money to buy movie tickets. They've *got* to be interested in national recovery."

"I'm sure they are," said Jack.

Governor Roosevelt arrived about half an hour later, exhilarated by the reception he had received in the park and along the streets of the city. "I saw ten thousand people! More to the point, ten thousand people saw me."

"I may as well come right to the point," said Jack. "Open motorcades . . . are dangerous. One nut with a rifle—"

"One nut with a bomb," the Governor interrupted. "One nut with a pistol. One nut with a knife." He shook his head. "But you can't isolate yourself. Maybe Lincoln shouldn't have gone to the theater, Garfield shouldn't have gone to the railroad station, McKinley shouldn't have gone to the Pan-American Exposition. What should they have done, holed up in the White House as if it were a fort—or a prison?"

"Los Angeles may be particularly dangerous," said Jack. "There are some gangster labor leaders allied with some dishonest producers. A 'labor bill of rights' would cost them millions. They—"

"Everywhere we go there are dangerous possibilities," said Governor Roosevelt. "I can't hide. I have to show myself to the people. It's especially important for *me* to show myself to the people, so they can see I'm not a helpless cripple."

"I'm flying back to Los Angeles this evening. I don't know if I can do anything to find and frustrate an attempt to shoot at you, but I'll do what I can. I don't have much time."

"You're a marvelous friend, Jack."

It didn't surprise the Flynn brothers when Siegel returned from driving Marfeo to Mexico, not having been gone long enough to drive halfway to Mexico let alone to come back. They were not surprised when the newspapers on Saturday morning carried stories saying the notorious mobster Carlo Marfeo had been found dead, "executed gangland style," on a mountain road. What did surprise them was that Siegel handed back their seventeen thousand dollars.

"I'm an honest guy," he said blandly. "I don't keep other people's money."

He surprised them again by saying he was returning immediately to New York and asking one of them to drive him to the station. He'd come to L.A., he said, to look into the possibility of opening a carpet joint, but he could see there wasn't room for another one—not without offending Big Dick DiCalabria, which he didn't want to do.

Jimmy drove him to the station and watched him board a Union Pacific train for Chicago. He noticed that Siegel let the porter handle his suitcase but shook his head emphatically when the porter offered to carry his valise, too. He wondered what was in the valise.

Leaving the station, Jimmy drove out to the mountains to meet with Scotty Oakley. He, too, had a valise, locked in the trunk of the car. In it was fifty thousand dollars in cash.

Scotty looked different. He was newly shaved and had had his hair cut. He was not wearing bib overalls but a khaki suit, cut in a Wild-West show style with decorative stitching on the seams. He wore his expensive boots and a white Stetson hat. He sat on his front porch as usual. He had a table in front of him and was loading ammunition. He squinted over the meticulous measuring of gunpowder, and only when he was satisfied to the last grain did he pour the measured amount into a brass cartridge.

Jimmy sensed that the man didn't want to talk until he took a break, so he stood and watched him until finally Scotty looked up at him. Then he asked, "Going somewhere?"

"Goin' into town if you brung the money," said Scotty.

"I want to talk with you about that," said Jimmy. "My people will go along with your fifty thousand, but they think we should give you only half in advance and half when the job is done. How do we know you won't take our fifty thousand dollars and scram?"

"You don't," said Scotty, his eyes narrowing.

"Well . . . You'll agree it's an awful risk."

"Don't figger I could hide from you guys forever. I figger you'd catch up with me sooner or later."

"We'll trust you for twenty-five thousand," said Jimmy.

Scotty shook his head. "Look at it from *my* point of view," he said. "Or— Better way to put it, I look at it from *your* point of view. Like I mentioned one time afore, if I was you guys I'd hire Scotty to shoot Governor Roosevelt—for whatever reason you got, which I don't understand; the money is the reason for me—and I'd give Scotty just part of his money. Then when Scotty comes to collect the rest, I'd kill him. That's what I'd do if I wuz you fellers. I wouldn't leave no witness alive to connect the deed to you. I don't know who you are, but I can kind of guess. If I wuz you, I wouldn't leave Scotty alive."

"You said we could hunt you down."

"I'll have a head start," said Scotty wryly.

"You won't do it if we don't give you the fifty thousand in advance?"

"Right. Y' see, I've got two options. I kin go on livin' right here the way I've done fer years. It ain't a bad life. Or I kin do this job fer you and make fifty thousand. If I do that, it's th' end of Scotty, don't y' see? I'll have t' go somewheres and be somebody else. An' I won't dare ever touch a gun for the rest of my life. Anybody see how good the man is with a rifle, that there'd make him a suspect in the murder of Governor Roosevelt."

"You make a good case for yourself," said Jimmy.

"So?"

"So I'll take a chance on you. There's fifty thousand in that satchel. You want to count it?"

"No need to do that right now. I'll count it and look it

over before I leave for town. If it's short, I won't do the job. You kin come back and get the twenty-five or thirty or whatever. No, I figger you wouldn't short me. I'm not worried about that."

Jimmy pushed the valise across the porch floor. "Is what you're loading there what you're going to use?" he asked.

"Yep. I load more careful than what the companies that makes it does. When I git the rifle sighted in and ready, every shot'll go exactly the same. Store-bought ammunition kin vary just a teensy from one ca'tridge to another, which means your shots can stray a little. I don't take no chances."

"Do you need any help? I mean, do you want me to drive you into the city?"

Scotty shook his head. "What I want you to do is scat. I thank ya for the money, and I don't ever wanta see you ag'in. You don't wanta see me, neither. I ain't tellin' ya where I'll be. You'll read about me in the newspapers. That is, you'll read about what I done."

Jimmy nodded and rose. He did not offer to shake hands. "Good luck," he said, and he walked back to his car.

He drove about a mile, then pulled into a filling station and general store. Two men waited for him in a Buick.

"He's back there," Jimmy told them. "Now. Whatever you do, don't lose him. And whatever you do, don't let him figure out that you're following him. Don't forget, he's a dead shot, and dead is what you'll be if he decides he's being tailed. You're supposed to be smart boys. Now's the time to be smart."

Jack's return flight to Los Angeles was aboard a Boeing 40B, a single-engine biplane. He was not the only passenger. He and another man occupied the two-seat cabin in the fuselage, while the pilot flew from an open cockpit above. In the rear of the fuselage, the Boeing also carried five hundred pounds of airmail.

The flight was not comfortable. The roar of the radial engine made conversation with the other passenger impossible. The cabin was not lighted, so it was not possible to read. The noise and bumpiness of the flight prohibited sleep.

All a passenger could do was stare out the window, and over the expanses of the West he might stare for a long time without so much as seeing a light. Jack knew the pilot was following beacon lights, but they were ahead, where passengers at side windows could not see them. From time to time he spotted a green-and-white flash on the northern horizons: a beacon for some other route.

At Salt Lake City they got out and stretched their legs. They went to the bathroom, which was not possible on the plane—though of course wide-mouth bottles were supplied.

The flight landed at Los Angeles a little after midnight.

Charlotte was waiting for him inside the little building that served as a terminal for Boeing Air Transport.

"A pleasant surprise," said Jack.

"Maybe," she said. "Tony DiCalabria is waiting for you in the car."

"Trouble?"

"Well . . . news."

DiCalabria waited in his Packard. A driver and another man sat in front. Jack and Charlotte entered the rear to sit with DiCalabria.

"How's the Governor?"

"Well. The campaign is going well. Hoover's in trouble.

Jack Garner told the Governor all he has to do to win the election is live through November."

"Gotta talk about that."

"Uh-oh."

"Things have changed," said DiCalabria. "To start with, Marfeo is dead. They found his body beside a mountain road southeast of town, shot in the back with a .45 automatic. That ain't suicide."

"Executed for fouling something up," said Jack.

"Yeah, but . . . Why drive a hundred miles to do it? There's gotta be something more to it than that. Somethin' else. Benny Siegel caught a train for Chicago this morning. He came out here to see me, and he never even called me."

"He's a nut," said Jack.

"I called Meyer Lansky and asked him how come Siegel comes out here and doesn't even call me. He doesn't know. I asked him what kind of gun Siegel carries. He said a Colt .45. I'm guessing Siegel killed Marfeo . . . for the Flynn brothers."

"Why?"

" 'Cause Marfeo made a big mistake in the Norma Jean business. If the cops had got him on the charge of corrupting that girl, he'd have talked his head off. Couldn't risk that."

The driver had pulled the Packard out of the parking lot at the airport.

"Late, but let's go home and have a drink," said DiCalabria. "There's more to this than what happened to Marfeo. Meyer talked hard to me about it."

Half an hour later they sat at a table behind the DiCalabria villa, facing the crashing surf at high tide.

Angela DiCalabria came out, and as if she had been cued for this, she asked Charlotte to go swimming with her.

"Don't get many chances to go in the surf at night," she said. "Too cold, too dark— But with a little moon like we got . . . Hey!"

"I . . ."

"Hey, c'mon! Night like this, no suits. Private. The guys here won't be able to see us."

Charlotte took a cue from Jack, who nodded almost imperceptibly. She understood that Tony DiCalabria was not accustomed to trusting a woman.

"Meyer told me more about the Governor," said DiCalabria when the two women had walked beyond hearing. "More about you. The Governor is the next President of the United States. Little guys like Marfeo and the Flynns don't see it. Some of them even got it in their heads they can influence the election. Influence? Make it come out different." He shook his head. "We can't, you know. Guys like me, guys like Meyer Lansky, guys like Frank Nitti, like Charlie Luck, we can't do things like that. Some guys believe their own press clippings. Hey . . . No matter how smart we are, we only make money off things we're *allowed* to make money off of. Off things the public *lets* us make money off of. I mean, hey, the public *wants* booze, it wants to gamble. Guys want whores. All that's against the law, but it's not against the laws the public cares anything about. Meyer told me the murder of Governor Roosevelt would bring the hardest crackdown this country has ever seen. I believe him. It can't happen. We've got to stop it."

"Do you think they're going to try?" Jack asked.

"Yeah. They're going to try. I figure they're going to try."

"What do we do?"

"I could eliminate the Flynn brothers. That wouldn't be

too hard. But I'm not sure it would help. They wouldn't be working alone. There has to be others."

"Vogel," said Jack.

"Possibility," said DiCalabria.

"He was definitely a part of the Norma Jean business. He threatened me with it."

"We don't have time to fool around," said DiCalabria. "Why don't you go swim with the girls while I make a little arrangement?"

Swimming was what Jack needed. Before many more hours, he would have been twenty-four hours without sleep. Plunging into the surf and fighting the power of the water did not tire him; it exhilarated him. When he, Charlotte, and Angela came out of the water they found towels lying on the beach waiting for them, and they dried themselves and dressed. On the terrace a table was set with coffee, sandwiches, and pastries.

He drank coffee and ate, but even so he needed sleep, and he lay back on a chaise longue and went sound asleep. When Charlotte woke him, he checked his watch and saw it was after 3:00 A.M.

"Vogel wants to talk to you," said DiCalabria. "In the house. We'll see you in a few minutes, girls."

Jack carried a cup of strong dark coffee with him as he followed DiCalabria through the house. They went down a flight of steps to the cellar. It was damp down there, being too close to high-tide level. The rooms were crowded with crates of wine and liquor.

They came finally to a small, square room. Two men sat on flimsy old chairs. A third man, stark naked, hung from the ceiling by a rope tied around his ankles. His hands were free, but he was not athletic enough to rise and untie the rope. He hung there groaning. He was Benjamin Vogel.

DiCalabria glanced at Jack, and Jack nodded and walked into the room.

"H'lo, Vogel," he said. "I guess you see, now, what happens to a man who falls into bad company."

Vogel blinked and twisted his head back and forth. He didn't at first recognize the man speaking to him. Then he mumbled, "Endicott?"

"I have a question for you, Vogel," said Jack coldly. "Straight out. You're in no position to play games. I want to know if there's a scheme to murder Governor Roosevelt when he's in Los Angeles on Monday."

"How would I know?" Vogel wept.

One of the men rose from his chair, seized Vogel's testicles, and squeezed.

Vogel screamed. Then he choked. "Yes!" he shrieked. "*Yes!*"

"Who?"

"Marfeo."

"Marfeo's dead."

"Then the others. Sean Flynn. Jimmy Flynn."

"How?"

"Oh God, I swear I don't know. Marfeo talked about a rifleman. He said, 'rifleman.' That's all I know. I don't know what rifleman. Or where. Or when."

The man who had squeezed Vogel got up and reached for him again.

Jack shook his head. "No. He really doesn't know. He hasn't got the guts to hold out on us." Jack sighed. "You know Marfeo's dead."

"Yes. I saw it in the paper."

"Did you give him some money to help pay this rifle-man?"

"No. Oh, no. He demanded it, but I wouldn't get involved in anything like that."

Jack backed out of the room and spoke to DiCalabria. "What are you going to do with him?"

DiCalabria shrugged. "Take him home, I guess. If we work him over a little more, we might get more information."

"I doubt it," said Jack. "He's a coward. He's not holding out on us."

DiCalabria nodded. "Rifleman . . ." he said thoughtfully.

XII

―

"Rifleman."

No matter that Jack had had little sleep. The word *rifleman* kept him awake. Frank Roosevelt's train was moving across Utah. Chief of Police Jackson had said he wished the Governor would not ride through the streets of Los Angeles in an open car; a rifleman on a roof could kill him. Now, Vogel. Vogel had used the word *rifleman,* had said he heard it from Carlo Marfeo.

Jack risked annoying Chief Jackson and telephoned him at home at seven o'clock. It was Sunday morning, and he apologized, then told the chief why he was calling.

"No need to apologize, Mr. Endicott," said the chief. "I'm concerned about that possibility. You say the Governor refuses to ride in a closed car?"

"Yes. He has his reasons. One reason is that he thinks he ought to let people see him, see that he's not a slumped cripple."

"He's not going to be persuaded otherwise?"

"I don't think so."

"What can I do for you, then? I'll put as many men around him as I can, but I can't promise it will help."

"Are there any known riflemen in the area? I mean, do you know of anyone who might take money for killing someone with a rifle?"

"No, sir. I can't think of anybody. There are two gun clubs in Los Angeles. Two rifle ranges. But the members are a pretty straightforward, respectable bunch of men . . . businessmen. Anyway, there are at least two hundred of them, and I don't know how we could check them all out."

"Among the mob people?"

"Not that I know of. Rifles aren't their style. You mentioned Marfeo. I don't know how much you know about Marfeo, but he was killed the way the gangsters kill people: pistol, a shot in the back or head."

"All right. That leaves one other group I've heard about. The movie sharpshooters. There aren't many of them, and somebody mentioned one in particular: an eccentric named Scotty Oakley. Have you ever heard of him?"

"No, I never have."

"If I get from the movie studios the names of ten or twenty men, could you put them under surveillance? Also, I've given you one name: Oakley. Can you run him through your files?"

"Yes. Yes, I can."

"I'll have to make some calls. I'm sorry to disturb you on a Sunday morning, Chief, but I guess you can understand the urgency."

"I certainly do," said Chief Jackson.

* * *

Ordinarily, on a Sunday morning Scotty Oakley would be sleeping off the monumental binge he'd been on the night before. Saturday night was when he chased his whiskey with beer, which ordinarily he didn't bother with. Saturday night was when he went to the Rose Garden, a fancifully named shack where friends gathered and drank and danced and sang. They played a game there that involved a quart milk bottle. It was placed in the middle of the floor, and anyone who wanted to could try standing above it and urinating through that two-inch mouth and into the bottle. The result was poured into a measuring cup and marked on a blackboard on the wall. The winners received a free bottle of whiskey.

Winners . . . The women competed, too. Separately. Betty, whom Scotty favored and who favored him, usually won the women's competition. Sometimes they managed to stagger home. Sometimes they slept on the floor at the Rose Garden. Sometimes they lay down by the path and slept on the ground.

But last night he had not gone to the Rose Garden. In fact, Scotty had not had a drink since Friday.

He sat on the hillside across the creek and above his house. He was something like one hundred fifty feet from the house and maybe twenty-five feet above the level of the stream. He had taped a paper target on a rock on the house side of the water. Now he was sighting in the Savage rifle, with his hand-loaded ammunition that he expected to give him greater accuracy.

This would be like the shot down on the car. He would be above the street, above the motorcade. Firing down on a target required adjustment of the sights. Bullets flying from a barrel at a down angle would have a different trajectory from bullets flying from a level or almost-level barrel.

Scotty did not take long to aim. He set the cross hairs on the X ring of the target and fired. Then he stared through the scope at his bullet hole. The windage was right, but the elevation was too low. He adjusted.

He fired again. Almost right. He made a tiny adjustment and fired again. Bull's-eye! He fired three more shots, then clambered down the slope to take a close look at the target.

Perfect. His last four shots had not made separate bullet holes. They had gone through the original hole, only scalloping out its edges and making a big, chrysanthemum-shaped bullet hole.

Scotty picked up the rock that had backed his target and heaved it into the rushing stream. Usually a man wouldn't shoot at a rock. The bullets ricocheted and whined away in all directions, as these had. But a smart investigator, if he suspected Scotty, could come out here and dig slugs out of trees and boards, looking for silver-tipped hollow-points. And he might find them and match them to the slugs dug out of the corpse. Not these. These had hit the rock, fragmented, and spanged off in all directions, hundreds of yards.

He returned to the Savage rifle and carried it down to the porch. Of all the weapons he'd ever owned, this was his favorite. Now he'd have to give it up. He was close to tears as he removed the screws and bolts that held the stock to the rifle. It was in some way like giving up a favorite dog.

He had wiped its every component free of fingerprints and had since touched the rifle only when he was wearing thin white cotton gloves. He had cleaned the ammunition the same way.

Stock separated from action and barrel, the Savage rifle fit into a gladstone bag. Scotty laid in some clothes, then the rifle and its stock, then more clothes with hand-loaded ammunition in the pockets. Finally, he stuffed fifty thousand dollars in cash into the bag, dispersing it through the clothes.

He didn't lock his house. Why bother? He would not be back. Carrying the bag, he walked up to the road and waited for the bus.

Charlotte tried to encourage Jack to get some sleep during the morning. Tomorrow might be a tough day, she said. She took the calls from DeMille and Goldwyn, giving the names of the studio sharpshooters. About eleven o'clock, Chief Bryan Jackson called. She wakened Jack.

"Got something for you," said the chief of police. "I don't know if this is going to be any help, but maybe it's better than nothing. Your man Scotty Oakley . . . It turns out he does have a record. He was arrested in 1925 on a charge of possession of whiskey, a violation of the National Prohibition Act. All of which means nothing much, except this: that his real name is not Scotty Oakley but James Collins. He was born and reared in Los Angeles. The record shows that he was bailed out by a brother named Dennis Collins. James was fined ten dollars."

"Do you have anything on Dennis?"

"Nothing. I did look in the telephone book. He lives in Beverly Hills. It may not be the same Dennis Collins."

"Where does the one who calls himself Oakley live?"

"We've got no record of it," said the chief.

* * *

"Never heard of either one of them," said DiCalabria. "Can tell you this, though—the brothers Flynn are holed up at Captain Frank's, which is their headquarters, when normally they'd be home. Sundays are big family days with the Flynns. The wives and kids are at Sean's, in the pool and picnicking, and the brothers are not there. That could mean nothing. I guess it means something."

"The Governor's train will be across the Nevada line before long," said Jack.

"What can I do for ya?"

"Let me have a car and driver," said Jack.

At their table at Captain Frank's, the Flynn brothers huddled with a man they called Paddy—an odd name for a swarthy man who had to be either Italian or Mexican.

"No question," said Paddy. "We never lost sight of him. He caught a bus on the road, came into town, and checked into this little hotel called McKinley's, on Fourth Street. Doug's sittin' in the lobby. The guy can't come down and go out without Doug seein' him. Fer sure."

Sean nodded. "Okay. Don't you guys lose him. *Don't lose him!* You understand me?"

"Gotcha."

"Get back to it. Keep your eyes peeled."

"Gotcha."

The brothers watched Paddy walk out of Captain Frank's.

"Okay," said Sean. "It's gonna work out. Either Oakley will kill Roosevelt or he won't kill Roosevelt—"

"He'll kill him," said Jimmy. "I can just sense it. The guy's a pro. Hell, he takes pride in what he does. He—"

"*Awright!* Either way . . . Either way, he's gotta be made dead. To start with, my boy, I want our fifty grand back. That's dough, brother! That's dough. But more important, I don't want a witness left alive. You know what he'll do. He'll blackmail us."

"I don't think so," said Jimmy. "I think the guy's just nutty enough to be honest. But I don't disagree with you. It's a chance we can't take."

"All right. This is *my* part of the deal. You can't get anywhere close. If he saw you— But he's not goin' to see you. He's not goin' to see me, either. Once he makes his move—he's got the Governor or he's not got the Governor— I'm gonna kill him. He's got the money on him or he's not got the money on him. If it's not on him, it's in his room at this McKinley Hotel. Which is where you're gonna be. Soon as Oakley leaves the hotel room, you move in and get the money, if it's there. Paddy or Doug will tell you when he leaves. When he leaves, I follow him. That's when Paddy and Doug go home. I don't want either one of them around, figurin' out what's goin' on. This is your deal and mine, little brother. Nobody else's."

Black homburg set squarely on his head, banker's suit fit well over his husky frame, walking stick authoritatively in hand, carnation in his lapel, John Lowell Endicott touched the electric bell button on the door of the Beverly Hills home of Dennis Collins.

A moment later he shook the hand of Mr. Collins, one of the city's more successful insurance brokers, as a couple of telephone calls had revealed. Collins still squinted at the engraved card that announced the Boston banker and plainly wondered why he had such a visitor on a Sunday afternoon.

"If I were you, Mr. Collins," said Jack, "I expect I should wonder what on earth possessed a certain Mr. Endicott to pay you a call at such a time."

"I cannot deny that I am curious," said Collins. He was a white-haired man—hair thick and healthy and wild, since it had just come out of the swimming pool behind the house. He was wrapped in a thick white terry-cloth robe. "I don't often receive calls from Boston bankers in any circumstances, much less on a Sunday afternoon."

"And so you shouldn't," said Jack. "And I don't often pay them. I have a question or two I should like to ask, and then I will apologize for interrupting your Sunday afternoon and depart."

"Well . . . Sit down, sir. Would you like a drink?"

"A light Scotch if you don't mind."

Collins went to his bar and poured a Scotch for Jack, a gin for himself. "So, what can I do for you, Mr. Endicott?"

"Would you be so kind first as to tell me the address of your office," said Jack.

Collins shrugged. "It's on Broadway, between Third and Fourth," he said. "Why?"

"For no reason at all, p'raps," said Jack. "The next question is a bit more difficult. Do you have, Mr. Collins, a brother who calls himself Scotty Oakley?"

"What's he done now?"

"Nothing. Nothing at all. But I should like to know a bit more about him. Most of us have, in our families, someone who is potentially embarrassing. A great-grandfather of mine, Mr. Collins, made a great deal of money trading in African slaves. I don't mean, really, to suggest that your brother James is embarrassing. But could you tell me anything at all about him?"

Collins looked miserable. "My younger brother is a drunkard, Mr. Endicott. He showed a propensity for it from the time he was a boy. My father came to regard him as, uh . . . As, uh—"

"A black sheep?"

"Precisely. On the other hand, he had and developed an odd talent. He is a marksman, Mr. Endicott. He is an excellent shot with a rifle. He could have gone to Africa and become a white hunter. He could have become an officer of the army or . . . He chose to shoot for show, in Wild West carnivals. To give himself an interesting name, he began some years ago to claim he was the illegitimate son of Annie Oakley. As you may know, Annie Oakley died in 1926. That is what my brother became: false claimant to the name Oakley, a skilled sharpshooter, a heavy drinker, and an eccentric. When my father died, he left half his estate to me, absolutely, the other half to me also, in trust for James's benefit. In a sense, James owns half my business."

"But it is within your discretion as to whether or not you disburse any funds to him."

"Exactly. But please tell me, Mr. Endicott, why do you ask these questions?"

"It's nothing you need concern yourself with, Mr. Collins. He's done nothing wrong, and I'm hoping to be able to prevent his doing anything wrong."

"He *is* my brother. He never married. He lives out in the Santa Monica Mountains. I haven't seen him in six months."

"How can I find him?"

"I can write down directions to his place."

"I should be grateful."

Collins scribbled a note, telling how to find the road and the lane leading to his brother's home. While he was at it, he wrote down the address of his office and the telephone number. "Please call me if there's any trouble with James."

"It's outside our jurisdiction," said the plainclothes police detective who drove Jack in an unmarked car.

"I don't expect to make an arrest," said Jack. "Put it this way, Sergeant: If I have to do anything, I'll shoot him, and you can pretend you didn't see it and you didn't bring me out here."

They walked the last fifty yards down the rock-strewn lane to the ramshackle house on the swift stream. Within a minute they knew that Scotty Oakley—James Collins—was gone.

"What do you say, Sergeant? Do you think this man is ever coming back?"

"Why you ask, Mr. Endicott?"

"House unlocked. Valuable guns lying about. Whatever else the man has, lying about. Does that suggest to you that he absquatulated? Or that something dreadful happened to him?"

"You could look at it that way."

"I *look at it* that way. Let's get back to Los Angeles!"

In the garden apartment at the Ambassador, Jack found Charlotte and DiCalabria waiting.

"All right, kid," growled DiCalabria. "The time has come. You gotta have some sleep, or you're gonna get some sleeping medicine in your drinks."

"Man's life's at stake . . ." Jack muttered.

"The guy who's gonna save him has to be halfway able," said DiCalabria.

Jack handed DiCalabria the note Dennis Collins had written. "Is it some kind of coincidence," he asked, "that the Collins office is in a building on Broadway, on the motorcade route between Union Station and Pershing Park? Is that a coincidence?"

"Sure. Maybe. Could be. Let's don't get too excited."

"One hell of a fine marksman could be in any window of that building, or on the roof. What'd Vogel say? 'Rifleman.' Well, Scotty Oakley—James Collins—is a *rifleman.*"

"I'll have boys all around that buildin' in the morning," said DiCalabria. "Right now is beddy-bye time, Jack. Or you're not goin' to be part of whatever happens."

"Christ . . ."

"Jack . . ." Charlotte whispered. "*Eat.* Then bed. You can get up in the middle of the night. But— Tony's right. You won't be worth a damn tomorrow if you don't get some sleep. Now, eat, goddamnit!"

A little later she stretched out on the bed beside him and made going to sleep memorable.

Scotty Oakley did not sleep well on Sunday night. If he overslept, he could spoil his plan, so he slept fitfully, checking his watch every fifteen minutes. At 3:00 A.M., he got up. He shaved, wet his hair with Vitalis and combed it flat, and dressed carefully in his best outfit. He left the hotel. He had paid cash in advance, so the dozing night clerk took no notice of him. Even so, he explained his early departure. "Gotta catch an early train," he said.

He walked to the building on Broadway where his brother had his office. If the sons of bitches had changed the locks, he'd have a big problem. But they hadn't. He had a key to the Collins Brothers Insurance Agency office—after all, he was one of the Collins brothers—and keys to the office were also keys to the building. Dennis had given him the key so he could, if ever he needed to, come to the office and sleep on the couch. It had not been an innocent invitation. It meant, Don't get yourself locked up in the drunk tank.

The building was four stories high. The Collins offices were on the third floor. He didn't stop there but went to the roof. He couldn't shoot from an office window. There'd be people in the office. But from the roof— It was the way he had planned this job from the day when that fellow who called himself Bob Wallace had first tried to get him interested.

Wallace . . . Scotty had a good idea who he was. He was a gangster. And he wasn't just a soldier in the ranks; he was a man somebody had trusted with fifty thousand dollars in cash. He looked sort of Italian, but Scotty didn't think he was; his hair was too light. A newspaper story Scotty had once seen said that the Flynn brothers, who ran the crooked Wiring and Lighting Workers Union, were onetime boxers. He'd guess this man was a Flynn.

He'd guessed that early. That was why he also guessed they'd kill him after he did the job, or failed to do it. The Flynn brothers were not nice people.

The roof was a perfect place for this job. The walls of the building rose three whole feet above the roof—so somebody wouldn't fall off—and a man could squat behind the brick wall and be completely out of sight from the street or even from other roofs. The buildings on this block shared party walls, so a man could move from one building to another with ease. Two buildings up the street, a fire ladder ran down the back to the alley behind.

He would fire his shot—two shots at the most—drop the Savage, strip off his gloves, and slip across the roofs to that fire ladder. He knew the neighborhood. He'd walk in the back door of a hardware store just up the alley, make some small purchase like a can of saddle soap, and walk out the front door. He'd be on Spring Street. He'd board the first bus that came by, and in ten minutes he'd be a mile away from where Governor Roosevelt got shot.

Right now he had a little job to do. Somehow he had to jam down the trap door in the roof, so no one could come up here. There was nothing on the roof he could use, so he left the bag, the money, and the rifle and went back down into the building.

A ringing phone woke the Flynn brothers. Paddy reported where Oakley had gone.

"Okay," said Sean. "Stick with it for another hour or so. Then Jimmy and I'll come take up the watch and you guys can go home and get some sleep."

The Flynn brothers favored Colt automatic pistols. Jimmy's was a .32, small enough to be tucked inside almost any clothes. Sean's was a .38. He carried it in a shoulder holster.

Charlotte insisted Jack eat breakfast. She also insisted she would go with him, at least to sit in the police car. The driver was to pick him up at eight o'clock, two hours before the

Governor was scheduled to ride down Broadway in an open car.

The Governor, too, enjoyed a hearty breakfast. He liked ham or bacon, with eggs, toast and marmalade, and coffee. James A. Farley, his campaign chairman, was with him, as was Louis Howe and Missy LeHand. All of them were eating breakfast.

At Barstow, California the train had been switched from the tracks of the Union Pacific to those of the Atchison, Topeka & Santa Fe, so they were less than two hours out of Los Angeles.

Farley briefed the Governor on the people he would meet in Los Angeles. "Upton Sinclair is going to want to see you. The author, you know. Keep a distance from him. He's unstable. The people we want to talk to are the movie people. We want them in our corner."

When the Governor finished his breakfast, Missy knelt before him and helped him with the painful and laborious process of strapping the leather-and-steel braces on his legs.

The telephone rang in the garden apartment just before eight o'clock. It was Chief Jackson. "I've got great good news for you, Mr. Endicott. We've caught him! The rifleman. Some of my boys spotted him on a rooftop on Broadway and plucked him off."

"That's great news, b'god! Is it Oakley?"

"Whoever he is, he won't talk. So I don't know who he is yet. We'll get fingerprints and try to identify him."

"Congratulations, Chief. It's a great relief."

"A car and driver is at your disposal. I've assigned Sergeant O'Dwyer to drive you. Just tell him where you want to go. Since we've got the rifleman in custody, I told him he didn't have to pick you up quite so early."

"Thanks very much. Being in a police car, maybe I can get close enough to see the Governor."

Sergeant O'Dwyer did not arrive until 8:45. The man was a uniformed sergeant—white-haired, flush-faced, but trim and hard—and the car was a marked police car. Jack sat in front with Sergeant O'Dwyer. Charlotte sat in the back.

"Where to?" asked the sergeant.

"Well . . . why don't we drive the whole route? I'd like to see exactly where the Governor is going."

Sergeant O'Dwyer drove to the railroad station. A crowd had already gathered there, and the police had stretched ropes to set a limit on how close people could come. Jack and Charlotte got out of the car for a few minutes. Jack knew he was no expert on security. He was interested, even so, in how the police would protect Frank Roosevelt. Of course, they would be protecting the mayor, too, plus a lot of other dignitaries.

It might be difficult to leave the station, even in a police car, once the train was in, so when the word came that the campaign train was only five minutes away, Jack and Charlotte climbed back into the car, and Sergeant O'Dwyer set off down the motorcade route.

A crowd had formed along both sides of the streets. Policemen were taking control of the intersections now, allowing only a few cars to pass onto Broadway, clearing it of traffic.

"They turn off Broadway at Fifth," said Sergeant O'Dwyer. "Then Pershing Square." He pointed at two police cars sitting in front of a five-story building. "That's where they caught the rifleman, incidentally. He was on the roof of that building."

Jack stared at the building. *"M'god!* Not the right building. Turn around! The rifleman *I'm* worried about will be on top of a building between Third and Fourth!"

"You sure?"

"Damned sure! Here!" Jack handed the sergeant the paper on which Dennis Collins had written his office address. "On top of *that* building!"

Sergeant O'Dwyer switched on his flashing emergency lights, sounded his siren, and made a U-turn.

Jimmy Flynn stopped at the desk at the McKinley Hotel.

"Lookin' for a fella named Oakley. Checked in here yesterday."

The desk clerk shook his head. "Got no Oakley registered, yestiddy or today."

"Cowboy-type fella. Carryin' a gladstone bag."

The clerk nodded. "Mr. Doak. Checked out early this mornin'."

Jimmy slipped a ten-dollar bill across the desk. "Like to see his room."

Damn! Scotty Oakley *had* checked out. He hadn't left the money in his room. Well . . . Jimmy would try to catch up with Sean. Two men were better than one.

Sean had climbed on top of a car and reached the lower rung of the fire ladder on the rear of the building two doors up the street from the building where Scotty lay in wait on the roof.

Reaching the top, he peered cautiously over the rim of the wall. He saw no one. So, okay, Scotty hadn't seen him, either.

Sean knew he was over there—unless he'd taken the fifty thousand and lammed. When he fired a shot, Sean would know where he was and could move. So far, so good.

Jack, Sergeant O'Dwyer, and the building manager took the elevator to the fourth floor. The building manager opened the door to the ladder that led up to the trap door in the roof. The sergeant drew his revolver and climbed the ladder.

The trap door was jammed! He shoved and couldn't open it.

Scotty heard the commotion under the trap door. He'd tied the door down the best he could, with rope he'd found in the cellar. He'd tied rope around the handle and looped it around a vent pipe, pulling it as tight as he could. The door would open a little but not enough for a man to come out on the roof. A man could see the rope and could reach out with a knife to cut it—and get a rifle stock in the face. The trap door wouldn't hold long. But it didn't have to.

Sirens and the roar of motorcycle engines told him the motorcade was coming.

Scotty raised his face and peered over the wall. Yeah. There it was. A wedge of police motorcycles led the cars and cleared the street. First car, that was more police. Then a car with big newsreel cameras on tripods and cameramen standing and making film of the next car, which had to be the car with the Governor of New York in it.

Sure. There he was, sitting in the back seat of the big, open automobile, waving and smiling. A man rode the running board on each side of the car. Plainclothesmen trotted alongside.

But the Governor was an open target. He'd pass by no more distant from the muzzle of the Savage than the paper target had been. It would be so easy that for a moment Scotty considered trying a head shot. But no . . . That wasn't what he had planned. A shot to the middle of the chest. A silver-tip hollow-point would tear apart everything that counted. There might be time for a second shot, maybe that one to the head.

"We haven't got time!" Jack yelled.

He meant they didn't have time to break open the jammed trap door. That it *was* jammed was ample proof that Scotty Oakley was on the roof.

"We can stop the motorcade," grunted Sergeant O'Dwyer.

"*You* can," said Jack. "And you may be in time. While you're trying that, I've got to get to the roof." He turned to the building manager. "Up from an adjoining building?"

The building manager nodded and trotted down the steps, not waiting for the elevator.

Sergeant O'Dwyer ran into the street. Jack followed the building manager in the front door of the next building down the street. A shoe store occupied the ground floor, and they ran through the stockroom to a door opening onto stairs. Jack shoved his way past the manager and ran up ahead of him.

* * *

Scotty was ready. He crouched on his knees behind the wall, the Savage cradled in his arms. Fifty thousand dollars . . . Yes, but damnit, he could take *pride* in this job. He was sorry he would have to leave the rifle behind. But . . . Nothing for it. He looked down fondly at the beautiful stock and steel he had lovingly cared for for years.

What was going on? Some kind of disturbance down on the street. He raised his head and looked down. The motorcade had stopped. A cop was out in the middle of the street yelling, and the cars had stopped a hundred feet or so up the street.

No matter. Now he had a stationary target instead of a moving one. He adjusted his sight one click. A good time for it, while they were stopped.

Scotty rose, rested his arm and the front stock of the rifle on the top of the wall, and looked through the sight.

How could it be easier?

"*Scotty!*"

He jerked his head around. A dude, an eastern-type dude, knelt on the roof of the next building and rested an automatic on the wall between the roofs, aiming square at him. Something wrong here. Hell, he hadn't even got off a shot.

"Put the rifle down, Scotty, or I'll kill you."

Looked like he would, too. The dude had the automatic sighted right, and the distance wasn't much.

Scotty pulled the Savage back. "Who you?" he asked.

"A friend of Frank Roosevelt," said the dude. "Friend of yours, too, probably better than you'll ever figure out."

Scotty glanced down at the street. Cops were all over the car. You couldn't even *see* the Governor of New York. He looked back at the dude, who kept the automatic leveled at his belly.

"Damn . . ." he muttered.

Holding the Browning pointed at Scotty Oakley, Jack stepped over the party wall that separated two buildings and walked toward the disgruntled rifleman.

"Step away from the rifle. Open your jacket. I want to see what else you're carrying."

Scotty laid the rifle down on the roof and stood up and stepped away from it. He opened his western-style jacket and held it back to show that he was not carrying a pistol. He glanced warily around, first over his left shoulder, then over his right, as if he expected to see someone. Maybe he was looking for a confederate, and help.

"*L'k out!*" screamed Scotty.

Jack saw what the rifleman was screaming about a second before a burly, red-haired man fifty feet away on another roof pulled the trigger on a big automatic. It was time enough to jump aside. The bullet whizzed by.

Jack dropped behind the wall, scrambled along a few yards, and raised his head for a look.

Scotty had dropped face down on the roof to be out of the line of fire. But he wasn't. The redheaded man held his automatic extended in both hands and aimed at Scotty. He pulled the trigger and shot the recumbent rifleman in the back.

That gave Jack time enough to take aim. He took time to steady the Browning and squeezed away a single shot. The burly redhead yelled, threw his arms in the air, throwing away his pistol, and sprawled on his back.

Jack jumped over the separating wall and ran to where Scotty Oakley lay in a spreading pool of blood. He had just knelt beside him when he heard thumping and banging on the trap door. He ran to the door and stood behind it, on the side where the hinge was. A hand thrust out a knife and began to saw on the rope that held the trap door shut.

Help? A police detective? Or—

"Sean? What the hell . . . ? Sean!"

That answered his question. Jack waited until the man finished cutting the rope and threw the trap door open. Then he pressed the muzzle of the Browning against the back of a man's neck and asked, "Jimmy Flynn, p'raps?"

Epilogue

Sean Flynn was dead.

Scotty Oakley was dead.

The rifleman earlier arrested on a rooftop in the next block was an anarchist named Constantinescu who meant to shoot what he called "a bigwig"—any bigwig in the motorcade, Governor of New York, Mayor of Los Angeles, it made no difference to him. He was held in jail until he could be deported to Romania.

Jimmy Flynn was sentenced to death on two counts of felony murder and attempted murder. Under the law of most states, when anyone is killed during the commission of a felony or an attempt to commit a felony, every participant in the crime is guilty of murder. Ironically for Jimmy Flynn, he was guilty of felony murder in the death of his brother, because Sean died during their joint attempt to assassinate the Governor of New York. It made no difference that Blackjack Endicott had killed Sean. Jimmy was guilty of felony murder in the death of Scotty Oakley, even though Sean had killed Scotty. He was to have been put to death in the gas chamber on November 3, 1932, but since he had actually not killed either of the men who died on the Broadway rooftop, and because he promised to keep his silence about what had really happened on that roof, the governor commuted his sentence to life imprisonment. He died in San Quentin Prison in 1971.

Edna Bascombe was sentenced to ten years imprisonment for corrupting the morals of her daughter. She was paroled in February 1938. She became a shoplifter and was returned to prison as a parole violator. Released again in 1941, she became involved in an automobile-theft ring. In April 1942, she was sentenced to ten years. She died in prison in 1950.

Antonio DiCalabria was murdered by one of his subordinates, who shot him and dumped his body off a fishing boat, in 1935. Angela DiCalabria married a cowboy star who used the name Tex Wright. After Wright's movie career ebbed, they moved to a ranch in Simi Valley and became prosperous breeders of palomino horses.

Bugsy Siegel was murdered in a Beverly Hills apartment in 1947—at which time he was one of the nation's most notorious gangsters.

Meyer Lansky died in bed in 1983. Second only to Lucky Luciano, he was the nation's best-known gangster. In his entire life, he served only sixty days in jail.

Norma Jean Chandler was released in the custody of Charlotte Wendell. Jack and Charlotte took her to Boston, arranged for her child to be born at Boston Lying-In Hospital, and arranged with her consent for the infant to be adopted. They changed her name and enrolled her in a school for troubled adolescents in western Massachusetts. After she was there a year, she was enrolled in a girls' boarding school in New Hampshire. When she was twenty-three years old, she graduated from Smith College with a degree in mathematics and psychology. She married a young instructor on the Amherst faculty. During World War II, he served in the Pacific in the navy, and she joined the WAVES. After the war, they returned to Amherst, lived there for many years, and had three sons. She never knew what became of her mother and never asked.

Jack picked up the fifty thousand dollars that had been in Scotty's gladstone bag. At police headquarters, he made a suggestion about it to Chief Jackson. The chief agreed. No record was made of it. It was deposited in First Boston Provident Trust as a trust fund for a young woman who had a new name. Jack did not reveal its existence to her until 1946. He explained to her husband that it was a trust fund established for her by her maternal grandfather.

Jack's day was not over when he came down through the building and returned to the police car. The motorcade had moved quickly on after the sound of shooting on rooftops above Broadway had frightened everyone. At Pershing Square, the sergeant edged the marked car through the crowd and brought Jack and Charlotte close to the platform where Governor Roosevelt spoke.

They were joined there by Chief Jackson.

"The big thing now is to keep it quiet," the chief suggested to Jack.

"The best we can," said Jack.

"Suppose O'Dwyer here gets a citation for breaking up the brouhaha on the roof?"

"Absolutely," said Jack. "He deserves it. Personally, I was flat on my face, hoping the bullets would fly overhead."

The chief and the sergeant chuckled.

Frank Roosevelt spotted Jack while he was speaking and acknowledged him with a friendly wave. At the luncheon for fat cats, he asked him to bend over his chair and give him a briefing on what had happened. Later, they met on the campaign train, and Jack gave a fuller report.

Missy wept. She put her arms around the Governor, kissed him on the neck under his ear, and sobbed, "Oh, Eff Dee! You might have—"

Frank patted her back. "Don't you worry," he said. "When a man's got a friend like Blackjack Endicott watching out for him, he's got little to worry about."

When they returned to the Ambassador, Jack and Charlotte found an invitation waiting for them. William Randolph Hearst and Marion Davies loved to host costume parties. The ones at San Simeon could be most elaborate. The invitation was accompanied by a note, written by Marion, asking them to stay over the rest of the week and be guests at San Simeon as soon as they could get up there.

It had been a trying two weeks, so they went—being careful to pack plenty of Scotch and brandy, supplied by DiCalabria. This turned out to be unnecessary. Hearst did not trust his Hollywood guests not to get disgustingly drunk and embarrass him. He trusted John Lowell Endicott and Charlotte Lanier Wendell. He offered more than they wanted.

If there was a price for his hospitality—and there really wasn't—it was an account of what had happened in Los

Angeles. They told him much of it, emphasizing the help they'd had from himself and the *Examiner*.

They spent the middle of the week at San Simeon, lounging around the several swimming pools, playing croquet, essaying an occasional game of tennis, and examining the fascinating and revealing collection of artifacts Hearst had shipped to his hill.

Toward the end of the week, his guests began to arrive. Jack and Charlotte began to understand that—circumstances being equal—people Hearst liked and trusted were invited to come earlier.

One of the guests who came early, on Thursday in fact, was Fred Astaire. He was a wholly charming man, although his complete dedication to his art was never invisible. He was a little naïve as well, and as the other guests arrived they began to play small practical jokes on him. Even when the jokes were crude, they did not diminish Astaire's good humor.

Clark Gable arrived for this weekend, too. He was a favorite. Then came Constance Bennett, acknowledged the most beautiful actress in Hollywood—acknowledged also as the best poker player in California and the most foul-mouthed woman in America. Charles Chaplin arrived. Jack had supposed Chaplin would be interesting, but Chaplin was in a dark mood and seemed unwilling to say anything. Cary Grant came—Archibald Leach, with his English accent out of control.

The costume party was held on Saturday night. Few guests supplied their costumes. Most were supplied.

Jack found himself dressed in the uniform of an 1890s naval officer—or Masonic Knight Templar. His bicorne hat was adorned with gold braid and ostrich feathers, the broad lapels of his knee-length blue coat gleamed yellow, his buttons were big and brass. He wore a sword, and on drawing it out he found it was indeed a Knights Templars sword.

Charlotte had expressed herself to Marion Davies two weeks ago as admiring her comic-opera uniform, so tonight she wore one very much like it. Marion wore one, too. Their distinguishing feature was the skintight pants that displayed every turn of a woman's legs.

Constance Bennett wore a silver-lamé gown that seemed to have been poured over her like a coat of paint. She was meant to be Constance Bennett.

Gable was dressed like a cowboy, Chaplin like one of the Three Musketeers, and Cary Grant in a tramp costume, as if he were supposed to be Charlie Chaplin.

Other guests looked like devils, angels, Roman senators, and ancient Greek soldiers.

The lights in the walls of the swimming pools were turned on. Guests milled around, sipping their ration of liquor.

A man approached Jack. He wore a costume meant to represent a sixteenth-century king, maybe Henry VIII. "Good evening, Admiral Endicott," he said.

Jack glanced, then stared. It was Benjamin Vogel.

"I have something for you," said Vogel, handing over a slip of paper.

Jack looked at it. It was a check for five thousand dollars, written on Birdsong Productions and payable to James A. Farley, campaign chairman, Roosevelt campaign.

"You look a little happier than you did the last time I saw you," said Jack.

Vogel did not even wince. He deftly plucked two glasses of champagne off a passing tray and handed one to Jack. He raised his glass in toast. "To Franklin D. Roosevelt," he said. "The next President of the United States!"